The Jasmine Sari

The Jasmine Sari

PHILIP TUCKER

Matador
9 Priory Business Park,
Wistow Road, Kibworth Beauchamp,
Leicestershire. LE8 0RX
Tel: 0116 279 2299
Email: books@troubador.co.uk
Web: www.troubador.co.uk/matador
Twitter: @matadorbooks

ISBN 978 1785898 624

British Library Cataloguing in Publication Data.
A catalogue record for this book is available from the British Library.

Printed and bound by CPI Group (UK) Ltd, Croydon, CR0 4YY
Typeset in 11pt Adobe Garamond Pro by Troubador Publishing Ltd, Leicester, UK

Matador is an imprint of Troubador Publishing Ltd

TO MY FRIENDS IN BANGLADESH

Dhonnobad.

*In memory of Mrs Sullivan and Pritilata
Waddedar.*

ACKNOWLEDGMENTS

Thanks to Mark Hardie, Robert Chatterton, Sarah Armstrong, Saira Hamilton and Helen Tucker.

In memory of my friends and hosts, Nadira and Habib.

Singapore Free Press,
6 October 1932

The raid was carried out with lightning-like rapidity and almost perfect organisation.

The band, including a girl dressed as a Bengali boy, surrounded the club at about 10.30pm while the members were engaged in a whist drive. Without any warning they launched their attack.

The first bomb was flung into the hall through an open window and was immediately followed up by others and a succession of shots from guns, rifles and revolvers. An elderly European lady, Mrs Sullivan, fell mortally wounded and thirteen others were injured, necessitating their removal to the Railway Cottage Hospital.

Having carried out their purpose, the raiders disappeared into the night, but subsequent investigations resulted in the recovery 100 yards from the club of the body of a girl. She was later identified as Pritilata Waddedar.

The discovery of Government-marked ammunition shows that the terrorists were armed with revolvers and muskets which had been stolen during the raid on the armoury in April 1930. A further intensive search resulted in the discovery of leaflets of a revolutionary character calling upon youths to join the terrorist campaign and kill Europeans and 'white-skinned' Anglo-Indians: 'Whoever may get Europeans or Anglo-Indians dead or alive to the Headquarters of the Indian Republican Army will be amply rewarded.'

PART 1

CHAPTER ONE

The reinforced steel door closed with a deep thud behind him and he was free. The oppression, the threatening chaos of colour, noise and movement, unceasing, was locked safely outside.

Upstairs, although the bar was open to the heavy air and the heat, the cold Heineken and the calm order of the club were curative. The newcomer picked a seat at one of the empty tables, each of them shaded with a large green umbrella. The only other occupant was a slim woman dressed in a loose white shirt, linen trousers and sandals that showed pretty brown toes that had been many weeks in the sun. She sat listlessly stroking a computer tablet, sorting multicoloured images that sparkled in the twilight. Below, out of sight, a tennis match was taking place.

'Do you live here?' he asked the woman.

'Yeah.' An American.

'It can't be an easy place to live. I don't think I've ever been anywhere quite like it.'

Instead of answering, she looked vacantly at the sky and then began to speak to the tablet. 'Hi, honey. You home now? Are the kids home, honey? Great – put them on.'

She was low in her chair, almost lying, long legs stretched out beneath the table. Her neat face shone with moisture and the thin material of her shirt slid over her as she settled into her call. She was confident and comfortable, perhaps in her late forties.

The tennis pairs arrived at the bar, wiping racquets and towelling their heads, chatting and laughing. Two of them were thirty-something white men; the other pair were Bangladeshis: a shapeless woman in a grey tracksuit and an older man in whites, whose bowed and gnarled legs looked too frail for sport.

The visitor listened to their chit-chat for a few moments and then walked over to the edge of the terrace. The noise of the wild exterior – voices babbling, cars, horns and bells – intruded through the razor wire hoops atop the smooth grey wall, carrying with it an unfamiliar aroma of…? He tried to identify the constituents of the unique cocktail: something floral, perfumed; cooked onions; rotting meat. Could he smell these aromas, or were they simply suggested to him by the things he had gaped at as he had picked his way along the precarious pavement? Rickshaw riders waving their dark fingers close to his face to entice him as a fare, black running water flowing beneath the concrete, glimpsed here and there below the shattered grey lumps from which reinforced wires protruded like damaged nerves. A dog picking at the mangled remains of some black-feathered fowl, the rubbery orange feet pristine, apparently indigestible. A pile of sodden rubbish heaped across the pavement, so that he had to step into the road to avoid it. People. Everywhere, people: squatting with a few packs of cigarettes to sell, sitting with a hand held up for alms, on bicycles and rickshaws, walking, in cars, in shops. Everywhere, brown people.

His mobile phone rattled and he hooked it out of the tight pocket with difficulty.

'Guv'nor? It's Joe Pritchard here. Mr Thorogood asked me to give you a call.'

'I'm in Dhaka.'

'Yes, I know, guv, but Mr Thorogood said you wouldn't want to find out about it when you got back.'

'Go on.'

'You've been allocated forty nominals. The Service sent them over. I'm the case officer.'

'Terrorists?'

'Yes. Well, no, not exactly.'

'Yes or no?'

'No. Activists. G8 protesters.'

'Why has Counter-Terrorism Command got them then?'

'I, er, don't know, guv.'

Cadman looked out into the bewildering anarchy of the city. 'I've got enough on my hands at the moment.'

'Mr Thorogood said to tell you, guv. I'll crack on, shall I?'

'Yes. You do that. And tell Thorogood to shove his forty nominals—'

'I'll crack on, guv. Thanks.'

He looked at the phone and puffed out a lungful of hot damp air. Below, a bearded youth jigged through the filthy gutter playing on a wooden flute a refrain like that of an ice cream van. A net bag full of the home-made instruments dangled from his shoulder.

'It's an odd feeling, isn't it?' The soft voice came from behind him.

He turned and looked into the smiling brown face of the elderly tennis player, who had his hand outstretched. The Bangladeshi took his hand and held it softly, not releasing it as he spoke.

'Welcome to Bangladesh. It's an odd feeling, I think, when you first arrive from the order of the West. I am Akbar. I think you are Mr Cadman, are you not, sir?' His smile was wide and white, his head to one side, wobbling almost imperceptibly, thin black hair streaked across a round, shining dome of a head. His spectacles were slightly steamed and a trickle of sweat ran down an otherwise dry and clear face.

'Rector? I didn't expect to meet you until Sunday morning, sir. Yes, I'm Alex Cadman. And yes, Bangladesh feels very odd.'

'Call me Akbar please, Alex. Dhaka is not a beautiful city' – he pronounced it with a heavily emphasised 'H' and with the 'D' sounding like a 'T' – 'but the people here I hope you will find to be welcoming and hospitable. If we have time, perhaps we will get to see the beauty of my country together. Come and meet your colleagues.' He released Cadman's hand at last and touched his heart through his pristine white tennis shirt.

A tall man in a fluorescent green T-shirt pulled a sweatband from his head as he spoke. His white teeth flashed as he said in a loud voice with an unmistakably antipodean accent, 'Canada should have a cricket team. What's going on there? Australia and Bangladesh both play cricket. India. The Windies – Chris Gayle is the best batsman in the world. I'm sure he's really an Aussie.'

'You must be Sam. Nice to meet you at last. Alex Cadman.'

The Australian threw a strong, sweaty arm around Cadman's shoulder. 'Why don't the Canadians play cricket, Alex? I thought the Brits made all the countries they invaded play cricket.'

'I have no idea. Weren't there a lot of Scots in Canada?'

'Fair point, Alex,' Samuel Kanoski grinned. 'You never quite anglicised the Celts, did you?'

'I'm not sure that I've ever tried.'

'Ignore him, Alex.' The other man shook Cadman's hand with an exaggerated up and down motion. 'I'm François Sutherland. Call me Frank. I'm the project manager. Welcome to Bangladesh.'

'And I'm guessing you're Canadian?'

'You'd be right too, my friend. RCMP. Seconded to the UN for this project.'

'So you're the boss?'

'Royal!' Kanoski bowed towards the Bangladeshi woman, a sweeping dip of the shoulders accompanied by a dramatic flourish of his right hand. 'Do you notice that, Jasmina? RCMP – Royal Canadian Mounted Police. They couldn't prise the Canadians away from their ice hockey but they left their bloody queen behind.'

She smiled shyly beneath her large white tennis visor, her shiny black hair gathered into a long ponytail that almost reached her waist. It was a touch of feminine beauty adorning her otherwise plain, slightly plump body. 'I don't know about such politics,' she replied, her voice soft and melodic, a mere hint of a South Asian accent. 'Perhaps we will learn more of this on the course.'

'Jasmina is one of your students. She's the Rector's daughter,' said Sutherland.

'I hope we're not going to get too bogged down in politics,' Cadman started.

'Terrorism *is* politics, Alex,' asserted Kanoski, 'the politics of the oppressed.'

'I've always rather considered the victims…'

'That's where you've been going wrong. The victims are random. Motivation is everything in terrorism. Haven't you read Hoffman? Basic stuff, Alex.'

'I don't study terrorism. I investigate it.'

Jasmina reached across and took the orange juice that her father was holding out to her. As she did so, she rested the fingers of her left hand on Kanoski's forearm.

'I tend to agree with Mr Kanoski,' she said.

'So what do you think of the club, Jasmina?' asked her father. 'Is it not a good place to come and relax?'

'Yes, Abu. It has good facilities and it's cosmopolitan, just as you said. Here in this little group even we have an Australian, a Canadian and a British man.'

'Then you should come again.'

'We are the only Bangladeshis, Abu,' she said, twisting her body to look all around her. The barman approached when she looked in his direction. He was a local man of about Akbar's age and wore a smart white shirt and black trousers.

'Another drink, madam?' he asked quietly.

Jasmina shooed him away dismissively, without speaking, and he faded back towards his bar.

'Well, here is to everyone's good health,' smiled the

Rector, his face now free of any sign of exertion, 'and may you have great successes over the next three weeks.'

'Cheers!' Alex Cadman chinked his thick mug of beer against the four stemmed glasses of orange juice, the heavy head of foam slopping onto the concrete floor. He looked around at his new friends and smiled broadly.

'Alcohol on a Friday?' asked Kanoski.

CHAPTER TWO

The tricycle rickshaw wobbled dangerously as it bumped across the uneven road surface. The puller ceased pedalling for a moment to keep the machine stable, then, standing out of the saddle, using all of his weight to maintain momentum, he swung right, through the darkness and into a relentless flow of oncoming traffic. An orchestra of horns blared aggressively, their users unseen behind a glare of blazing white headlamps amongst which there were no gaps and no hope of survival. The rickshaw puller responded by ringing his bell and waving his left arm, like a thin brown tie whipping in the wind, his right hand gripping the handlebar, and they hurtled into the blaze.

'Way-hey!' yelled Cadman, clinging to Kanoski's right arm. His right buttock could not fit into the narrow seat and he perched perilously on his left. The puller's feet were clad in flimsy sandals that slipped painfully on the pedals, wasting energy, his bare calves scratching against the oily metal.

'Poor sod!' Cadman said loudly, above the noise of the traffic.

'Oh, he's alright. He'll be pleased with the fare. They pay 500 taka a day to hire these. He'd struggle to make that if it weren't for the occasional fat Englishman.'

'Oi! Less of the fat please, Sam. I'm twice your age, aren't I?'

'Twice my size anyway, mate.'

There was still the uninterrupted babble of voices from the crowded streets. Everyone seemed to be shouting at once in some barbarian language that resembled the barking of dogs in kennels. Great thick swathes of black insulated cables draped hammock-like between the numerous telegraph poles that sprouted out of the pavements. Lethal-looking exposed ends of wires hung down lower than the heads of the pedestrians, who dodged them with expert nonchalance. A boy, no more than four years old, naked below the waist, with filthy face and hair, ran alongside the rickshaw, his hand held out, palm upwards. 'Dollars mister, money mister?' he sang. As they passed a busy side road, with cars and rickshaws seeping in and out of it into the main road, the child ran straight across, his dark eyes fixed on the heavy white wealth that trundled along beside him.

'This is fantastic!' Cadman hollered. 'I've never seen anything like it in my life.'

The rickshaw suddenly careened to the side of the road and the puller was looking back towards his fare. 'Keep your eyes on the fucking road, mate,' screamed Kanoski.

But then they had stopped and the puller had broken into a grin. The begging child ran into the knees of a uniformed porter, who ushered him away. The puller's smile was unhealthy, skeletal and unshaven. His skin was very dark and the dirt of the streets was engrained into the creases around his eyes. He had a rough, do-it-yourself haircut. He was perhaps thirty years old – a touch younger than Kanoski. A drab, colourless T-shirt hung over his thin chest and his legs were draped in a faded tartan sarong. He looked deliriously happy and proud to have delivered his charges safely, though he said nothing. He just grinned.

'Is this Road 11 already? Quite a journey!' enthused Kanoski as he sprung to the ground.

'Did you see that taxi that nearly hit us?' asked Cadman ardently, as he pulled a 500 taka note from his wallet and thrust it into the puller's eager hand.

'Let's get a photo,' Kanoski suggested and handed his smartphone to the porter.

The two teachers clasped their arms around the puller, who grinned with them into the camera.

'Welcome back, sirs,' said the porter, handing back the phone and opening the door.

'I've got a good feeling about this course, Alex,' said Kanoski as the door closed behind them and the rickshaw eased its way back into the melee. 'Shall we grab a beer before we turn in?'

'Will they do a beer on a Friday, do you think?'

They found a roof terrace bar and settled into some comfortable armchairs. A small swimming pool shone its blue glow into the darkness. Above the drone of the streets came the clashing, banging and drilling sounds of the neighbouring construction site. Young workmen clambered barefoot, unprotected, across a network of bamboo scaffolding from within which the new concrete shell of some hotel or factory was emerging. Cadman watched them as they worked, wondering how they managed it in the unceasing wet heat.

'This hits the spot alright,' said Kanoski, settling back comfortably with his drink. 'So, tomorrow... I guess we should get some preparation done for Sunday, don't you?'

'Do you know anything about the students?'

'A bit. The Rector told me we've got some from National Security Intelligence, a handful from DGFI – I think that's military intelligence – and the rest are cops. What do you think of Mina, by the way? I'd give it one, wouldn't you?'

'Mina?'

'Jasmina. The Rector's daughter.'

'I didn't really think...'

'She's a cop.'

'What's their knowledge level? Do you know?'

'Last time I was out here they didn't know a thing. The cops were the worst. Like kids. They hadn't a clue, even though they were all in CT.'

'Then they're well-chosen students, aren't they? That's why we're here, after all. It'd be pretty pointless coming all this way if they already knew everything.'

'I suppose you're right, mate.' Kanoski clonked his empty beer glass onto the table and fingered the bill. 'Crikey. Twelve hundred.'

'That's alright, I'll get these.'

*

Back in his room, Cadman collapsed onto the crisp white sheets and listened to the muffled chaos of Dhaka's traffic seven floors below and the clatter of the workmen who seemed to be right outside his window. He thought of the rickshaw puller, wondering if he had a family and where they might live. His mind switched to his own boys and for a moment he considered ringing them, but before he could work out the time difference he had drifted off to sleep.

CHAPTER THREE

'What's that?' Kanoski asked.

'Fried eggs, sir,' the waiter replied, in a matter-of-fact manner that suggested he was unable to interpret the heavy tone of irritation in Kanoski's voice.

'They're not fried eggs, that's a bloody omelette, mate.'

'No, sir. Fried eggs,' the waiter insisted.

Kanoski looked at them for a long time and then sighed. 'Give them here,' he conceded.

'I don't know what's wrong with them, do you?' Cadman blurted, somewhat emotionally, pointing to the front page of *New Age*. 'It's got nothing to do with Nigeria and nothing to do with the French ambassador.'

'It's not the reaction that we should be looking at, it's the root cause,' responded Kanoski. 'What's wrong with the bloody French artist who drew the thing in the first place? That's what we should be asking.'

'It's terrorism, pure and simple. Boko Haram has claimed responsibility. Evil. I hope they hang the bastards. His wife and four members of staff were also burnt to death. They were probably Muslims. I'd like to run the investigation myself.' Cadman did not look up from the newspaper.

'The artist is responsible. When he insulted the Prophet, Peace be upon Him, he insulted all Muslims. The reaction is entirely predictable and understandable.' Kanoski spoke with the smooth assurance of an academic who knew his subject.

'Forty-seven people killed in riots in Pakistan. They would have been Muslims too. Do you think that's reasonable?'

A gentle female voice responded. 'It might not be reasonable, but it is to be expected. The Muslim world feels much anger at the West when it shows such indifference to the principles of Islam.'

Cadman looked up as Kanoski pushed aside his uneaten eggs. He had no idea how long she had been standing there and his mind raced as he tried to recall whether he'd said something he shouldn't have. 'Good morning, Jasmina. I'm sorry, I didn't see you there. Can I get you a coffee or anything? Tea?'

Jasmina remained standing. She wore a striking shirt and trouser suit of light cotton, turquoise and white, adorned with tiny sparkling stones that glittered, sending shards of light across the breakfast table. In the centre of her forehead was a turquoise circle, the size of a Ludo counter. Her hair rose in a gentle arch from her face, and then fell heavily across her shoulders.

'No. Thank you, sir,' she smiled. 'I won't stay. My father asked me to come to tell you that we will collect you from the hotel tomorrow morning. The opposition has declared a *hartal* because of this insulting French cartoon.'

'A strike,' Kanoski said quickly.

Jasmina looked at Kanoski. 'You know Bangladesh well, Mr Kanoski.'

'It's only right to study a country if you're going to work there,' Kanoski responded, leaning back in his chair.

Jasmina continued, 'But not everyone will abide by the opposition's declaration and then there will be demonstrations. The Police Staff College is in an area where there is often trouble. My father wants to ensure that nothing happens to his guests. He believes very much in this counter-terrorism course.'

She smiled. Her teeth were large and white, perfectly arranged. Cadman stood with his napkin in his hands. 'So do I,' he said.

*

'Do you play tennis, Alex?' asked Kanoski when Jasmina had left.

'Not really. I did at training school, but most of my sport just fell away when I joined CID.'

'That's a pity. I could have called old François le Celtic Frog and we could have made up a four. No worries. You're welcome to come and watch, mate.'

'You're playing today?'

'Certainly am. Mina and me are playing at the club at six. Come and have a cold one and watch.'

'I might well enjoy a beer later on. That sounds good.'

'How old do you reckon she is?'

'Jasmina? I don't know. A bit younger than my oldest boy. About twenty-seven?'

'I thought you probably had kids.'

'Yes. Two boys. Men.'

'I bet they miss their old dad when you're abroad?'

'I don't think so. I haven't seen them for a couple of years. I don't suppose they know I'm in Bangladesh. Unless their mother told them.'

'Their mother? That's a funny way to talk about your missus.'

'She's not my wife anymore.'

'Shit, mate. Divorced?'

'Yes. Not quite. Nearly.'

'Ah well. Better off without her, I reckon. You got grandkids?'

'No. The youngest boy's wife's pregnant.'

'The youngest boy's wife? You don't use their names? You've got to start to get to know your kids, Alex mate, otherwise you'll never see your grandkids.'

'It's awkward.' Cadman paused, studying Kanoski's face, before he said, 'You know what, Sam? I should know my kids better. There just might be some sense in that antipodean head of yours.'

'Something decent that the Brits left in my genes, do you mean?'

'You married, Sam?'

'Yep. Lisa. She's a cracker. Want to see a photo?'

*

When Kanoski appeared in the hotel foyer dressed for tennis, Cadman was again reminded of his sons. Alexander had been the more sporty of the two. He probably still was. Kanoski wore a garish orange basketball vest and loose green shorts. He looked young and vital; his strong brown calf muscles and forearms were decorated with a layer of virile blond down and his shirt hung straight and loose from a firm chest across a belly that showed no sign of existence.

'Do you want to walk or shall we get a rickshaw?' Cadman asked.

'No. The hotel will get us a car.'

'A car? I thought you were a rickshaw man?'

'Sometimes. But the car will have AC and it's bloody hot, mate.'

Cadman watched the younger man as he strolled to the reception desk and then returned.

'Car's coming now. Out the front,' Kanoski said.

Cadman looked at his own reflection, miniaturised in Kanoski's sunglasses. 'I've just thought of something I've forgotten to do tomorrow,' he said. 'I hope you don't mind. I can't get through the first session without it.'

'Shit, mate. You'd better crack on.' Kanoski looked towards the door. 'There's my car. I'll catch you at breakfast, Al.'

CHAPTER FOUR

The porter opened the car doors and the Rector eased himself out of the front passenger seat.

'Good morning, gentlemen,' he beamed as he shook their hands in turn, a slow, deliberate process with the same gentle pressure as the day before. He wore a smart dark blue uniform: a tight-fitting short-sleeved shirt adorned with epaulettes and badges and matching trousers. 'The *hartal* started at dawn this morning,' he continued, as the driver loaded their bags into the car. 'I'm not expecting any trouble. We might even arrive earlier than normal because there is less traffic. Still, it is better to be safe than sorry.'

'I'll go in the middle,' Kanoski offered as he, Cadman and Jasmina shuffled around each other at the rear doors. 'Nobody likes going in the middle.'

'That's very kind, Samuel,' Jasmina responded as she pressed in next to him. She pronounced each of the three syllables of his name with precision, slightly emphasising the 'U'.

They had waited inside the hotel until they had seen the car draw up, but even so Cadman's shirt had already begun to stick to him.

'It is the hottest time,' the Rector said, 'before the rains come. The temperature will climb over the next couple of weeks. When it rains you must come up to the village.'

'Yes, you must,' said Jasmina. 'It really is something to see. What are now all fields will be water as far as the eye can see.'

'How did the tennis go?' Cadman asked.

'We were unable to play, because of Samuel's shoulder, so we just had a juice and chatted. It was a pity that you couldn't join us, sir.'

'Please, call me Alex, Jasmina.'

'Oh no, sir. I cannot do that. You are a more senior police officer than I. The police in Bangladesh are quite traditional when it comes to rank. It is the same in the army. Something we inherited from the British, I think.'

'Something else the British invasion left. The Queen and stiff upper lip. Jolly Ho!' Kanoski contributed.

'You can expect everyone in the class to call you sir, Alex,' the Rector confirmed, 'though they may call Samuel by his name. Perhaps Mr Kanoski.'

'Jesus Christ. I've got to put up with everyone calling you sir for three weeks! Well, I'm not calling you sir, that's for sure.'

Jasmina giggled. 'Oh, your sense of humour, Samuel!'

Cadman could not take his eyes from the window. It was as if all life had been amplified: colours were brighter; noises were louder, jangling and reverberating; speeds were faster – everything seemed to be careering past him as he tried to take it all in. Spaces were reduced; life was touchable – a begging child tapping on the window with some strange necklace made of teeth or pieces of bone, his round, dark eyes peering insistently. Exotic writing looped across doorways. Old skinny men crouched, selling packets of cigarettes they had not sold the night before. A bearded, shirtless ancient dressed in a Gandhi-style loin cloth and carrying a crooked stave limped past, his tired eyes staying on the white man's face for a long time. A boy of about nine with a foot missing hurtled by on a crutch. There were many slim young men, dapper, clean shaven, upwardly mobile and confident. They wore Western dress, open-necked office shirts and dark trousers, and they strode purposefully between the moving vehicles, holding up a disdainful hand towards the drivers to ensure a clear passage. A few wore beards and white *topis*, with long white shirts. Women, dressed in a bewildering range of coloured long shirts and trousers, shuffled rapidly along in droves – glowing hues of blues, pinks and greens.

'You don't wear saris, Jasmina? The women in Bangladesh?'

'In the country we do. If you come to my village I'll wear one for you. Also on more formal occasions. But for everyday use, we find it much easier to wear these *shalwar kameez*.'

'*Shalwar kameez*,' Cadman mouthed silently.

They were crawling in traffic, hemmed in by rickshaws and decrepit, colourless buses which bore the scars of thousands of accidents: scrapes, dents, amputated bumpers and wheel arches, bodywork filled and pasted with fibreglass, patch upon patch, layer after layer. Kanoski's hot leg pressed against his own and the door jutted into his midriff, and Cadman squirmed to try and find some comfort.

'Do you like Dhaka?' asked Jasmina.

'I don't know. I don't hate it,' Cadman replied. 'It'll take some getting used to though. This is the first time I've been out during daylight. It's quite a city.'

'This is not the real Bangladesh, sir.' Jasmina leaned forward across Kanoski. 'The real Bangladesh is in the village. This is just like any city.'

They had stopped and the driver was talking to a man standing by the side of the road who was pointing back the way they had come. He was wearing a white military uniform, like that of a naval officer. They were speaking earnestly and the sailor bent and peered into the car. His eyes briefly met Cadman's before he looked down at his clipboard. Rickshaws, cars and buses streamed past them. The Rector snapped something at the man and then at the driver; the naval officer was clearly instructing them to go a different way. At last the driver looked over his shoulder, span the wheel and took the diversion.

'This is an inconvenience,' the Rector muttered, clearly embarrassed. 'There is a power-play taking place between the military and the police. A sort of cold war. Today, because of the *hartal*, they will not let us through the cantonment. This is a nuisance, because the Staff College is just the other side of there. The driver is a bit worried for our safety.' He rubbed his eyebrows with his finger and thumb as he spoke. 'It is just as well we left early. It will take us about forty-five minutes now. We will have to get permission today and we must go through the cantonment this evening, because there may be riots.'

'But everyone else went through,' Cadman pointed out. 'You wouldn't even know that it's a military base if there wasn't a guard. The road looks exactly the same beyond the barrier.'

'Something else left over from the British Empire, I suppose,' whined Kanoski.

'Yes, it's a little frustrating, isn't it? But in theory you should have permission, and if you get stopped...'

They had turned back the way they came. The road was straight and wide – a dual carriageway with a concrete surface and pavements either side. Flat-fronted factories rose to several storeys. There was a high central reservation upon which groups of urbane young men gathered, waiting for gaps in the traffic. Rickshaws dominated the road in front, behind and beside them, their pullers standing up in the saddles in the stop-start traffic. From this metropolitan highway they turned into a narrow lane of dry dirt that snaked this way then that, so that there was never more than 20 metres of road in view before the next sharp turn. Though it was two way, on the bends there was only room for one car to pass at a time and progress was made only by means of noisy cooperation between drivers, a business that involved shouting and waving and heavy-handed sounding of the horn. The cut-through was lined either side by workshops where bony men dressed only in shorts could be seen squatting in the gloom, welding or planing. Their products were displayed all along their route: wooden bedsteads and steel reinforcing rods for concrete buildings. Though the workshops seemed to be independent of each other, they all produced either wooden beds or steel mesh.

Their car crept a few metres forward, but would then meet another vehicle at a 90° bend and they were forced to reverse back before trying again. Heavy-looking tricycle rickshaws with large wooden flat-backs plied their way carefully amongst the cars, often being hauled along with a boy at the front and another behind, the rickshaw overladen with a ton of steel mesh, the ends of which oscillated dangerously close to unprotected arms and naked backs. On every other bend there was a little tea stand: an urn, an ancient man and a few deeply stained china cups. The vendors and customers sat good-naturedly, pinned by the traffic against the protruding backs of factories and walls of houses that seemed to have been thrown up randomly and to have seeped into the inner city byways as unpredictably as spilled liquid. It was these that determined and shaped the route of their passage, the very existence of which was under constant threat of disappearance from the ever-encroaching buildings.

The tiny lane finally began to widen before spilling out onto a major road junction. A market on the corner was running as if there was no strike. Open-topped hessian sacks of spices, dried chillies and pulses nestled against the legs of the ladies selling them, and brightly coloured cotton clothes dangled from makeshift stalls. They were trying to join another straight concrete dual carriageway that came from their left, but the traffic was virtually stationary and there was no sign of it giving way to them.

'All this traffic has come through the cantonment,' the Rector said. 'It is just two or three minutes that way. We would have saved much time if we could have gone through.'

'Is it far to the college?' Kanoski asked.

'No. But this traffic is extra busy here. I think there must be a demonstration nearby.'

They had edged into the slow-moving flow and the driver was now jerking on and off the accelerator, trying to make ground wherever he could. Each time there was a hold-up, he yanked the wheel in irritation, swapping lanes, blasting his horn at every rickshaw that slid in front of him. As he turned and spoke to the Rector, Cadman saw that a trickle of sweat ran from his sideburn and down his cheek.

'He is worried about having white men in his car in this district,' said the Rector. 'He thinks it will make us a target of the demonstrators.'

'And will it?' asked Cadman.

'Possibly so. Though we're close to the Police Staff College, this is a volatile district. After all, the *hartal* is called because of the foreign cartoon. There have now been more than sixty people killed in Pakistan during demonstrations against it.'

'You'd have thought that the Danish one was enough. Why did the bloody French have to do one?' Kanoski's voice reminded Cadman of his children.

'It's a freedom of expression thing that we cherish in Europe,' he retorted.

'Insulting my religion is not freedom of speech, sir. It is wrong to insult the Prophet.' Kanoski edged away from Cadman and towards Jasmina as she spoke.

'These people have never even seen the cartoon. None of us has. We don't even know if it was insulting. Someone on Twitter, who hasn't seen it either, says it was and it triggers terrorism and rioting. The response is inappropriate and disproportionate.'

'Good luck with that one in class, sir,' Kanoski chuckled, looking at Jasmina.

There was a sudden crunch and simultaneous jolt. Craning to see through the screen, Cadman saw that the driver had collided with a rickshaw and that one of its rear mudguards was hooked into the front bumper of the car. The angry puller leapt from the machine, jerked it free and, wheeling it by the handlebars, manoeuvred it sideways to block any forward passage. The driver, his mouth open, looked left and right for a way out. His dark eyes were wide and alert. A grey bus hemmed in the nearside and the high central kerb, much too high to mount, blocked the offside. Behind, four or five rickshaws had already taken up any possible reversing space. Cadman's shoulders were squashed in against Kanoski's on one side and the window on the other, with no room to escape.

The driver rattled out something to the Rector, who did not reply. The puller, a sinewy man, perhaps in his mid-twenties, wore a colourless shirt and a grubby sarong. He spat angry words and wagged his finger aggressively as he walked towards the car. The driver wound down his window just enough for his slim arm to be able to protrude out and counter the puller's advance with a dismissive wave. The puller, glaring into the car, lashed out at the driver with amazing speed and accuracy, punching him full in the face, even through the limited window space. The driver's head jerked sideways with the force and he held it there, cringing in silence as the puller ranted noisily, shrugging his shoulders and flapping his hands in anger.

Cadman's shoulders were jammed against Kanoski's, his back hunched, the top of his head pushed into the roof lining. Turning his neck with difficulty, he saw through the rear screen that two of the rickshaw pullers from behind were stepping from their tricycles to join their angry compatriot.

One stooped and looked closely into the car, his face pressed against the glass, his hand shielding the morning sun so that he could see in. His juvenile moustache and curly lashes revealed that he was no more than a boy. Kanoski twitched as the thin teenager looked into his face and then hollered out to the others, waving them towards the window with an urgent gesture, just as a child at a zoo calls his parents. Abruptly, Jasmina wound down her window and shouted with irritation at all three pullers. She sounded like Cadman's wife scolding Alexander and Thomas. Far from being perturbed, the stooping youth grabbed the door handle and it flew open. Jasmina, under pressure from Kanoski's shoulders, tumbled out onto the road, landing inelegantly on her shoulder, her legs splayed. Cadman pushed open his own door.

'Stay there!' the Rector ordered. 'It is dangerous if you get out.'

The Rector skipped out of the car and the driver reached across and slammed the door behind him, using the additional space to cower away from the violence near his window. Cadman pulled his door closed. The Rector slid between the pullers and his daughter, who was picking herself up from the ground. Smiling, he confronted the first puller directly, looking into his face, moving his own head to prevent the man looking beyond him. Jasmina squeezed back into the car. The second two pullers drifted back to their own rickshaws and, the bus having now moved off, they disappeared into the traffic. The Rector's head was bobbing positively as he spoke to the man, whose demeanour was changing so that he appeared to be anxious to get away. Together, the two men walked to the rickshaw. The puller stepped up to his saddle and, with a slight wave to the Rector, he cycled off.

'What did you say to him?' asked Cadman as the elderly man got back into the car.

'I told him sorry,' the Rector said calmly. Then, speaking and gesticulating angrily to the driver, he urged him to continue the journey.

'He is admonishing the driver for not saying sorry immediately,' Jasmina explained. 'He's saying that the driver nearly got us all killed because he was too proud to apologise. One day I hope to be as good a police officer as my father.'

*

The Police Staff College was set back from the main road along a straight and narrow driveway. A young uniformed officer wearing baggy fatigues slumped at the raised barrier. An antique wooden-butted Lee Enfield bolt action .303 rifle, with fixed bayonet, was set alongside his leg. It stood straighter and taller than its bearer, though it must have been eighty years older. As their car approached, the sentry looked lazily into the vehicle then, abruptly, the rifle seemed to pull him upright and he came untidily to attention, throwing up a worried-looking salute.

They stopped under a grand portico beside a green square lake. Workmen carrying baskets of mud on their heads were building a low wall on the lakeshore and they paused and looked with interest, unabashed. The air was thick with humidity and Cadman could feel it in the palms of his hands the instant he stepped from the air conditioned car. It was the hottest he had ever been. Three large flags hung exhausted from the portico roof. They crumpled against the dreary sky and stroked the cracked concrete, the orange sun and green fields of the Bangladesh emblem portraying a colourful view that wasn't reflected in the grey reality of Dhaka.

'Good morning,' Cadman said to the workmen. They exchanged glances amongst themselves and then laughed with gusto.

'Welcome to the Police Staff College,' the Rector said proudly, as a young officer dressed smartly in dark blue uniform opened the door for them. 'I think you will find that this is a wonderful training facility.'

Kanoski sauntered close to Cadman. 'It's a fucking shit-hole, mate,' he whispered.

CHAPTER FIVE

Coming in from the sun, Cadman could just make out a dark reception desk where a gang of men, dressed in what looked like blue factory uniforms, were fussing over papers and boxes. Beside them, a sweeping curve of concrete staircase led up towards a dim first floor.

'Good morning,' Cadman said to the group, as he shuffled behind the Rector up the first few steps. They looked at each other in bewilderment.

The college was built on a grand scale, with large open floor spaces and lounge areas. A high, rather grand wooden desk was laid out with a selection of daily papers for students to stand and read. The roof of the portico was a wide and bright outdoor rest area, with views between the flags over the tepid lake, though it was unshaded and sweltering in the morning heat. In contrast, the functional rooms, arranged around the outside of the building, were small and dim. Several classrooms stood empty and dusty, home to broken furniture and old telephones. Conversations spilled out from hidden offices embedded into the darkened corners. On a second level there was a sumptuously fitted conference room where concentric horseshoes of plush chairs awaited delegates. There was a complete absence of students and Cadman guessed that their internationally funded course was the only one running. He got the impression of a business on the verge of collapse, or of a British high street in which the butcher's and baker's had closed and charity shops had opened in their stead.

Their own classroom was well appointed and had a computer, a screen and an impressive-looking sound system that included microphones for the students. A bottle of drinking water, a blue notepad and nameplates were neatly arranged on each desk. Mercifully, funding had stretched to air conditioning and the classroom was a haven of coolness. The Rector left them for one of the troglodytic offices and his voice could soon be heard amongst the others drifting through the heat. Jasmina settled into a desk in the front row.

A tall and powerful man of about sixty wearing a white lab coat bustled noisily into the room, the door swinging back and smashing into the wall under the charge of his wide shoulder. 'Coffee,' he barked, in English, as if it were an order, the two syllables delivered with equal strength and impact. His short jet black hair stood on end like the bristles of a shoe brush.

'Good morning,' Cadman said. 'Alex Cadman,' and he held out his hand. Kanoski sidled away and began unpacking his laptop.

The white-coated man took Cadman's hand seriously and squeezed it in his own giant brown fist. 'Tea,' he shouted, no hint of it being a question.

'Tea. Yes, tea, please,' Cadman replied. The serious face broke briefly into a white smile and the man blundered out again. Thirty seconds later he reappeared with a saucer on which rocked a china cup of steaming black tea with a chunk of fresh lime floating in it.

The students began to file sullenly into class, one every few minutes or so, dressed in smart plain clothes, the men in shirtsleeves with ties, the four women in *shalwar kameez*, two with their heads covered. Men and women alike looked nervous and untrusting. Cadman introduced himself to each one as they came through the door, smiling and shaking their hands, whilst Kanoski fiddled with the computer. The Rector returned; he made a brief formal introduction and then a pasty-faced, grubby-looking man in a grey-white ankle-length shirt appeared at the door. Looking towards the Rector, he raised his hand, by way of a vague salute, towards the lace-trimmed greying *topi* that rested atop a mass of curly hair, as he took up a position behind the lectern. Though beyond youth, he wore a boy's beard that curled sparsely across his cheeks and below his thin lips. His face was the same washed-out colour as his robe. His mouth opened and his throat rippled as if he were finding it difficult to speak. But instead of speech came a beautiful song, his voice pure and thin, high and nasal, in perfect pitch, like some exotic reed instrument. Finishing rather abruptly, the Imam read from the Holy Koran, first in Arabic then in English. He spoke mechanically, as if no one were listening, but also soothingly and hypnotically, gently urging Cadman, Kanoski and the students to find peace in their learning. Then it was over; he again acknowledged the Rector with his version of a salute and slopped unceremoniously out of the class. The Rector declared the Advanced Counter-Terrorism Course to be officially open before he again left the classroom for his dark office.

Cadman and Kanoski stood shoulder to shoulder at the front of the class. Twenty-odd pairs of suspicious dark eyes stared back at them.

'Good morning,' Cadman said, loudly, his voice cracking slightly.

The class was silent. A few heads nodded politely, nervously.

Kanoski spoke. 'Assalamu Alaikum,' he said, sincerely.

'Wa Alaikumus Salaam,' the class replied in respectful unison, Jasmina's voice loud amongst them.

Cadman retreated to the back of the class as Kanoski began an engaging lecture on the history and meaning of terrorism.

CHAPTER SIX

'Well, that wasn't so bad, was it?' Kanoski said, loosening his tie. They were standing under the portico waiting for their car.

'No, it was a good first day, Sam. You were good.'

'I've been studying terrorism long enough. It's what I do.'

A canvas-topped truck pulled up, its back open. Four bemused-looking police officers sat on benches that ran the length of the vehicle, like soldiers in a World War II film. Three of them carried Lee Enfields between their legs whilst one toted an AK47 assault rifle. They each wore different variations of police uniform: one in pale blue and dark blue camouflage fatigues, one in khaki, another in the smart dark blue that the Rector wore and that Cadman had seen around the college, and the fourth in a green and orange shirt not dissimilar to Kanoski's tennis outfit. The four young men looked towards the two teachers but avoided eye contact. Even when Cadman said 'Good evening' they evaded his efforts at communication.

'Ah, here is our escort,' the Rector said as he and Jasmina emerged through the doors behind them. On seeing the Rector from some unseen vantage point, the driver drew up and they followed the police truck up the road. 'We have permission to go through the cantonment, so this journey will be a short one, I trust.'

'How was the course, my darling?' he asked after they had pulled out of the campus.

'Oh, it was very good. Samuel has taught us about the history of terrorism. He is a very good teacher.' As she spoke she seemed to notice a speck on Kanoski's shoulder and brushed it off with her fingers.

Cadman stared blankly out at the streets. There was an industrious air, everyone seemingly carrying out some task or bustling to get somewhere. They swept through a right-hand turn and passed a market set beside a narrow track that spread out to flow into the major road. He recognised it as the same market they had passed that morning, at the end of the snake-like road they had been forced to take. Blank-faced men and women sat with hessian sacks between their legs, whilst shoppers wandered from sack to sack examining the contents. It was difficult to understand how there could be a general strike in progress.

'Has there been trouble today, sir?' he asked.

'Yes, there has,' the Rector replied. 'Ah! What is this?'

The traffic had slowed to a creep. Looking through the screen over the Rector's shoulder, Cadman could see a fire. People, mostly young men wearing T-shirts and jeans, were flocking towards or away from the scene. Some carried sticks. Cadman thought he saw a machete in the hand of one youth and could not prevent a shudder rippling across his back and up through his neck. They were jumping the central reservation and cutting across the road or appearing from small side turnings with excited, inquisitive faces.

Others pushed against the flow and disappeared down the same small alleys, either to avoid trouble or to arm themselves. The police officer with the AK47 was hanging by his left arm from the rear of the truck, peering over the roof to get a view. Cadman unwound his window and could hear shouting and chanting and the smell of burning rubber or of some synthetic material. Now they were engulfed by thick black smoke, which caught in his lungs and burnt. He quickly closed his window again.

It was a bus. Well ablaze, deep orange flames leapt from every glass-less window, and the smoke belched out in great rounded wafts. All around it, young men, some standing on abandoned cars, beat it with sticks as if it were some dying creature whose life they wanted to be a part of destroying. There were cheers each time the flaying led to the smashing of a wing mirror or the perforation of a panel. The bodywork had turned a dull orange as though it had rusted at the sight of the fire. The police lorry continued slowly past, the officers waving frantically at the driver to stay close. Cadman could feel the heat of the flames through the glass and he put his palm to it to see how hot it had become. As he did so, he saw a person burning inside the bus. A small body – a child, a young woman, an old man – charred beyond recognition, brown and moist, a few odd wisps of hair amongst the sizzling flesh, the hands and arms curled in front of the face, steaming and smoking, fingers melded together into wide, meaty hooks that bubbled in the midst of the furnace. In front of the bus, a distraught woman lay screaming on the road in agony, half kneeling, reaching towards the bus with an outstretched hand and wide-open mouth as if in some melodrama. Two younger women, in shocking pink and blue trouser suits, knelt either side of her, holding her back, sobbing with her. Suddenly, the bus rocked and fell on its side amidst a victorious cheer.

There was silence inside the car as they entered the cantonment and the police escort peeled off. Cadman wanted to make a comment about the appropriateness of such killing and destruction of fellow men as a response to a cartoon, but he made it only to himself. A few moments later they were pulling up outside the hotel.

'These people are not patriots, Jasmina,' the Rector said. He spoke in the manner of a reprimand. He could have waited until Cadman and Kanoski had left the car, but had clearly chosen not to.

'No, Abu.'

'A protest against anti-Islamic literature is one thing. But to destroy public property is not patriotism. These fanatics do not love their country. That is one less bus that will be available to take these poor people to work after the *hartal* is over.'

CHAPTER SEVEN

It was too hot to sit outside. Just as they had arrived at the club, a few large drops of rain had fallen, and the full sky had looked then as if it might dowse the heat, but nothing had come of it. Frank Sutherland was waiting for them in the small downstairs dining room, sitting below one of the ceiling fans that were doing their level best to cool the space. The room was full of foreigners like them, eating English pub food from tables covered with red and white gingham cloths. Cadman noticed the same solitary woman he'd seen on his first night. As before, she was sitting with only her computer pad for company.

'Hi, fellas, how'd the first day go?'

'Good, thanks, Frank,' said Cadman, shaking the project manager's hand. 'This guy's good, you know.'

'Yeah, he's not bad for a whingeing Australian, is he?'

'You bought the beers yet?' Kanoski replied.

'And you're on tomorrow, right, Alex?'

'Yep. The IRA. That's my thing really. It's terrorism you can understand. They just want their country back.'

'It usually comes down to territory in the end,' Kanoski said. 'Get out of Iraq, get out of Afghanistan and a lot of this Islamist terrorism will drift away. But it'll be replaced by another wave, sooner or later. Always is.'

The Bangladeshi waiter had already arrived and Sutherland ordered three Heinekens. 'Tennis the day after tomorrow, guys, if you're up for it,' he said, apparently satisfied with the updates on the course. 'Akbar and Jasmina are keen to win back some pride for Bangladesh.'

'Alex doesn't play,' Kanoski said quickly, 'but count me in.'

'I thought your shoulder was playing you up?' asked Cadman.

'Get out of it, mate! There's nothing wrong with my shoulder. I just thought I'd have a crack at Mina.'

Sutherland nearly dropped his beer. 'Oh, for Christ's sake! Don't you go upsetting the Rector's daughter, Sam. How much do I not need one of my tutors being involved in a scandal?'

'She's a grown woman. And very beautiful at that – when she bothers.'

'She's also, as you well know, the daughter of the main sponsor of this project in Bangladesh. If we lose the support of the Police Staff College, we might as well all pack up and go home.'

'And there's Jasmina's reputation to think of too,' Cadman added. 'I don't think you should take her friendliness as a come-on. She's just being hospitable. She's not just a local, she's our hostess.'

'Sam-u-el,' said Kanoski, mouthing the syllables slowly. 'I love the way she says my name.'

'You should be careful. There are cases where women who bring shame on their family have been punished. I'm talking about abductions, mutilations, beatings. And murders.'

'Christ. You coppers. Do you ever unwind?'

'Just drop it, Sam,' Sutherland said. 'Alex is right. Jasmina trusts you. Don't let her down.'

'You know there was a body in that bus today, don't you?' Cadman said suddenly.

'Like I say. Coppers. They never unwind. Especially Brits.'

'A body? There's been no reports of any deaths on the TV,' Sutherland replied.

'Well, there might not be much left of it to find. But I saw it. And I saw the grieving mother. Or sister, or daughter, whatever she was.'

'Well, I never saw any bodies.'

'It was my side of the car. I tell you what, I'm pretty sure Akbar saw it too.'

'He never said.' Kanoski spoke without moving his beer can from his lips.

'No. He didn't. I think he just wanted to protect his daughter.'

'But Mina's a cop.'

'She's also his daughter.'

'Don't pretend you care,' Kanoski said with spite.

'What are you talking about?'

'You haven't called your own kids in years. I'm sure you don't care about someone else's. She's too young for you, mate, let's face it.'

Cadman stood and Kanoski too rose to his feet. Cadman looked up at the young Australian who backed away, knocking his green wrought iron chair over. Sutherland stepped in between them. 'Come on, guys. Enough.'

Cadman's mobile phone rattled into life on the table and he swept it up and walked over to the perimeter wall.

'Hello, Joe,' he said, running his finger along one of the blades of the razor wire. 'Just in time.'

'Hello, guv. Just thought I'd update you on progress. Mr Thorogood's authorised an online operation. I can't say more than that on this. But we've started dialogues with a couple of the most tasty-looking nominals. One in particular looks interesting. Calls himself Higher Ground. An angry young man looking for a cause. He'll be dangerous if he finds one. An anti-globalisation agenda.'

'Any terrorism?'

'Er, no, guv.'

'So why SO15? Remind me again why Counter-Terrorism Command are involved?'

'It's just that…'

Cadman watched Sutherland pick up Kanoski's chair and the two of them sat down at the table. Kanoski looked towards Cadman and smiled unconvincingly, as if Sutherland had told him to do so. 'Look, Joe,' Cadman said into the phone, 'I've got plenty on my hands here. Stick at it for the time being. When I get back we'll see if we can't offload this load of old crap to the Public Order Intelligence Unit, alright?'

CHAPTER EIGHT

'So, this morning we're going to be talking about the terrorist group the IRA. The Irish Republican Army.' Cadman clicked onto his first slide and turned his back for a moment to check that it had appeared on the screen. 'The IRA…' he started.

'Or Indian Republican Army.'

'Pardon?' Cadman turned towards the class. 'Did somebody say something?'

A young man at the back of the class had his arm in the air. Cadman walked nearer to him and looked at his name plate. 'Shah-ja-han,' he read aloud, syllable by syllable.

'Yes, sir. IRA also stands for Indian Republican Army.'

Cadman looked over to where Kanoski was sitting, but the academic was preoccupied with something on his shoe and did not make eye contact. 'Well, I must admit that I've never heard of the Indian Republican Army. Can you tell us something about them?'

'They were inspired by the Irish Republican Army. They took their name from them. Like the Irish, the Indian Republican Army was also trying to get you out of our country.'

Some of the class members looked down at their laps. 'Well, it wasn't me…' Cadman started.

Shahjahan continued. His wide, flat face was full of earnestness. 'It was the British invaders, sir, who had occupied India by force and are responsible for what we find in the Indian subcontinent today.' Cadman thought he heard Kanoski laugh.

'Well, I think that the Raj wasn't quite like that…'

'It was quite like that, sir. Gandhiji led the passive non-cooperation movement, but in Chittagong there was a heroic violent uprising against the British police cantonment. Just as in Ireland, we Bengalis wanted our country back and not all of us were happy to wait for Gandhiji. Taking their inspiration from the Easter Uprising of 1916, the Indian Republican Army seized the armoury in 1930. They were just boys, sir, but they outwitted the British.'

Cadman looked up at his slide for inspiration. It was a photograph of some 1970s wall graffiti in Belfast that said, 'If you are not confused, you don't understand the situation.'

'Chittagong is in present-day Bangladesh, sir,' Shahjahan finished.

'Well, thanks, Shahjahan. You've told me something I knew nothing about. I was about to talk about the motivating factors for the terrorism committed by the IRA, so it's great to hear that these factors mean something to Bangladeshi police officers today.'

'It didn't end there, sir,' Jasmina called out.

Cadman shrugged slightly and indicated that she should continue.

'The final act was by a national heroine: Pritilata. After the Indian Republican Army had all been captured she made a lone suicide attack on the European Club in Pahartali.'

'Well, this is even more evidence of their ideological links to the Irish Republican Army. Their terrorism was also characterised by martyrdom. The hunger strikes of…'

'They weren't terrorists, sir,' she said flatly, 'they were freedom fighters. Pritilata was a freedom fighter.'

Cadman looked at her and then again at his slide: *If you are not confused, you don't understand the situation.* He turned again towards Jasmina but did not speak.

The pause was long enough to be noticeable. His face was hot and he felt sure it was reddening. 'Is the air conditioning on?' he asked and there were a few titters from one or two of the bowed heads of the students.

Kanoski stood up at the back of the class. 'Well, this is an interesting debate that always crops up in counter-terrorism courses. The maxim "one man's terrorist is another man's freedom fighter", whilst overused, is nevertheless central to your understanding of the issues and Alex and I are delighted that our inputs have drawn this out of you so early in the course.' He paused with his right index finger hooked over his top lip and then said, 'During Alex's presentation on the IRA, look for the indicators that suggest whether they were terrorists or freedom fighters and we'll return to this theme after tea. OK?' He cast his learned eyes about the class and there was a general murmuring of approval. Heads that had been fixed on their laps were now facing the front again. 'That's great,' Kanoski concluded, 'so thanks, Shahjahan. And, of course, thanks, Jasmina.'

*

'Chicken,' the white-coated man shouted, his hair standing proudly. 'Rice. Naan. Dhal.' He smiled broadly, his arms hanging downwards as if they had nothing to do.

A glorious aroma of spices filled the immense dining hall, the size of an aircraft hangar. A buffet lunch was laid out on a white-clothed table. In striking contrast to the delicious smell, the food lacked colour, everything being a similar hue of dirty yellow-brown. There was an absence of steam and the dishes, displayed in oblong aluminium tins as in a school, had a stagnant, tepid look. Three or four long, wide tables, each able to seat about forty or fifty diners, were laid. Ceiling fans the size of helicopter rotor blades swept efficiently through the warm air. The students were all hanging back from the food and Kanoski had disappeared, so Cadman helped himself to a little of each of the unappetising dishes and wandered vaguely towards the dining tables. His host quickly overtook him and, his arms back in use again, pulled out the chair at the head of the table.

The students were not slow to join Cadman and he was soon surrounded by a quiet throng of enthusiastic eaters, their heads bent towards their food. He bit into the chicken curry, served on the bone, and instantly discovered that all the colour was in the taste. Rich blends of spices – turmeric, cumin, coriander and chilli – excited his palate. The chicken, cooked to perfection, fell easily from the carcass. He scooped some dhal onto the stodgy-looking rice and, using a spoon as the students did, took a mouthful. Again, the taste was superb; the garlic in the lentils was smooth and rounded and the pieces of fried onion and dried chilli were aromatic, not pungent. The thin naan bread was light, buttery and flavoursome. Food that looked as if it should be served in a prison tasted better than any Indian restaurant he had ever been in. His host, laughing rather manically, surrounded his plate with little bowls, each with extra portions of the buffet food items. 'Chicken,' he yelled in his deep, rounded voice. 'Rice. Naan. Dhal.'

Shahjahan was the nearest student to him, sitting carefully and earnestly consuming his meal. For a long time Cadman ate in silence, wondering how to apologise for the behaviour of his country during its occupation of India, frightened of bringing up a subject about which he knew so little. 'Thank you for an excellent presentation on the IRA, sir,' Shahjahan said at last, as his plate was taken away. It was replaced by a small bowl of cold, sweet rice pudding. Cadman looked at his own full plate of food and realised that he was the only diner to have been provided with his own little bowls of extras. 'We found it useful to know the tactics that were used that time by the terrorists and the police to bring about the Good Friday Agreement. I think it remarkable that Martin McGuinness should now shake hands with Queen Elizabeth.'

'Well, thank you, Shahjahan, that's very kind of you to say so.'

'My seniors in the class have ordered me to apologise to you for my comments on the British occupation of India.'

'You needn't do that. The truth is that it did lead to a very good debate.'

'You must understand that, whilst I speak English, I do not know many words. This means I am direct in my speech.

This is normal, I think. But I am your friend, of course.'

'I like your directness, Shahjahan. I'm pleased that you're my friend. The point of this course is to learn. Please speak freely at any time.'

Kanoski joined them. His plate contained a piece of naan bread and some rice. 'What's that meat?' he asked, pointing to the bones on Cadman's side plate.

'Chicken curry. It's delicious. You should try it.'

'On the bone? I'm not sure about that. What's the soupy stuff?'

'Dhal. Lentils in spices and garlic.'

'Lentils? I don't think so.'

'Didn't you eat here last time?'

'No. I stayed in the class. I just thought I'd come over and find you.'

Shahjahan was hovering above his seat, his palms on the table, as he prepared to leave. 'Excuse me. I must pray before class starts again. Hospitality is very important to Bangladeshi people. When you come to our country, we must treat you like it is your home. It is important that we share our food with you. So welcome to Bangladesh, sir. You are our friend.'

'What was all that about?' Kanoski asked, dropping a half-eaten piece of naan bread onto his plate. 'That was all a bit formal, wasn't it?'

'Shahjahan was apologising for insulting me. He's a good lad.'

'He did launch into you, didn't he, mate!'

'And you enjoyed it!' Cadman laughed with Kanoski. 'Thanks for bailing me out there, Sam. I wasn't expecting that at all. Have you ever heard of the Indian Republican Army?'

'Honestly? No. Never. It didn't come up at all on the last course. Mind you, we didn't have a bloody ex-colonial trying to tell the locals what to do either!'

CHAPTER NINE

The following morning, the return to normality after the *hartal* was not immediately apparent. Road 11 street life seemed just the same as before. The old men still crouched with their packets of cigarettes; rickshaws streamed ceaselessly up and down, the pullers desperately trying to catch their eye as he and Kanoski waited for their car. Something warm touched his foot and, instinctively repelled, he withdrew it. A naked baby was crawling along the teeming concrete pavement, its bald head and chubby bare bottom the same shade of brown. A skinny woman, her cheeks drawn and lined, her teeth large, misshapen and protruding, her head covered with a shawl that she clasped to her slender belly, held out her hand for money. She nodded towards the child and then to her hand and from her mouth rattled a sound that was not words of any language, but a kind of resigned whimper for alms. She looked beyond the age of childbirth yet also could have been the child's mother. So unhealthy was she that she was ageless; she could have been anywhere between twenty and eighty. Cadman quickly slipped her a 100 taka note before the porter shooed her away.

'You don't want to start that,' observed Kanoski, 'you'll be mobbed now.'

'I know. I don't give money to beggars in England. It just encourages more. But a baby crawling naked up the road? Come on!'

'Life's back to normal alright! What did you give her?'

'A hundred.'

'Jesus Christ. She'll be waiting for us every day now.'

'I know. Sorry, mate. I couldn't help myself.'

'The driver's late. Shall we go inside?' They started to move back towards the cool of the hotel foyer when the now familiar low white Toyota cruised up to the kerb.

'You know what 100 taka is?' Cadman asked as the porter opened the car doors for them. 'It's about 80 pence!'

'But you can't give a dollar to every hungry person in Dhaka, mate!' Kanoski shouted through the noise of the traffic as he lowered himself into the front passenger seat.

'You could do on the money you earn from the UN!' said Jasmina. She was sitting in the back of the car.

'Good morning, Jasmina. We weren't expecting you today.' Cadman shook Jasmina's hand.

'You alright in the back there, Al? If there's not enough room for your legs…'

'I'm fine, thanks, Sam.'

'Good morning, Samuel.'

'Yeah. Morning, Mina. What you doing here?'

'My father gave me permission to travel in the car with you. The driver lives near to us, so it's easy for him to collect me before coming to the hotel – as long as you don't object.'

'Of course we don't. Whose car is it?'

'I'm not so sure we don't mind,' Kanoski cut across Cadman, 'we're not a bloody taxi service for the Bangladesh police.'

'Oh, Samuel. Your sense of humour.'

It was as they emerged from the cantonment that Cadman noticed the difference. Even then, it was only a gradual realisation that there were more women on the streets. The closer they got to the college, the more there seemed to be. Thousands of women, mostly young, many very beautiful, were walking with purpose along the sides of the road. Some held hands, like school friends making their way to class. Their *shalwar kameez* were as bright as the yellows, blues, greens and pinks of the fluorescent highlighting pens that Cadman used to mark his lesson plans. Some wore coordinating scarves draped loosely over their shiny hair, a sensual gesture that fascinated him. Though he assumed it was a symbol of piety, the immaculate and pretty faces smiling from beneath the veil were framed and projected by its presence. Perhaps it was worn simply as a means of protection from the sun.

'Beautiful aren't they, sir? Do you like the Bangladeshi fashion?'

'I'd never have said so,' Cadman replied guiltily. 'Where are they all going?'

'They are going to work.'

'Where?'

'They make clothes. Bangladesh is the second biggest producer of ready-made garments in the world,' she said with obvious pride.

'Exploitation,' said Kanoski.

'But these women want to work, Samuel. They would not give up their jobs for anything.'

'It's just slave labour,' Kanoski insisted. 'Global brands selling Bangladeshi clothes for a hundred times what they pay these girls.'

'But, Samuel, you don't want to pay more than a few dollars for your shorts or your tennis shirt. Why would you pay more, when you can buy a Bangladeshi-made shirt for such a low price?'

'Prices don't need to go up,' said Kanoski. 'Profits need to come down. They should invest in higher wages and some decent working conditions. It makes me bloody angry.'

'It's beyond me,' Cadman said. 'How did we emerge from the industrial revolution? Wish I knew. Think I'll stick to catching terrorists.'

'You're a bloody idiot, Cadman,' Kanoski retorted. 'Conditions in Britain only improved because of colonial slave labour. When the Brits didn't want to do it themselves, they got their bloody colonies to do it for them. Why the bloody hell do you think you took slaves from Africa? To pick your bloody cotton to make these things in the first place. Shahjahan was right. The Brits are responsible for this. Take a good look at all your beautiful slaves, Alex. They're something else the bloody Brits left behind.'

'Samuel! You're making it sound as if Alex is responsible. Say you're sorry.'

'You're an arse, Sam,' Cadman said, as the sentry came lugubriously to attention. 'But you don't need to say sorry. I get it. Ever since Shahjahan told me about the IRA yesterday, I've been wondering what on earth a British police officer is doing here teaching them about terrorism. We wouldn't go to Ireland and do it.'

'It's because they like the Yanks even less, mate.'

*

'You are a very honest man, sir,' Shahjahan said, as he and Cadman walked between the classroom and the dining hall.

On the lake, a boatman drifted past, kneeling in an old wooden barque that might have come from a romantic tableau on a restaurant calendar. He was carrying out some task that involved throwing a yellowy liquid from the boat into the lake, presumably to clear the water or feed the fish. But he did not take his eyes from Cadman wandering along in the heat. The remaining students walked in groups of two or three in front of or behind them, their heads towards the ground as they chatted.

Jasmina caught up with them as Shahjahan continued. 'I do not think the class was expecting that you would acknowledge the role of your country's foreign policy in creating terrorism.'

'No, this was remarkable, sir,' Jasmina said, as the two men parted to allow her between them. 'The class really enjoyed your lesson this morning. They are all talking about it now.'

'Well, I was simply reflecting my country's honesty,' said Cadman. 'Many Muslims believe that the UK and America have caused suffering and anger in the Islamic world. I just wanted to get that out in the open, because I don't think we could have a debate if you were all sitting there unable to mention what was on your minds. We call it the elephant in the room. If everyone can see there's an elephant in the room, then we should all acknowledge it, rather than trying to continue as if there was no elephant in the room.'

'An elephant in the room,' Shahjahan laughed. 'That is funny and clever.'

'I'm not a politician,' Cadman acknowledged. 'And the longer I'm here, the more I realise that. I'm a policeman. We're all cops together, regardless of our countries of origin. That's where our strength lies. I want us to be able to share our experience without being frightened of the elephant.'

'I had to deal with an elephant in a room once,' smiled Jasmina. 'Well, a garden. It was some kind of performing elephant and it had wandered away from a parade. It wanted food, we think. Of course, the police were called.'

'It is always the uniformed police that get the calls that nobody else can deal with,' agreed Shahjahan. 'That's why I changed.'

'I had to kill a sick rabbit once, with my truncheon,' said Cadman. 'Have you ever tried to kill a rabbit by bashing it on the head with a wooden stick?!' He mimed the action, his left hand grabbing an imaginary small throat, his right rising and falling. 'You're lucky if you can even hit the thing.'

By now they were filing along together helping themselves to the buffet lunch. Kanoski appeared carrying a bottle of Coke. He walked along behind them, looking between their backs at the food. Jasmina dropped some pieces of naan bread onto Cadman's plate. 'Of course, I didn't know what to do with the elephant,' she continued, 'but someone said that they eat… what do you call those groundnuts?' She hesitated a moment. 'Peanuts. So I called on the radio for some peanuts. "Where am I supposed to get peanuts from?" the radio controller asked me. "Get your own peanuts." Everyone heard it and was laughing at me for weeks. I felt so silly.' She laughed easily and Cadman and Shahjahan laughed with her.

'I don't have any animal stories,' Shahjahan said, 'but there is one funny story I remember.'

They had filled their plates and sat down with Kanoski. Shahjahan spooned in some dhal and said, 'There was this dead body under a blanket at the hospital. It was in the middle of the night. I was a new police officer and my seniors said to me that they were going to play a trick on another colleague.'

Their friendly host arrived and surrounded their plates with little bowls of food from the buffet. 'Chicken. Rice. Dhal.' Jasmina said something to him and he quickly placed more bread on Cadman's plate. 'Naan,' he shouted.

Shahjahan was enjoying his food and seemed to have lost his train of thought. 'So what happened then, Shahjahan?' Jasmina asked.

'So they told me to get under the blanket with the dead body and when my colleague arrived, I was to sit up and terrify him. So I got under the blanket and they left the room and it was very dark and it was just me and the dead body.'

Cadman scooped up some of the dhal with his naan bread. 'Ugh! I don't think I could have done that!'

'So there I was in the dark, lying under the blanket next to the dead body, waiting for my colleagues to come. Then suddenly the body moved.'

'Oh!' Jasmina gave a little scream.

'It turned to me and it said, "It's dark in here!"'

Cadman snorted and a piece of dhal shot across the table towards Kanoski. Jasmina reached over and mopped it up with her napkin. 'Of course, it was my colleague,' Shahjahan said, 'and I was the victim of the joke, after all!'

'I've got a great one about a body coming to life during the post mortem,' Cadman started.

Jasmina and Shahjahan crowded in.

'I've got to get back to class,' Kanoski said, putting the lid back on his Coke bottle. He scraped out his chair and walked away.

CHAPTER TEN

'What are this lot doing?' Kanoski asked, nodding towards the class. They were grouped around in little huddles, talking loudly amongst themselves, scribbling on large pieces of flip-chart paper.

Cadman looked up from his notes. 'I've split them into groups. I've asked them to identify a route to radicalisation.'

'What's the point of that?'

'If we can identify a person's pathway towards violent extremism, we can identify intervention points. If we can prevent a person from being radicalised we can prevent terrorism. We can save lives. That's what we're doing here. We're helping Bangladesh to save lives.'

'That's a copper's way of looking at radicalisation.'

'We are coppers.'

'So I've noticed.' Kanoski walked to his customary seat at the back of the class and began to scratch away at some notes of his own.

Cadman clapped his hands. 'OK. Everyone, please. What I'll do now is talk through the New York Police Department radicalisation model and we'll see where the similarities are with the steps you've identified.' He checked his notes and presentation as the students reluctantly left their groups and returned to their seats. 'Now the question is:

what turns unremarkable people into terrorists? According to the NYPD, there are four distinct phases that a person has to go through before they strap on a suicide vest and blow themselves and their innocent victims to kingdom come.'

Jasmina and Shahjahan, like many other students, were scribbling furiously. Cadman clicked on his next slide. 'These four phases are: Pre-Radicalisation, Self-Identification, Indoctrination and Jihadisation. The first, Pre-Radicalisation, is easy: that's where we all are now. It's where an unremarkable person is before he or she takes the first step towards violent extremism.'

Kanoski was scrutinising the slide from the back of the class. His pen moved around his page as if he were scribbling a diagram. 'So let's look at Self-Identification,' Cadman continued. 'This is where a trigger of some sort – it might be economic, social, political or personal – acts as the catalyst for a person to begin to identify with a new extremist ideology, for example, this might be Salafi Islam.' There were a few murmurs around the class. 'Any questions?' Cadman asked. He looked towards Shahjahan and then towards Jasmina.

'In starting to explore this new identity, people in this phase tend to move away from their old identity and gravitate towards…'

'I've got a question,' Kanoski said, standing up. Walking down the side of the classroom towards the front, he asked, 'How many people in this room have explored Salafi Islam?' No one answered. 'Let me ask this another way then,' he continued. 'You don't mind, do you, Alex?'

Cadman looked at Kanoski and then perched on the desk at the front of the class.

'How many people in this class have *not* explored Salafi Islam?' Again, no one answered. 'Just assuming for the sake of argument for a moment that most people in this class are Muslims, I think it's probably true that most of you have considered the tenets of Salafi Islam at some stage. Please put up your hand if you have considered Salafi Islam.'

About ten hands hovered in the air, and several more elbows rested on their desks in a half-hearted attempt at being raised. 'This is quite normal, of course. Now, how many of you consider yourself to have taken the first step towards violent extremism.' All of the hands went down.

'Some of the finest scholars in Islamic history have a Salafist perspective,' ventured Shahjahan.

'And here we see one of the many major failings of the NYPD model. Each of the steps can just as easily be attributed to an innocent, non-violent exploration of faith or ideology.'

Shahjahan began rapidly scribbling in his notebook. Several more of the students began to do likewise as Kanoski continued speaking. He was standing now in the centre of the front of the class, his back entirely to Cadman. 'The NYPD model is referred to as a phase model of radicalisation. It describes the phases one apparently passes through on the way to violent extremism. There are other phase models; the well-known terrorism writer Sageman uses one, for example. The problem is that he describes different phases, so the models instantly become useless. Imagine two different maps each purporting to lead from where you are to the same location. How would you know which to choose? Are they both right? They take you in different directions, so how can you be sure they'll both lead you where you want to go?'

Jasmina spoke up. 'So is there a way of identifying the pathway of radicalisation?'

Kanoski turned slightly towards Cadman, but, instead of making eye contact, he looked thoughtfully at a space somewhere near the power sockets beneath the screen, his right index finger hooked over his top lip, his elbow cradled in the palm of his left hand. 'The short answer is: no. But the longer answer is that a different type of model, a root cause model, is a much more academically sound model to use. The root cause model described by the Institute of International Relations, for example, concludes that macro factors, such as the British and US invasion of Iraq and Afghanistan, combine with micro factors, such as the loss of a loved one, leading to the polarisation of a person from mainstream society.'

'I can see that,' said Jasmina.

'It is right to acknowledge the impact of foreign invaders in Muslim lands upon Islamist extremism,' said Shahjahan.

Cadman's face shone red. Large damp patches on his shirt extended from under his arms. He silently eased his buttocks from the edge of the desk and turned off his presentation. The light in the room dipped, but Kanoski did not appear to notice. Cadman walked up the side of the class and occupied Kanoski's seat at the back of the class. 'This polarisation, the feeling that someone is at the fringes of society, leads to radicalisation. The person adopts radical views outside of those held by the majority at the centre. In turn, radicalisation leads to more polarisation and so on. Once isolated in this way, a person is very vulnerable to violent ideology and, at that stage, a personal catalyst could easily lead to a person choosing to use violence against mainstream society.'

'Then this is a model of radicalisation towards all kinds of violent extremism, not just Islamist extremism,' suggested Jasmina.

'Exactly. And this is precisely why it's appropriate to use this type of model when trying to explain radicalisation to a Muslim audience.'

'But I think that the police in New York have a good deal of experience in this matter?' Jasmina asked.

'The NYPD version is a typical policeman's model,' Kanoski said. 'It lacks academic rigour. It's based on minimal quantities of data obtained from a handful of police officers' interviews with terrorist suspects.'

Cadman rose. 'So you don't think accounts given by actual terrorists to trained police interviewers are worthy of consideration?'

'No,' Kanoski asserted, holding up his open palm in Cadman's direction, 'I don't think they're worth considering. The police analysis of them is ill conceived and a gross over-simplification.' Addressing the class, he said, 'If you want to understand the route from ordinary frustrated anger to violent extremism, ignore what Mr Cadman has just told you about the NYPD.'

Shahjahan scratched his pen across his paper in exaggerated heavy lines.

*

'Guv? Sorry to bother you. Joe Pritchard.'

Cadman had just finished his lunch and most of his companions had left for prayers. He walked from the cool of the huge dining hall out to the lakeside. The gardens here made the hot air seem fresher. A row of young palm trees bordered the water's edge close to where the workmen were building a small wall. Pink blossom trees, perhaps azaleas, had been neatly trimmed so that their canopies formed big cushions propped up by a slender central trunk. Bushes of bay were sculpted into near-perfect half-globes and a disciplined low hedge stood perfectly straight and still, awaiting inspection. He plucked at its leaves as he listened to Pritchard's report.

'There's a bit of an update on that guy Higher Ground. But I can't speak over this, I'm afraid, guv.'

'What's the point of calling me then, Joe?' He felt the impatience bubbling up into belligerence. He'd once grabbed Alexander, a grown man, by the scruff of the neck, for some stupid impertinence that he'd long since forgotten. He could still see the look of contempt in his son's face, staring back at him from above the big pink fist.

'I've made an appointment for you at the High Commission this evening, guv. Sorry, guv.'

'Alright, Joe. The job comes first. What do I need to do?'

'If you go to the High Commission for six o'clock, I'll call you there at quarter past. Sorry to be a pain in the neck, guv.'

*

Cadman took a car direct from the college and was grateful for the opportunity to be away from Kanoski. He felt angry at his own weakness in letting the Australian walk all over him in front of the students. He wondered why he hadn't done or said something. Perhaps he was too unsure about his status, his right to be there in a Bangladeshi police academy, telling them how to do things. And he'd taken it out on poor Joe Pritchard. 'Oh, Alex,' he said to himself with a sigh as they came to a halt beside a guarded vehicle entrance. A small plaque on the wall told him he had arrived.

The British High Commission turned out to be not much different from the other office buildings in Dhaka, and he felt a little disappointed not to be standing outside a colonial palace. The beige concrete perimeter wall was mouldy and bland, the reinforced entranceway no different from that at the club.

He went through a series of barriers and body searches carried out by Bangladeshi security guards and then found himself sitting in an austere waiting room looking at a big Foreign and Commonwealth Office crest on the wall. It struck him that any terrorist attack on the British High Commission would result in the deaths of Bangladeshi guards – they were the ones in the front line. A young Englishman appeared and led him upstairs. He was perhaps no older than Alexander and here he was, serving his country abroad.

'Why do they call it a high commission and not an embassy?' he asked the boy's heels as they climbed the shiny grey concrete stairs.

'Commonwealth,' the small dark head said without looking back. The syllables fell out in rapid round tones as he accelerated away. 'Here we are. Mobile phone, please.'

Cadman dropped his phone into a little wooden compartment and passed through an open thick steel door that looked like it belonged on a bank vault. He was ushered past two more young men drinking tea in an office that was as untidy as a sixth form common room and then was sitting at a modern wooden desk inside a tiny square room whose walls were covered with blue carpet. The thick door shushed into place behind him. His chaperone sat opposite him, eyes hovering over the secure phone. The impression of a small face was enhanced by a long fringe that hovered just above his eyes. The boy could do with a haircut.

'Met?' he asked with no interest.

'Met who?' Cadman asked, wondering if it should have been 'whom' in a high commission.

'Met Police. Are you Metropolitan Police?'

The phone rang before he could answer and then Pritchard was introducing himself.

'Hello, Joe. All well there? You must have been up early this morning to call me at lunchtime here?'

'I was, guv, but no problem. We're in a chat room with one of the activists on the list. That guy Higher Ground.'

'Are they talking about terrorism?'

'Well, no, not really, guv. But Mr Thorogood says…'

'Alright, Joe. It's not your fault. What have you got?'

'Not sure who he is yet but he's an angry man. He's anti-globalisation, though he uses jihadist rhetoric too, sort of sees the globals as another arm of the war against

Islam. Really having a go about the way they're taking over, especially in developing countries.'

'Is he advocating violence?'

'He's sort of working himself up to it, trying to justify it, but can't quite get his argument right. Like he's rehearsing his views. Talking to an old-fashioned communist he met at G8 and a third world debt activist called Daina.'

'Third world debt.'

'Yes. And guess where Daina is?'

'I don't know for Christ's sake, Joe.'

'Bangladesh.'

'Bangladesh?'

'He's got a hang-up about the way Bangladesh is developing. Sees Starbucks as the enemy.'

'Any signs of attack planning?'

'The Bengali guy and the communist are both espousing non-violent direct action but Higher Ground is definitely embracing violence as a means of achieving his agenda.'

Cadman pondered the young man's practised phrase. The boy sounded younger than Alexander, younger than the MI6 lad sitting with him. Did his sons speak so professionally, so articulately? 'How do you know?'

'MARX15 (the communist one) accuses him of being a religious nut and not a committed Marxist. He takes the Mickey out of him a bit, saying he should go and train with ISIS.' There was a pause and Cadman guessed that Pritchard was searching through a document. 'Higher Ground says, "Why should I risk dangerous travel abroad when I can train at home instead? Open Source Jihad is America's worst nightmare, a disaster for the repressive imperialistic nations."'

'So what's your point?'

'This mix of ideologies is what makes him different. And maybe dangerous. He seems to want to apply an Islamist justification of the use of violence to the threat of globalisation.'

'Good work, Joe. Keep me posted.'

'What's more,' Pritchard continued, not quite ready to stop, 'the pattern of speech is different from his previous chats, as if he's copied it word for word from somewhere. So we've done an online search and the bit about jihad is more or less a direct quote from *Inspire* – an old issue, granted. It's a piece about how to operate an AK47. So he's not only comparing his anti-globalisation stance to jihadism, he's actually seeking solutions from Al Qaeda's online stuff.'

'That's good work, Joe. Is there any sense that the threat is imminent?'

'No, guv. But I thought you'd want to know about it.'

'Is Dave Thorogood around?'

'No, guv, he's gone home.'

'Alright, Joe. Good stuff. Keep me posted.'

'Are we all done?' his chaperone asked when Cadman put down the phone.

'All done.'

He was whisked through the common room and downstairs. A young Bangladeshi man sat alone, waiting in front of the crest, his back to Cadman. Cadman was saying goodbye to his charmless host when the waiting man turned and looked at him.

'Shahjahan? How are you?'

Shahjahan looked puzzled for a moment, then stood. He looked unsure about something. 'Hello, sir. I am delighted to see you.' He held out his hand for shaking, but he was looking at Cadman's chaperone, who was holding the door open. Cadman slid past him and out into the hot night. Looking back from the darkness, he saw the two young men climb the stairs together.

*

Jasmina and Kanoski were waiting at the kerbside in the car. They were talking about the causes of terrorism and didn't pause as Cadman got in. On the way to the club, they drove past the upturned remains of the burnt-out bus. Cadman's head was thumping and he was looking forward to a cold beer at the club, even if it did mean spending time with Kanoski. At least he could sit and drink on his own whilst they played tennis.

'Was anybody killed in the *hartal*?' he asked, interrupting some question Jasmina was asking the academic about root cause models. He had long since stopped listening to their conversation and instead sat glued to the window, the evening lights flicking past him like a migraine.

'No,' Jasmina replied. 'The newspaper said that seven vehicles were torched and that two policemen were attacked and injured, but there was no suggestion that anyone had been killed.'

'*Hartals* don't usually lead to deaths,' Kanoski put in.

Cadman did not reply. He had drifted into his own world, wondering about his boys, thinking of himself as the distraught father watching his sons burn only to find that their deaths were not even registered. He wanted to go home to his wife, but she would not be there. A sharp pain suddenly shot through his abdomen and he winced involuntarily at the acuteness of it, although it passed as quickly as it had arisen.

'Are you OK, sir?' Jasmina asked.

'Just tired,' he replied. 'Please call me Alex, Jasmina. At least out of the classroom.'

CHAPTER ELEVEN

The Rector was pristine in his whites; he looked like a Wimbledon player of the seventies. A wooden racquet would have been appropriate for his short shorts and tight Fred Perry-style shirt. Kanoski and Sutherland were both dressed garishly, whilst Jasmina wore loose-fitting white tracksuit trousers and sweatshirt. Once again her long hair was swept back into a ponytail and she wore the over-sized visor. Cadman leaned against the high wire fence that separated them from him and watched them play a few games. His mind wandered as he thought of Kanoski's behaviour in the classroom. One day he was a hero who'd come to Cadman's aid when he needed him, the next he had deliberately undermined him in front of the students. He pictured with embarrassment Shahjahan scratching out what the New York Police Department had learnt in favour of Kanoski's academic theories.

'Well done, Mina!' Kanoski called. Cadman looked up to see the Australian slap Jasmina's outstretched and uplifted palm with his own and then pull her into a celebratory hug. Cadman walked away.

The cool dining room was crowded and Cadman, seeking his own company, decided to brave the heat of the upstairs bar.

He was alone, except for a barman, who was watching a Bangladeshi news channel that was showing footage of burning vehicles and young men with sticks.

'A Heineken, please,' Cadman said.

'I have Fosters today too, sir?'

'Fosters?!' Cadman snorted. 'Australian beer? Brewed by convicts?'

'Heineken, sir?'

'Yes. Heineken, please.'

He picked a table at random. He had brought the next day's lesson plans with him and he sat with them on his lap without turning the pages. He had taken a few big swigs of beer, when he heard the voice of the American woman ordering a gin and tonic.

'Hello again,' he said, as she slid past him. She was wearing tailored trousers and a loose blouse that hung expensively from slender, square shoulders.

'Oh, hi,' she replied, smiling. 'We were about to talk the other night, weren't we?'

'Yes, you were interrupted by your call.'

'Oh, my daughter. I call when I can. There's good WiFi here. She has twin girls. I love to talk to them when I'm away. It gives me something to cling onto in this madness. I'm waiting for her now. They're in Boston. Do you have grandchildren? May I?'

Cadman stood up. 'Oh, of course. Yes, please join me. I'd like that. I've had a funny day.'

'Welcome to Bangladesh, honey. Can I get you a drink? Your beer looks almost done.'

'I'll have a Heineken, please.'

She called out the order to the barman. 'So?'

'So what?'

'So, do you have any grandchildren?'

'No. One on the way. My youngest son's wife… my youngest son Thomas and his wife Daniela have one on the way. About a month left to go, I think.'

'A boy or a girl?'

'I don't know. They haven't told me. I don't know if they know.'

'I'm Beverley,' she said, holding out a well-manicured hand with slender, slightly masculine fingers. The loose skin around the knuckles suggested she was a little older than Cadman had at first thought. 'I'm in water management. Trying to help Bangladesh manage the pollution and the loss of land to the shrimp industry. That sort of thing. My friends call me Lee. My husband used to call me Bev. He's dead, honey, you don't have to worry about him.'

'I'm Alex. My wife left me.' He said it simply, like she had. It was the first time he remembered saying it aloud.

'Alex! Why?!'

Cadman's beer arrived and he watched the waiter pour it for him. He was pleased to have something to do to fill the gap.

'I don't know,' he said.

'That's tough.'

'Not as bad as your husband dying.'

'I don't agree. I know why Jack died. Smoked himself to death. I've got the autopsy report. Lung cancer. It ain't easy, but I'd rather know than not. Another guy, maybe? Jack had a woman.'

'No. Not as I know of.'

'A girl? Is that better or worse? I don't know.'

'No. Nobody.'

'What does Thomas think? And Daniela? What do they think?'

'I've never asked them.'

'Oh, Alex, honey. You English guys. You wear it all inside.'

He took a sip from his beer and, as he did so, her computer tablet rang. 'Hi, honey!' she said and she swept off to a corner of the terrace and laid her long body out against one of the chairs. Her form described a more or less straight line, her backside on the edge of the seat, her slender legs stretched out, head reclined beyond the top of the chair-back. He picked up her drink and took it over to her table, then watched her take sips as she chatted. A deep, muscular pain gripped his stomach and he suddenly sat up and forward, clutching himself. It was stronger than before and lasted three or four seconds. Then it was gone again and, sweating, he downed his beer in one and looked up to see the barman already approaching with a fresh can and glass.

Presently he heard Jasmina's laugh on the stairs, as she made her way up to the bar with the others. 'So, we'll keep these new sides, shall we? You two will want your revenge against Samuel and me,' she giggled. 'Hi, Alex. Come and join us for a drink.'

'How's the beer, Alex?' Sutherland asked. 'Another?'

'I'd love a Heineken, thanks.'

'They serve Fosters also.'

'No, I prefer Heineken. Thanks.'

'Phew, it's hot up here,' Sutherland said, handing out orange juices. 'Shall we find a table downstairs?'

'It's very crowded,' Cadman said.

'Full of Brits eating fish and chips,' Kanoski said.

'They could just as easily be Australians,' Cadman pointed out. 'You eat fish and chips as well. Perhaps fish was all you could get on the prison ships.'

'What?' Kanoski put his drink down.

'Calm down, mate. Knowing that your granddad did twenty years at Port Arthur is bound to have radicalised you a bit. You're probably feeling polarised. I'm just pointing out the root causes.'

'Guys,' cut in Sutherland, 'this is sounding a bit personal. Come on, I don't need my two tutors falling out over fish and chips.'

'He knows what I'm talking about,' Cadman jabbed his beer towards Kanoski's chest, but, as he did so, his insides seemed to erupt. A massive bubbling somewhere in his lower intestine gurgled loudly up towards his stomach and a spasm gripped him like a big fist closing around tender internal organs. His face creased, his eyes closed and his knees buckled. He plonked his beer down on a table, clutching his abdomen with the other hand.

'Alex. It would be best to not drink any more beer,' the Rector said as both he and Jasmina leaned over him. 'Come and sit downstairs with us and have an orange juice. Perhaps we can get something to eat?'

It was gone again. Cadman opened his eyes and looked at the Rector and his daughter. He said, 'I don't know what you two are doing in here. Why would you want to be in here with us?'

Jasmina snapped at Cadman with ferocity. 'You think Bangladeshis should be banned from your foreigners' club?'

'No. That's not what I meant.'

'Like in the Raj? Is that what you want, Alex? You want your empire back? And your European Club with its sign "Dogs and Indians Not Allowed?"' She slammed her juice down on the table and disappeared down the stairs, her ponytail whipping behind her.

'That's not what I meant... What does she mean?' Cadman asked.

'The Indian Republican Army, the freedom fighter Pritilata,' Kanoski said. '"Dogs and Indians Not Allowed." That was the sign outside the European Club.'

'Rector, please,' Cadman begged, 'that's not what I meant at all, sir.'

'Look on the bright side, mate,' Kanoski chirped. 'She called you Alex.'

CHAPTER TWELVE

Cadman lay carefully on the edge of sleep, the cool of the air conditioning and of the sheets temporarily soothing him. His stomach felt sore and tender and he wondered if it was over. A creeping dull pain lurked on the left side of his belly. He took a sip of water from the bottle on his bedside cabinet.

On the other side of the planet, Alexander and Thomas were on duty in the Home Counties. Though neither had joined the Metropolitan Police, he was very proud of them. Perhaps their instinct to avoid London had been the right one. He had moved from London to bring up his family and they naturally wanted to police the area they knew. Why had he not made contact with them since their mother had left him? He knew that he 'wore it all inside' as his new friend had put it. Beverley's friendly, blunt words tumbled around inside his head the way that Bangladesh tumbled around inside his belly. He had never thought of his being deserted without explanation as being worse than if his wife had died. He didn't wish her dead, but he understood now how it might have been easier. Easier to explain. Easier to understand. As it was, he was left to presume that he bored her or made her unhappy in some way, but he didn't know what he'd done or not done. She'd said that she felt on the edges of the family once the boys joined the police, that she was no longer at their heart. She'd said they were all part of some police club and she was left on the outside.

Cadman awoke to the sound of his alarm. He had been sleeping very deeply. He pushed snooze and lay there drifting in and out of sleep. Now that he looked back on those ten minutes he could see exactly what had happened. He had harmlessly broken wind as he lay there curled up on his side – a soft, puffy fart that probably his wife would never have even noticed. It was not an explosion; that's not how it had happened. It was more as if that little trapped pocket of gas had been acting like a cork in a wine bottle that was lying on its side. When the cork came out, so the liquid flowed freely from the bottle. When you spill wine, you hope it will be white wine; red wine stains and seems to multiply as it spreads across the carpet. This liquid that seeped from him was equally damaging. As he dozed in those ten minutes, one little fart led to a growing pool of thick brown sludge that spread like a disease across and through the crisp white sheets. He didn't feel it until he put his hand in it to turn towards the alarm on his phone when it buzzed back into life.

He looked at his stinking, dripping hand in utter horror. 'Oh no,' he groaned aloud. Now he felt it down the back of his thighs and thick on the sheet. 'No! NO!!' The alarm blared louder and louder.

He sat up and dragged the liquid with him, infecting more of the snowy white sheet. He slid out of bed and the top sheet, as it must, drifted gently into the mess. The liquid ran down his thighs to his calves and smeared against the side of the bed. He tiptoed naked into the shower, and, using his soiled fingertips, eased the hose from its holder and turned on the water. The alarm, which he dared not touch until he was clean, seemed to be happily announcing his shame to the entire hotel. He sprayed his legs, backside and lower back. The rasping buzz was ripping through his brain – at last he cantered round to it and shut it off.

'Please, please, please,' he said to himself, opening each of the drawers in the wardrobe. 'Yes!' he whispered, as he discovered and then pulled on the fluffy white bath robe. He lifted one corner of the bedclothes and folded it into the middle of the bed, obscuring one quarter of his obscene, fetid mess. He repeated this for a second corner and could see that it had not yet soaked into the mattress. 'Thank Christ for that!' Folding in the next two corners, he rolled the whole lot up into a huge ball and slung it into the bath. Though he'd hidden it, he pictured the eager stain seeping treacherously out towards him.

He grabbed his key card from the little holder on the wall and sprinted out into the corridor. He ran along, past seven or eight doors before he found what he was looking for. One of the room doors was open, with a trolley of towels and toiletries outside. He rushed into the room and inside found one of the uniformed room cleaners gathering up a plate and cup from someone's late supper. 'Thank Christ you're a man,' he said.

'Come!' he said, and took hold of the boy by his arm. 'Come quickly! Please.' He dragged him off down the hallway, leaving the trolley outside the unfinished room. Reaching his own room again, he pushed the boy inside and, running to his wallet on the cabinet beside the bare mattress, Cadman pulled out 1000 taka. No, 2000. He thrust the money into the boy's hand and then led him to the bathroom. Cadman picked up the huge bundle of bed clothes, almost as big as the boy, and dropped it into the young arms, which extended automatically.

'Shit,' he said, pointing to his backside. 'Shit.'

The boy looked blankly, but whether he understood the cause or not, he did understand that he was to take the bundle away. Cadman slammed the door behind him and lent back against it in relief. Suddenly a sharp heat pierced his abdomen, his eyes clamped shut and he bent forward, his fists clenched. Ripping off the pristine white robe in panic, he shot nude into the bathroom and sank down on the toilet.

CHAPTER THIRTEEN

'How you feeling, mate?' Kanoski and he stood outside the hotel. It was very early morning and the heat had not yet percolated through the dull, cloudless sky. Instead it simmered above them in the monochrome grey, almost touchable.

'I'm better thanks, Sam. I think I can make this journey.'

'Did you take the loperamide?'

'Yes. I'm not risking anything.'

'It can cause stomach cramps sometimes, but it usually holds it in.'

'Then it'll do what I need it to. I can cope with cramps. I just need the diarrhoea to stop.'

The road was calm and there were few rickshaws to be seen. When the driver appeared in the car, he was alone. 'No Jasmina?' Cadman asked.

'She went ahead yesterday evening with Akbar. They wanted to make sure everything at the house was ready. They've not been up there for a couple of weeks.'

'Six hours of just you and me then. That'll be nice.'

With no English-speaking guide, Cadman had no idea in which direction they were heading. There was no discernible difference between boroughs or neighbourhoods; a map would have been useless to them. The chaos with which he had become increasingly familiar seemed to be homogenous, spread evenly and thickly across the city.

Crossing a low-sided railway bridge, Cadman looked down a steep embankment at a dark green train, stationary at a platform. The roof of every carriage was full of young men, at least twenty to a car, maybe more. They sat on the curving camber of the roof, their hands around their ankles, as calmly as if they were inside, waiting for the train to pull away. Cadman half expected to see a ticket collector wandering along amongst them. He vaguely wondered how they would get to the toilet if they needed it. He had horrific images of himself having to crouch by the side of the road if the loperamide capsules didn't do their job. Only bottled water had passed his lips since he had left the club two nights ago.

They did not speak for an hour or more. Then there was a break in the incessant collection of houses, shops, shacks and people: a tiny fleck of green field and the briefest glimpse of a distant horizon. It seemed to herald a thaw in their relations and Kanoski spoke at last.

'Do you think she'll forgive you?'

'I don't know. I hope so. I meant no harm at all.'

'She didn't speak in class yesterday.'

'What did you tell her about me?'

'Just that you were unwell. I think she understood.'

'She probably thought I was hungover.'

'No. I told her that you had…'

'You didn't! I told you that in confidence.'

'I told her that you had an upset stomach. That's all. Bangladeshis know that it happens to visitors.'

'How long is the journey?' Cadman asked the driver, who made no reply. He didn't seem to have realised that Cadman was talking to him and Cadman imagined that all he could hear was the 'bar-bar' of a barbarian. Cadman held out his arm so that the driver could see and tapped his wristwatch. The driver smiled and nodded at the wrist briefly, barely taking his eyes from the road. Then there was another break in the building line, this time larger: several flat paddy fields and a longer stretch of misty grey sky. There was a roundabout where sleepy rickshaw pullers waited for fares and men sipped tea in little roadside huts. After that, the traffic thinned and they began to drive faster, bumping along at a decent pace.

'Shouldn't take too long now that we're moving a bit,' Kanoski said.

Abruptly, the driver pulled into a petrol station. Instead of walking directly to the pumps, he came around and opened Cadman's door. Cadman climbed stiffly out. The driver took him by the arm and led him some 50 metres across a forecourt and then pointed out an unmistakeable drawing of a little black man on a green wooden door – toilets! As the driver walked away, Cadman gingerly lifted a grubby latch and went inside.

'How was it for you?' Kanoski asked, as Cadman crossed the forecourt again some five minutes later. He was waiting outside the car.

'I couldn't go. I think that's good news!'

Kanoski handed Cadman a hot, sweet and milky coffee; it was just right for his tender stomach. 'The driver bought it, not me,' Kanoski said, frowning into the little plastic cup.

They were now clear of central Dhaka and in an altogether more suburban area. The air was cool, carrying with it a freshness that Cadman had not experienced since he had arrived in Bangladesh. An orderly row of three-wheeled baby taxis, dark green with black vinyl roofs, scuttled like bugs towards the pumps. Beyond them the road was lined with tall and lush trees. In the early morning light, vapour could be seen rising in shimmering waves from their canopies. The driver returned smiling, holding out his empty cup for them to slot theirs into. Cadman finished his last drop whilst Kanoski threw his coffee onto the dry sand.

'Swap?' Kanoski asked, lowering himself into the front seat without waiting for an answer. Cadman eased his tender and unreliable body into the back. He started to speak, but the sentence would not quite form itself and he abandoned it.

As they swung out of the forecourt, the huge blue bonnet of an immense truck was suddenly bearing down on them, on the wrong side of the road, filling the windscreen. Its claxon blasted in the face of the small Toyota. Kanoski threw himself to one side and flung his arms up in front of his face. The driver, unperturbed, tooted his horn and slid carelessly onto the sandy track beside the road. The nearside tyre clattered and wobbled on the dry dirt. In a whoosh of blue and yellow paint the truck hurtled past, missing the Toyota's wing mirror by a mere centimetre. The driver nonchalantly swung back onto the road.

'What the hell?' Kanoski screamed at the driver, but his question went unfinished as he again shrank rapidly back from the windscreen and into his seat. This time the driver was himself on the wrong side of the road, so that his offside tyre was skipping through the dirt on the far side, as he overtook a heavy-looking pickup truck that was, in turn, overtaking a bus. Four workmen peered down from precarious perches on the back of the pickup, their faces inert. A baby taxi bumbling down the road towards them tweaked a little hooter and trundled down the remaining thin strip of rough sand, whistling against the leaves on the trees, its single front wheel wobbling. The youngster in the driving seat was so close that Cadman could have checked whether he'd brushed his teeth. Their own driver did not even glance towards his passengers.

'Glad you grabbed the front seat?' Cadman laughed.

'No, I'm bloody well not, mate.'

'Only another five hours.'

They passed many shops – shacks with great pyramids of fresh fruit and vegetables: watermelons, oranges, apples, coconuts, peppers and aubergines. Some of them boasted the heaviest bunches of succulent white grapes that Cadman had ever seen. Lorries loaded to the gunnels with hemp that bulged out of fat tarpaulins trundled along in front of them. On the verges, bamboo poles the length of lamp posts were stacked alongside great tubular bundles of logs and sticks. There was now no sign of the city and its suburbs; they were plunging through a flat, pale green landscape of paddies interspersed by small islands of healthy-looking darker green woods, amongst which little shacks and animal shelters rested. For some miles, a raised single-track railway line cut through the rice fields roughly parallel to the road. Men, women and children walked along it in both directions, alone or in little groups, some carrying loads on their heads.

'This road is higher than the fields,' Kanoski observed. 'I think that we're in the bit that floods.' The land he was talking about was vast. If he was right, everything in sight both sides of the road would be completely immersed, save for the railway line and the patches of woodland, which would become islets in a tremendous shallow lake.

'It will all look very different in a couple of weeks then.'

For an hour or more the paddies swept by until, without warning, the driver turned right into a single-track side road. It, too, was constructed on a high embankment overlooking paddy fields. Within a few metres they encountered a wide carpet of rice hay, obviously laid out on the road to dry. They drove across it and the farmer working to spread it by hand, a slim elderly man in a conical wicker hat, paid no attention to their passing. But the further they journied from the main road, the less accustomed to cars the people seemed to be. When the driver sounded his horn they started and leapt back, adults holding children clear of the passing menace.

The rice fields were divided into small oblongs, each not much bigger than an English suburban back garden, separated from each other by a narrow pathway, so that the whole resembled a perforated sheet of pale green postage stamps. Most of the patches had not yet been harvested, but where the rice had been cut, the field assumed a dull yellow colour, as if a stamp had been torn out from the middle of the sheet. Some of the little fields were given over to vegetables: peppers and aubergines, which hung bulging from their plants. Here and there were spread beside the road or draped down the embankment large tarpaulins, covered with bright red chilli peppers drying in the sun. Their acrid aroma infiltrated the car and made Cadman cough. A wave of embarrassment surged through him as the involuntary spasm made him lose control of his body for a moment. The loperamide plug did its job but, as the unpleasant sensation subsided, Cadman wondered why on earth he had so readily accepted this ridiculous assignment in this anarchic country where the food turned your stomach to pulp and the dead weren't counted.

He longed for the familiar security of London, his office at the Yard, his flat in Leytonstone – comfort. Not luxury; the 60s tower block in Broadway was way past its best with its flimsy partition walls and ill-considered windows; his office was freezing in winter and boiling in summer and there was nowhere near enough space to file the classified documents that he spent his life poring over. The canteen was too small for the workforce and the staff seemed to all be anti-police. But a cheese roll there did its job; it tasted good, it filled you up and it came out solid the next day. Comfort, that was all, not luxury. Not to be bumping along a South Asian backwater with a duplicitous Australian academic and a treacherous arsehole. His simple converted Victorian house with its spring garden, sprouting forget-me-nots, foxgloves and beautiful old roses. The rusty barbecue waiting to be fired up on summer evenings; hot dogs with his beautiful sons. His sons…

'Bloody hell!'

Cadman didn't respond to Kanoski's expletive. What was he doing pretending to be a teacher? He was a detective.

He'd never taught in his life, other than potty training his kids. Perhaps he should have learned a few of his own lessons? He'd never be as good as the arrogant Kanoski. He was a detective. A DCI. Counter-Terrorism Command. SO15, not a training sergeant. He couldn't abide that training sergeant type who avoided the real world, had given up operational work years ago, but who had been given guardianship of the moral compass of the British police – the responsibility to challenge the institutional racism that Cadman was supposed to represent. You have to be doing something to make a mistake, that was Cadman's philosophy. It's easy to be a wise old teacher who's never been provoked, never been lured into saying one wrong word by some smarmy civil rights geek. Something about it was all wrong. Cadman knew he had no capacity to be racist, he felt it inside himself. The police were not institutionally racist, they were institutionally terrified of being racist. That's why he'd been so keen to come. He had the portfolio for investigations in South Asia but had never been outside Europe. He was a good investigator; he could teach that, and he wanted to. But he also wanted to learn. To understand what it was like, to test himself. To see if he was racist. To confirm that he wasn't.

And yet he'd got it all wrong. He'd relaxed for just one moment and he'd blundered into a racist insult that had sent Jasmina running from the club, offended and in tears. And then he'd shit the bed.

They were snaking their way down a track not much wider than the car itself, between corrugated iron bungalows that gave the impression of being hurriedly thrown up and stacked against each other. Dung was drying outside each of the homes, either in golf ball-sized lumps squashed in rows onto slender wooden skewers, like shish kebabs, or perfectly round platters, the size of large pizzas. Here the farmers' smiles were tainted with bewilderment at the sight of the two white men. Hemmed in by the tapering raised track, pedestrians crammed against each other, their toes struggling for purchase on the steep bank that fell away behind them. They looked inquisitively in at the strangers; small children, whose eye level matched theirs, peered out from behind their parents' legs with startled expressions. There was nowhere else to dry the hay but on the dusty road surface and nowhere else to desiccate the chillies except on the escarpment either side. Ever narrower, they drove over many hay carpets until finally the track shrank down to little more than a footpath and, unable to go further, the driver jerked the car to a halt.

Chattering unintelligibly at his passengers, as if they could understand, he went to the boot and took out their bags. Kanoski jumped out whilst Cadman eased his delicate body upright, groaning as he did so. He stood with his hands on his hips in the intense unshaded heat and arched his back. He pulled his wet shirt away from his sticky shoulders. A group of children and young men gathered around the car, some of them slurping on juicy slices of watermelon. They smiled. The driver gave their bags to two of the group and the whole ran off, the bags disappearing with them down a pathway no more than a metre across, between the unpainted shacks of a rudimentary village. The driver was back in the car and was manoeuvring.

'What do you think?' asked Kanoski.

'We go with them, I suppose.'

The pathway led downhill through the shade of some big old trees, whose thick roots, shiny with wear, wormed in and out of the dry soil. Concentrating on his feet so as not to slip, and chasing his bag, Cadman had little time to take in his surroundings, though he was aware of being watched by a host of smiling faces that beamed out like lanterns from the gloomy hovels.

'We're there, I guess,' Kanoski called out from behind him.

Cadman stopped and Kanoski quickly came up beside him. 'But we've not been driving for even four hours, never mind five and a half,' Cadman observed. 'The roads must have been quicker than the Rector had planned for. I hope they're ready for us.'

'Hello!' an unseen man's voice called out, in English.

They had stopped near to a group of men sitting closely together in a dark shed, perhaps drinking or eating. Cadman got the impression of them sitting at a picnic table, as in an English pub garden. One of the men was grinning hard at him, whilst the others, less clear in the shadows, looked unsure, nervous even.

'Hello,' Cadman tentatively replied, uncertain now whether he'd heard correctly.

Now they all beamed. 'Hell-o!' the men sang in unison, laughing at themselves for their audacity.

Some movement ahead of them caught Cadman's eye. 'Our bags!' Kanoski pointed to the group of boys and youths who came briefly into view across a curve in the path and then disappeared again.

With Kanoski pushing at his shoulder, Cadman continued down the hill after them. 'Hell-o!' he heard the men shout again.

'Hello!' he cried back.

'Hello!' came another voice from another wooden room, followed by another peel of laughter.

'Hello!' responded Cadman as they hurried past.

'Hell-o!' came the happy chorus.

'Hell-o!' piped Cadman tunefully, every metre or so, not taking his eyes off the gnarled floor which dropped more and more steeply in front of them. All along the way he was enjoined by a chorus of friendly voices, practising their one word of English: 'Hell-o!'

'I wish you'd shut the fuck up,' said Kanoski, tumbling into Cadman's heels as he came suddenly to a halt at the bottom of the long dip. 'Can you see our bags?'

'Give it a rest, Sam. You sound like one of my kids embarrassed at his dad's singing.' Cadman surveyed the scene ahead of him. 'I don't think we're there yet.'

They were on the banks of a wide river. A group of four or five men, dressed in sarongs and sandals and wearing uneasy smiles, stood half in and half out of the water. The children had stopped on the muddy foreshore, which had been sprinkled with hay to allow a drier passage. Two of the older youths were placing their bags inside the corrugated iron hold of a low narrow barge. Dressed in Western-style T-shirts and shorts, their faces and hair immaculate, their teeth gleaming, the children bobbed up and down with glee. They were grouped in a shy semicircle around the white men's knees, smiling up at them, their long dark lashes fluttering.

Cadman looked down at the boy nearest to him. 'Do you want to take me to the boat?' he asked. He held out his hand to the boy who, with a questioning look, slid his little hand into the strange pink fist and began to lead Cadman across the hay. There was an instant battle for domination of his other hand and he arrived at the water's edge with three children hanging from each side.

One of the youths already on the boat helped Cadman step up onto the pointed wooden prow, which curved upwards from deck level. Once there, the boy pointed happily at their bags and handed Cadman an open, faded yellow umbrella. Then he pointed to one of two wicker stools on the deck and Cadman sat down. Kanoski stood hand on hips on the foreshore.

'Come on,' called Cadman, wiping his red cheeks on the shoulders of his damp shirt.

Kanoski picked his way across the hay and stood momentarily weighing up the safest way to clamber aboard. The youth offered his hand but Kanoski shrugged it off and stepped aboard unaided. At the rear of the boat, a diesel engine spluttered uncertainly to life. Taking his umbrella, Kanoski plonked himself down next to Cadman, who now flapped his hand in front of his face in a futile effort to fan himself. An older man with a neatly trimmed white beard came happily to shove them off but, when a quick comment was made by a surly-looking woman who stood up to her knees in the water, his face drained. The atmosphere had suddenly changed. The woman berated them all and waved her hand towards the village shacks. The smiles of the children waned and the men spoke in subdued, puzzled tones. The youth who had helped Cadman on board shouted over the corrugated roof to the helmsman, who killed the engine. The two of them sat with their umbrellas like wilting flowers whilst a gabbled conversation went on around them.

'Something's wrong,' said Kanoski nervously, sweat running down his cheeks from beneath his sunglasses.

Before Cadman could answer, the boy who had first held Cadman's hand came running pell-mell down the hill and onto the foreshore, clutching something green to his chest. The woman belted out an instruction to him. Approaching the boat, he reached out and handed each of the men a cold bottle of 7-Up.

The smiles and the launch were back on. The bearded man shoved off with aplomb, the barge drifted out into the river and the diesel engine was alive once more. The shore party waved and the children jumped up and down.

'Hell-o!' Cadman sang.

'Hell-o,' echoed the chorus, men and boys waving unabashedly.

'Shut the fuck up,' Kanoski growled, his 7-Up bottle fizzing as he twisted off the cap.

Kanoski reached for his camera, and the youth who stood beside them on the deck rapidly bent and handed him his bag. Then, 'Wow!' he exclaimed as they edged clear of the other craft at the water's edge.

'Isn't that something?' Cadman uttered, standing up.

The river was as wide as the Thames at Westminster and the water was the same greeny-grey colour. The banks were deep and they sloped rather steeply down to the water level, topped by a tree line and then big swathes of sky; the river ahead of them disappeared into the trees.

The banks and the shallow waters were alive with human activity. Men and boys swam or washed their bodies and hair. Women in saris carried baskets and bundles on their heads as they walked along the banks or wove their way towards the tree line. Others stood in the shallows, their saris dangling in the water as they stooped to wash clothes and metal pans and as they bent Cadman glimpsed their plump breasts. Every so often a man was cleaning a yellow cow, up to his chest in water, the beast passively enjoying the pampering. Their bow plunged through groups of ducks, too proud to hurry out of the way until the last moment, whilst boys and men swam for a closer view of the two umbrella-wielding pink men.

'Don't say it,' said Kanoski, and Cadman simply waved.

Narrow barges were tied up to long spindles of bamboo that protruded metres out of the water. Some of the boats were similar in construction to their own, which, apart from its elongated bow and stern, was not dissimilar from an English narrow boat. But others were giant enclosed arks that lay impassive on the shore like huge leathery cocoons, as big as a passenger aircraft's fuselage. These big boats were reminiscent of Chinese junks, with high pointed prows. The cocoons sat heavily over the stern end, giving the impression that they were unbalanced and should tip, or rock back and forth like a fairground swing boat. Smaller, canoe-like rowing boats lay sleeping on the beach, some upturned, others on their side. A neat file of children sat under one which had been propped up on its side with sticks, providing a shady eating place. More of these smaller boats bobbed in the water, their noses tied to the shore. Children stood in them, watching the toil that went on around them. Others plied up and down the river, each carrying a near naked fisherman, their dark brown skins shining as they crouched looking into the water.

Amidst all of this Cadman felt lonely. How he wished he could share this adventure with Tom and Alexander, their mother even. He remembered a sunny day when the four of them had taken out a rowing boat on the Serpentine, only to discover that Cadman couldn't row. Later the boys had paddled in the lido and they'd had a picnic next to Peter Pan's statue. They were happy then. Really they had been until about the time that he had joined the anti-terrorist branch, until about the time he'd investigated the suicide bombs on the London Underground. Until then he'd been just a copper, a detective doing his job and leaving it to the courts to decide. But that death and carnage on a summer day had made him see the world and his job differently. Being a detective on Counter-Terrorism Command was about keeping people alive, catching the terrorists before they killed. And he could feel the change in himself; he'd become dedicated to the cause. Before that he was indifferent as to whether his sons joined the police, even to the point of positively discouraging them. But after 7th July, everything changed. He talked to them about what he'd seen down there and how important it was to stop it from happening again. Before he knew what he'd done, he'd talked his sons into following his footsteps, had sold them an exciting and worthwhile career, an ideal. Once they were in, they talked about their arrests to each other, swapped their funny stories and confessed their fears in the face of violence. Their mother could not share in this, had no wish to know about the dangers that her husband had dragged her boys into. She felt outside of their circle, polarised. And now Cadman was alone, on perhaps one of the greatest adventures of his life, and he had no one with whom to share his experience except Kanoski.

They drifted into an ancient world that seemed to irradiate health and vitality. So perfect was this sensation, that Cadman felt he could have been in a theme park, a museum of a preserved rustic idyll. He was reminded of Walt Disney's portrayal of the halcyon days of a rural community at peace with itself, unknowingly on the brink of some disaster that the cinema goer knows is coming.

High concrete bridges sporadically spanned the river, their plain grey tubular stanchions plunging into the water like thick poles of bamboo. They added a touch of modernity, though even these spoke of rustic necessity. They were constructed plainly and honestly, not architecture but a means of crossing the river. They had the look of a child's simple design given limited choices of building blocks, or perhaps of military engineering. They were functional and were not adorned or decorated in any way. Fishing nets hung from their walls at either end. Single-storey corrugated iron houses were grouped together amongst the trees at the top of the embankment whilst the decaying façade of a Victorian silver stone fort could just be made out amongst the foliage. Through its once imposing arches and balustrades could be seen the tree canopy and blank sky.

On the banks, freshly cropped rice was laid out and women walked through it with a shuffling motion, presumably threshing. All around them, dried yellow hay was heaped or being heaped into stacks fashioned as pointed domes. These structures, in varying stages of completion, dotted the embankments, which were themselves yellow with layers of hay. Men and women lugged loads of rice on their shoulders and heads whilst great white cuboid bundles of wrapped crops were dotted about untidily.

The scene reminded Cadman of *The Hay Wain*. This seemed a ridiculous comparison to make, given that they were in the heart of Bangladesh, but it was this irresistible similarity with a classic image of rural England that led him to appreciate what he was seeing. He was watching the harvest, done by hand, but on a massive scale. He had been taken from a city struggling with its industrial revolution, to a countryside that had not yet witnessed the agricultural revolution.

'They've got to do all of this before it floods,' he observed, unable to stop himself looking up towards the sky.

'I've never seen anywhere like this in my life,' Kanoski enthused, his camera snapping manically.

The river was wider here and they were turning slowly, coasting towards the shore and a long concrete stairway of impressive dimensions that led to the top of the embankment. There was a gaggle of life around the bottom of the steps, whilst at the top stood a lone woman, tall and slim in a shocking pink sari and holding aloft a prim turquoise parasol.

A surge of embarrassment shot through Cadman, tumbling up through his belly and chest and hissing out from his open mouth as a loud sigh.

CHAPTER FOURTEEN

'Alex!' Jasmina cried out as the little band reached the top of the steps. 'I'm so pleased that you were well enough to travel. How are you?' She hugged Cadman and then stood back, bobbing slightly on the tips of her toes, as Kanoski joined them, his canvas overnight bag slung from his shoulder.

'Hey, Mina.'

'Samuel!'

Kanoski grasped her shoulders and kissed each cheek. 'What's with the Mary Poppins? You're not going all English on me, are you?'

'What do you mean?'

'The umbrella. It's a bit Empire, isn't it?'

'It's for the sun. My mother didn't like my skin to be too dark.'

'I thought she was dead.'

'Samuel! This is not a way to say hello.'

'Just joking, Mina.'

'Oh! Your sense of humour. Let me give your bag to one of the boys.'

'No, I'm good, thanks,' Kanoski said. 'I've already lost it once today. I've got my camera in here.'

'Where is your bag, Alex?'

'I don't know,' he said, looking around. 'One of these boys has it.'

'Good, let's go then. My father is looking forward to greeting you.'

Jasmina led the way through a dry mud street that was too narrow for three so that she had to keep turning her head and talking over her shoulder at her two visitors. She pointed out items of interest as she walked: the street food, the pharmacy, a place where they could buy craftwork, the mobile phone shop in case they needed a local SIM card. Brown faces, either beaming or bewildered, gazed back at them. The pink of Jasmina's sari was adorned with turquoise and black, the colours combining in zigzags, dots and triangles, with a black floral design along some of the edges. The skirt reached down to her feet, so that her heels were only occasionally visible as she walked. Over her left shoulder hung a swathe of material that reached as far as her calves before sweeping up and under her right arm. Her right shoulder, which otherwise would have been exposed, was covered by a tightly fitting turquoise T-shirt of similar material to the sari, except that it was not patterned. Cadman tried to recall whether the women working on the embankments had been wearing these little blouses. On her left arm she wore five or six plain gold bangles which, given that she was holding a parasol, had slid down towards her elbow. Her hair was tied like a whirl of smooth dark chocolate that might drip from her head at any moment.

'Do you like my sari, Alex?'

'You look wonderful, Jasmina.'

They were escorted by an ever-growing entourage of children, who skipped along behind them. When Cadman looked back, they wore guilty looks, as if they had been inspecting him from behind and exchanging comments about him. Cadman felt the urge to turn and shout 'boo!' but there was something in such an act which made him think of the stone-faced fort. He did not want to frighten them away, even in jest.

'Hello,' he said, smiling.

There was an instant fit of giggles, as if they had not really believed he could speak.

'Hell-o,' he crooned.

'Hello,' one of them plucked up the courage to reply.

'Hell-o,' Cadman led.

'Hell-o,' they all sang.

'Oh, for Christ's sake,' muttered Kanoski under his breath. 'We've had this all the way here.'

'Alex has a natural friendliness. I have also seen it in class,' she replied.

'Hell-o,' Cadman sang loudly, grinning into Kanoski's face, his teeth clenched, their noses almost touching.

The children rejoined with gusto: 'Hell-o!'

*

'Hello, Alex,' the Rector said. 'How are you feeling, my friend?' Cadman accepted the outstretched hand and the Rector held on to it. 'I am so pleased that you are well. I wanted you to see my village and now you are here. What did you think of the boat?'

'It was very special, Akbar. I feel privileged to have seen the river that way.'

'It is a great pity that you could not see the village after the rain. Then you would experience the real Bangladesh. Perhaps you will come next time?' He let Cadman's hand drop and, briefly touching his heart, shuffled to his seat. He wore a tartan sarong with sandals and an open-neck shirt.

'That looks a cool outfit,' Cadman observed. 'Perfect for this heat.'

'Would you like a sarong?' Jasmina asked. 'I can get you one later.'

'I doubt if it would fit me.'

'Sarongs fit everyone, Alex! They are just a roll of cloth. Anyway, you are not fat.'

'Well, yes then. Yes please. No photos though! My boys would kill me for showing them up.'

'And what about you, Samuel. You would look fine indeed in a sarong.'

'No thanks, Mina. I'll stick to my shorts, thanks.'

'So, we will have some lunch and you may rest,' the Rector announced. 'Then, when it is cooler, we will have a tour of the village. Are you able to eat, Alex?'

'I think so. I'm actually starting to feel hungry. I've not eaten since the day before yesterday.'

'Oh, Alex!' cried Jasmina, taking him by the arm and pulling him towards her. 'You poor thing. Come and let us eat immediately.'

The house was not grand. It was about twenty years old and resembled a Spanish villa of that era, having been built of concrete, with two large pillars which supported the comfortable terrace on the first floor upon which they were now standing. The exterior was painted stucco, white and pale blue, peeling around the tops and bottoms of the pillars and flaking in little dry patches here and there. Two portable fans provided a fragile coolness.

Jasmina led them into a small dining room directly from the terrace. The table was already laid; two Bangladeshi ladies stood nervously by the door, so that entering was a little difficult. Once seated, they began to serve.

'You have staff?' Kanoski asked.

'Yes, naturally,' the Rector replied.

'Great idea, I reckon,' Cadman said.

'You object to the hiring of staff, Samuel?' Jasmina asked.

'Well, yes. In my country nobody has staff. Egalitarianism is very important to the Australian people. It's why most of us don't want the Queen.'

'But I have dined with the Australian High Commissioner at his residence,' the Rector said. 'He has staff.'

'Bangladeshis,' Jasmina added.

'Well, I guess ambassadors and the Prime Minister and such do, but directors of training don't.'

'These ladies have no other work, Samuel. Without our paying them they would starve,' Jasmina said. 'They are our cooks.'

'I know. I just didn't think you…'

Jasmina cut across his answer. 'Are you able to eat, Alex? I know how ill you've been.'

'This is something special from Bangladesh,' the Rector announced. 'It's my favourite: little fishes curry.'

Cadman looked at the food that had been placed in front of him, served by the two cooks: a rather full plate of three small flat fish, rice, dhal and a vegetable curry of some sort. He was hungry and the food smelt good, but he didn't know how it was going to feel once it touched his mouth. He had a terrible feeling he was going to gag and that he would not be able to conceal it.

'You like aubergines, Alex?' Jasmina asked. 'They are very good at the moment.'

'I like them well enough,' Cadman replied honestly.

He picked at the little dry fish with his knife and fork. It was difficult to separate the sparse white flesh from the many bones. However, when he finally hoisted a forkful to his mouth, he was relieved to find that there was no regurgitation instinct. His mouth opened and the food was accepted.

'Mmm. That's delicious. Curry and fish and chips all in one little package. Well done, ladies. Thank you.' It was not until that point that he had noticed that the two cooks were standing anxiously awaiting his verdict. 'Thank you,' he said again to them, pronouncing the syllables slowly and clearly. 'Del-i-cious.'

Whether or not they understood his words, they understood his meaning and, clearly delighted, they backed out of the room, smiling and giving little bows.

'Thank you, Alex,' the Rector said quietly, 'your appreciation means much to them.'

'You're eating with your hands!' Cadman blurted. 'That's not fair!'

Both the Rector and his daughter were eating not just the dry fish, but the entire meal, with their fingers, which they grouped together around the thumb to make a dainty pointed utensil. Cadman was reminded of the burning body in the bus.

'This is custom,' the Rector said, nonplussed. 'You don't mind, do you, gentlemen?'

Cadman gingerly inserted some aubergine curry. The bitterness of the fruit was balanced by a sweetness that was infused with cinnamon and cumin. 'There is something that I must say,' he suddenly announced, rather formally.

'The elephant in the room?' Jasmina asked.

'Yes. I think it is the elephant in the room.'

'Then, as it was before, it is my job to lead it away,' Jasmina said.

'Why are you talking about elephants?' asked the Rector.

'Father, the elephant in the room is Alex's behaviour at the club.'

Kanoski looked up from his meal for the first time, his fork raised, his elbow on the table. His happy eyes connected with Cadman's.

Cadman went to speak, but Jasmina stopped him. 'I am sorry,' she said, looking towards her father and then back to Cadman. 'I am sorry that I did not give you the benefit of the doubt, Alex, before I ran away like an angry little girl. It is so clear to everyone that you are a friend, I should have spent longer understanding what you were trying to say.'

'My words were clumsy,' Cadman admitted.

'But you are entitled to be clumsy when you are with friends, Alex,' the Rector affirmed. 'Now is the elephant gone?'

'Not quite,' Cadman said. 'Let me just give it a big clumsy kick up the backside to make sure. When I asked why you would be in the club I only meant why would you want to be with clumsy people like me? That's all. Why would you choose to come and mix with us lot when you have these... these... beautiful people on your doorstep?'

'Was it an elephant or a bull?' Kanoski asked no one.

'I had never heard of that disgusting sign,' Cadman continued. 'I can barely bring myself to say it: "No Dogs or Indians".'

'Abu goes to the club to play tennis with friends,' Jasmina said. 'Since he introduced it to me, I also go there to play. But also to ensure that Bangladeshi people are seen as equals and not just as staff, Samuel. Yes, we have staff here, we give them jobs so they can live. But some of those rich people at the club, it's as if the occupation has never ended. They come to Bangladesh and make their dollars and their pounds and they sit in that club and mix with their own. They have never seen this village, Alex. They do not know Bangladesh. They don't speak our proud language. They don't try. Their self-imposed isolation and seclusion, it's insulting. I will continue to go to the club so that they can see a Bangladeshi woman playing tennis with a white man. To make them mix with me. So that they can experience passing me without asking me to get them a drink. The only Bangladeshis they know are those who serve them.'

'It seems the elephant may still be here,' the Rector observed.

'It is so important that you come here and see our village, Alex. And Samuel too. It is important that you accept our true being. That you accept our Bangladeshi hospitality. I am proud to eat with my fingers with you, my good friends. Abu is too. To show you with pride my true country, without feeling like… like a second-class Muslim who is only here to serve wealthy foreigners at the club.'

'I think I was trying to say the same thing, Jasmina.' Cadman raised his head from the food and his eyes met Jasmina's intense gaze.

'But your suggestion was that we would be better off outside the club,' she said.

'Only because we agree.'

'Then the answer is not to run from it. The answer is to dilute it. The answer is for me to be in the club as an equal paying member.'

'And because I didn't want you to see me argue with Sam.' Cadman looked towards Kanoski. 'That's the real elephant.'

'It's getting like a bloody zoo. What's your elephant?' Kanoski asked.

'You should know. But it doesn't matter,' Cadman said. 'It only matters that Jasmina and Akbar understand that I did not suggest that they weren't welcome in the club.'

The two cooks returned and began to clear the plates. One of them placed a large bowl of beige-coloured yoghurt in the centre of the table.

'And after this we shall have a tour of the village,' Jasmina announced. 'Samuel! You haven't touched your dinner.'

'I'm not really keen on fish,' Kanoski said.

CHAPTER FIFTEEN

Jasmina sat curled up next to her father on an upholstered bamboo sofa on the terrace. She had possession of his arm, which she wrapped herself around as a child with a comfort blanket. The two fans whirled noisily and Cadman's sarong flapped precariously. He hadn't dared to ask what one wore underneath, in case the answer had been nothing. He had made it through dinner, but he would never trust his backside to be uncovered again. Kanoski was showing them his photographs on a computer pad.

'How do you feel, Alex?' Jasmina asked.

'A little fragile, but I think I'm over it now.'

'And what did you think of the village?'

'Super,' Kanoski replied. 'Look at this one of the old guy's bungalow.'

'They seem so happy,' Cadman observed. 'Are they?'

'They have food and water and, as you have seen, in their small homes they have television and mobile telephones. What they lack is opportunity. Young men leave the village to become rickshaw pullers in Dhaka, because they think they can earn more money that way. Some of the pullers there are just country boys. They do not know the dangers of the roads even. The best the young women hope for is to leave their families for work in the clothing factories. There is no education here beyond an elementary level. They see what the world has to offer on their televisions, but these things are not open to them.'

'Yet you and Akbar have made good,' Cadman said.

'No, Alex. I was born wealthy, in comparison to these villagers. I have been to a good school and to Dhaka University. I did my MSc in business studies in London. Abu has worked hard to make a good life for me. We come back to the village as often as we can because we provide for so many people here. We have sent seventeen village children, mostly boys, but now some girls too, to Dhaka to get a full education. Some others do even more. Much of the land you see is owned by two doctors: an elderly man and his wife. After they graduated, they went to England to practise and they brought up their sons as English boys. They built a complete hospital here, right in this village, and each time they came they worked here and they saved many lives. They tried to save my mother, but there was nothing anyone could do about her breast cancer; even a rich foreigner would have died from it. That old man, Samuel…'

Kanoski held up his picture.

'He cut off his finger in the fields. He ran to the doctors at their home and they sewed it back on again and it worked.'

'So where are they now?'

'They are old. One of them is very sick. They can no longer do their work. They thought they could hand over the hospital to someone new. They tried to. All the equipment and everything. They tried to give it away. But nobody wants to come here. Now the hospital is gone.'

Cadman experienced a flash of vulnerability as she spoke. He had never lived more than fifteen minutes from an accident and emergency unit.

'This is why I don't like the club. The wealthy foreigners there don't know what the real Bangladesh is. They don't know that there is no hospital here. They sit in their designer clothes, made by poor village ladies who work in terrible, dangerous conditions, and they ask for a gin and tonic and use the WiFi to make calls to say what a tough place Dhaka is to live in.'

'You are forgetting that some of those club people are good friends of Bangladesh, my dear. There are some who are here for profit, but others who work for the NGOs and do their best to help. Or international organisations – like Alex and Samuel here – to teach us how to stop terrorism.'

'The way to stop terrorism is to stop the poverty and inequality. These are the root causes of terrorism in Bangladesh, Abu.'

'I agree,' Kanoski said. 'You can have all the arrest strategies you like, but unless you deal with the root causes, you'll only make a martyr of those you arrest and the problem will have been exacerbated.'

'I'm starting to think it's you that over-simplifies, not me,' Cadman said. 'The IRA, the Irish one I mean, only came to the negotiating table because police tactics had made it so difficult for them to operate. You have to investigate terrorism and arrest the perpetrators if you're going to prevent the killing of innocents.'

'So said Chief Inspector Heat.'

'Who's Chief Inspector Heat?'

'You've not read Conrad?'

'Conrad who?'

'Joseph Conrad, Alex,' said Jasmina. 'The British author.'

'He's Polish by birth,' Kanoski put in. 'Heat is one of his characters. He's happy catching thieves but is out of his depth with terrorists.'

Cadman studied Kanoski, who was still flicking through photographs and had not looked up as he spoke. 'You're an insulting...' Cadman stood and his chair rocked noisily. Looking down at his fists, he saw that the knuckles glistened creamy white under the dim lamps. 'I think I'll go to bed now, Akbar, if you don't mind. Before I say something clumsy again.'

CHAPTER SIXTEEN

The large ornate fan on Cadman's ceiling turned lazily. Little oblongs of grey light had formed around the edges of the window shutters. The bed was a large, unsprung slab of wood of the type he'd seen being made on his first morning abroad in Dhaka. Upon this a thin mattress had been laid, covered by an ageing but clean grey sheet. He had slept well and he now lay there happily, amongst friends. He turned and looked at his phone: not quite six. He heaved himself over onto his side and, as he began to curl, he suddenly remembered. Leaping from the bed, he put his hand between his buttocks. Dry. He pulled back the top sheet: nothing; spotless. He relaxed again and, pulling on his shirt and slipping into his sarong as if he'd been wearing it all his life, he padded out onto the roof. Akbar was already there, leaning against the rail, his back to Cadman, looking out above the tops of the palms towards the huge expanse of paddies.

'Good morning, Alex. I'm happy you are up early. This is the best time of the day. You look as if you would like a cup of tea.'

They descended the narrow staircase that led to the terrace and from there, the grander, curving one that led to the ground. Between the pillars was the doorway to the kitchen. The two ladies were there, crouched in their saris barefoot on the tiled floor, surrounded by six or seven large pewter pans, some of which had brown clay lids. They were without handles and were shaped like the baskets that story-book snake charmers use. The room was filled with the luscious, heady aroma of fresh garlic, onions and chilli. It was almost too much for the time of day but it made Cadman's mouth water nevertheless. The women looked up from their haunches and beamed at Cadman. One of them – plump, young and bashful – stood effortlessly, and Cadman's eyes were drawn to a gap in her sari that revealed a roll of young feminine flesh about her midriff. She moved towards a large pewter kettle that was steaming on one of two gas rings.

The tea was hot, strong and milky. Cadman and the Rector wandered out into the garden where there was a small circular seating area, surrounded by tall palms. As the grey sky lightened, strange bird calls, long and shrill, entertained them. The air was fresh and refreshing. Cadman imagined the soldiers on early duty parading at the fort. It must have been the best time of day for them too.

'You seem to have a happy life, Akbar. What a beautiful way to start the morning.'

'Yes. We are happy. Now that I am Rector of the college, my work is not too difficult. I worry about Jasmina, naturally.'

'My boys don't give me any cause for worry, thankfully.'

'Now they are men, you mean?'

'Yes. My work seems to be done.'

'No, Alex. Your sons need you still. There is no stage in life when a child cannot benefit from the knowledge of its father.'

'But they're married. They have lives of their own. They don't need me.'

'I disagree with you. I do not mean you should interfere. But your presence should be close, so that when it is needed, it is not like interference. You need to be close enough to be the first one they turn to.'

'But what can I teach them?'

'Not teach, guide. We all need guidance. If we are not there, our children get it elsewhere. Even when we are there, they get it elsewhere, but then we are there to provide balance.'

'But what if we're wrong? I don't know anything about life. Look at my marriage. I didn't even know she was unhappy.'

'Then you already know more than your children. Have you told them they need to consider the happiness of their wives? This is guidance.'

'Does Jasmina need much guiding?'

'Yes. It is one of the reasons we come here together. She uses the time to help the village, and I use it to listen to her opinions and her grievances, just to moderate her temperament. As you see, she is quick to judge. I think the English would say that she's a live wire.'

'She's just passionate about the things she cares for: the village, her country, equality. She's beautiful and intelligent. You must be a very proud father.'

'Yes, I am. And I would say the same if I were to meet your sons. You have a great influence over them. You need to continue to guide.'

'I'm not sure they are influenced by me. As they grew older they just seemed to be embarrassed by me.'

'They followed you into the police, did they not?'

'You and me have that in common,' Cadman observed. 'And we're alone.'

'You are more alone than I, Alex. I have my daughter.'

One of the cooks appeared carrying a teapot. She took Alex's cup and saucer from him and refilled it, then did the same for the Rector. As she faded away towards the house, the second appeared and placed a plate of sliced sponge cake in front of them.

Cadman raised his cup to the Rector. 'This is the life, Akbar! You don't want to change places, do you?'

'No. I could not live elsewhere now. But Jasmina could learn much from you.'

'Like what?'

'Your professional experience. Terrorism can become a theoretical subject, discussed only in terms of causes and grievances. But these discussions sometimes forget the truth. Have you ever been to the scene of a terrorist bomb, Alex?'

'Yes. London 7/7. Others…'

'Then you know what a bomb does. We have had bombs in Bangladesh. In 2001 I was the most senior officer on duty in Dhaka for the Bengali New Year celebrations. A bomb in the park killed ten people. More than fifty were injured. I will never forget what I saw there.'

'No. I feel the same about what I've seen.'

'It was I who arranged for you to come on this course, Alex.'

Cadman looked up from his tea. 'Oh?'

'Yes. I like Samuel very much. He has more knowledge about terrorism and its causes than anyone I have ever met.

And he is a good teacher; I could listen to his lectures for many hours. But he has not seen the severed head of a suicide bomber grimacing in its death mask. Nor witnessed people with no arms and legs, their clothing blown from them, screaming as they die. After the last course, I asked François if he would change the second to have a more practical, counter-terrorism aspect to it and some emphasis on victim care. I think you are the result of my request.'

'Well, I'm really grateful that you said something. I wouldn't have missed this experience for the world.'

'And we wouldn't want to miss your experience for the world. When I saw your CV, I arranged for Jasmina to attend the course. There are benefits to being the Rector of the Police Staff College.'

'It's been a really fantastic time. I'm so grateful for you having arranged it.'

'Well, don't thank me. You should thank Jasmina. My easy job is to be the host. Jasmina had to make the arrangements for the driver, the dinners and the boat and so on.'

'I would like to buy her a gift, to thank her,' Cadman said. Fingering his sarong, he said, 'She gave me this. Would it be appropriate for me to buy her a sari?'

'Yes, it would. Of course it would. I think a sari would make a wonderful gift. She could wear it at the course closing ceremony. Unless you are asking students to attend in uniform?'

'No. Plain clothes. Suit and tie for the men.'

'Then a sari would be appropriate.'

'How would I go about buying one?'

'Tell me what you want and I'll go and get it. I can easily go during the day while you are in class. There are factories close to the college.'

'There are benefits to being the Rector, aren't there?'

'Now, I think I can hear Jasmina and Samuel talking. It is time for breakfast.'

CHAPTER
SEVENTEEN

The white-coated host looked most concerned when Cadman walked into the dining hall with Shahjahan. He led Cadman away from the buffet and, pulling out his customary chair, sat him down without food. Thirty seconds later, he returned with a little bowl of rice and placed it next to Cadman's empty plate.

'Rice.' His face was full of anguish and even his boot brush hair seemed a little wilted.

'Chicken,' Cadman shouted at him.

'Chi-cken,' the host repeated doubtfully, slowly. He looked around the room for guidance.

'Chicken,' Cadman said again, straight faced. 'Chicken. Dhal. Rice. Naan.'

The host beamed pure happiness, his white teeth glistening. He skipped away and returned with three little bowls of food that he arranged around Cadman's plate. 'Chicken. Dhal. Naan,' he shouted. He stood upright and smiled at the rest of the students who were spread the length of the dining table, looking at him.

'Chicken. Dhal. Rice. Naan,' he announced to them, triumphantly, moving his fingers above the tops of the bowls with a flourish. The students dropped their cutlery and erupted into spontaneous applause amidst calls of congratulations and good health.

'What did Mr Kanoski tell you about my being ill, Shahjahan?' Cadman asked, when the fuss had died down.

'He just said that you were very ill,' Shahjahan said gravely. He took a spoonful of dhal and added, 'and that you had shit in your bed.'

Jasmina joined them. 'Hello,' Cadman greeted her happily.

'Hell-o!' she sang and then added, 'sir.'

'It was a marvellous weekend. Thank you.'

'What have you done?' Shahjahan asked.

'Mr Kanoski and I visited Jasmina's village. It was a great experience. You said I should get to see the real Bangladesh.'

'Now you must invite Jasmina to your village,' Shahjahan said.

'You are more than welcome to my village any time.'

'What is your village called, sir?' Shahjahan asked.

'London,' Cadman replied. 'Have you heard of it?'

Shahjahan looked at Cadman for a second and then smiled. 'Yes, I have been to your village,' he said.

'You said you studied there, Mina?' Cadman asked.

'Yes. I lived with my uncle – Abu's brother – in Limehouse. He sells clothes.'

'I like Limehouse,' Cadman said. 'My favourite Indian restaurant is there, though I think they're from Pakistan, not Bangladesh.'

'Better than Brick Lane?' Shahjahan asked.

'You know Brick Lane?'

'I know it well. My uncle has a restaurant there.'

'They're expensive these days. Brick Lane has changed over the last ten years.'

'I think my uncle is not a poor man,' Shahjahan smiled.

'So. When will you come to my village, Jasmina? And you, Shahjahan?'

'I am there in June,' Shahjahan said. 'Perhaps we can meet in my uncle's restaurant?'

'That would be great! And you, Jasmina?'

'I would love to come also,' she said, 'but I am thinking of visiting Australia.'

'Australia?'

'A masters course in terrorism. Samuel…' she glanced at Shahjahan as she corrected herself, 'Mr Kanoski says that he can get me a scholarship.'

'Are you sure he can?' Cadman asked.

'Alex! How can you say that?'

'Sorry. Sometimes people promise things they can't deliver.'

'I don't think Samuel would lie to me, sir.'

'Just be sure. That's all.'

'I will ask him again this evening. Now we must pray.'

They stood to leave and met Akbar helping himself from the buffet. 'Ah, Jasmina,' he said, a plate with a small portion of steamed rice in one hand and a large serving spoon in the other. 'I cannot make tennis this evening, after all. There is something I need to do. Will you apologise to Samuel and François for me? I will try to come for drinks later.'

'Yes, Abu. Of course.'

'Oh, and watch that backhand return. You are still slicing far too often.'

'Yes, Abu.'

Akbar winked at Cadman, so that Jasmina could see. 'I think she will beat Samuel soon, Alex, don't you?' Jasmina smiled with delight and kissed him on the cheek.

They left Akbar to his lunch; Jasmina and Shahjahan wandered off to the mosque whilst Cadman walked past the manicured trees and the green lake back towards the portico and main entrance. He practised his backhand return as he walked, imagining that he kept slicing the ball into the water. But his mind was only partially on tennis. As he swung his arm, he wondered what Kanoski had said, what promises he'd made and what lies he'd told.

*

Cadman looked at the phone. He would just have time for a snooze and a quick shower. He laid back on the bed with his arms behind his head and his eyes started closing. Then he shifted and looked again at his phone. It would be midday there. Sitting on the edge of his bed, he dialled.

'Not interference, guidance,' he said to himself as the phone at the other end rang.

'Tom? It's Dad.'

'Dad?'

'Yes, Dad. How are you?'

There was a rustling sound and perhaps a muffled whisper before his younger son's voice came back on. 'It's been two years, Dad.'

'I know. How are you? How's Daniela? Is she well?'

'Are you well, Dad?'

'Yes. I'm well. I'm in Dhaka.'

'Dakar? Where the rally is?'

'No, Dhaka,' – he pronounced it the way that Akbar had taught him – 'Bangladesh.' There was a silence. 'What shift are you on? I'm glad I caught you.'

'I'm lates.' Tom spoke hesitantly. 'I've got to leave soon. Is everything OK? Nothing's happened to Mum, has it?'

'No. Nothing's happened. I'm working in Dhaka and I thought I'd give you a call.'

'Two years?'

'Two years too long.' There was no reply. 'For me, anyway,' he added.

'Me too, Dad. Daniela's having a baby.'

'I know. Your mother told me. In an email.'

'You gonna come and visit us, Dad?'

'If that's an invitation, Tom.'

'Yes, it's an invitation. Don't make it harder, Dad.'

'I'm sorry, Tom. I don't know what to say. I want to see you. Daniela too. And the baby. I want to…'

'Dad, come and see us. We want you to come. When you get back from Bangladesh, call me. You haven't seen our house. You haven't seen the village. You'll love it, Dad. I'll buy you a beer. My long weekend is three weeks' time.'

Cadman wiped the moisture from his cheeks. 'I'll be there, Tom. I'll call you. When I get back from Dhaka.'

'I've got to go, Dad. Everything alright? Are you on your own?'

'No. Yes… I'm alright. I'm with friends. Don't worry about me. I didn't call to make you worry. I called to say I'm sorry.'

'Thanks, Dad. It's the best call I could have had. See you in three weeks?'

'Yes. Three weeks. Be careful, Tom. Wear your body armour.'

'Dad! You have to. There's no choice. I'm safe. See you in three weeks. Love you.'

'I love you too, Tom. Be careful, son.'

Cadman wiped the tears from his cheeks with the backs of his hands and stood. He undressed and dumped his clothes on the floor in one movement and stepped into the shower. He held his face up to the gushing water and felt it invigorate him. He squinted at the tiny bottle of gel, opened it and poured it over his head. Before long he realised that he was singing.

*

At the club, the barman, dressed in a white cotton jacket, was pouring a small bottle of tonic into a glass of gin on the table beside Beverley, who was talking to her family. Cadman sipped his beer and hoped that she would finish soon. He was proud of himself for calling Tom and he wanted to tell her about the call and to thank her for her frankness. She caught his eye, smiled and held up her hand. She wore a striking red silk blouse that went well with her tanned skin and blonde hair. The thin material clung to her breasts. He looked at his own phone on the table in front of him and span it with his finger. Suddenly it rang, making him jump: Akbar.

'Alex…'

The voice was very weak and Cadman could not recognise it. 'Hello? Akbar?'

'Alex…' This time it was softer still. It was a voice like Akbar's, but it was a mere gravelly whisper.

'Get Mina…'

'Akbar? Are you alright?

'Get Jasmina.'

Cadman tore down the stairs, through the dining room and onto the tennis court. Kanoski served and the ball smashed with a sting into Cadman's thigh.

'You did that deliberately!' he shouted without looking towards the Australian. 'Mina! It's your dad. Something's wrong.'

He held the phone to his ear. It was dead.

'Alex?' Jasmina's voice came breathlessly as she jogged to him. 'What is it?'

'Your dad just called. He's hurt.'

Kanoski sauntered over to the net. 'What's going on, Alex? I was winning.'

'Shut up, for Christ's sake, will you? It's Akbar. Something's wrong.'

Cadman's phone rang again. Akbar's voice croaked weakly, the words dragging themselves slowly and painfully from the depths of his throat. 'Alex… tell Mina… I'm trapped. Fourth floor.' There was a loud rattle and scraping sound and the words stopped coming.

'He's dropped his phone.'

'What did he say? What's wrong, Alex?' Jasmina snatched the phone and spoke urgently in Bangla. Then she stopped and just listened. Her dark eyes widened. 'I can hear women. Screams. Moaning.'

Cadman took the phone and keyed it onto loudspeaker. The

three of them huddled around as it wailed thinly, desperately, transmitting the unmistakable sound of human misery.

'A bomb,' Cadman said. 'But where?'

'He was only going home.'

'Can you locate his phone?'

'Me? I'm here.'

'Bangladesh. Can the police track a mobile phone?'

'NSI do that.'

'Shahjahan,' Kanoski said. 'He's National Intelligence.'

Cadman thumbed his way through his contacts. 'Here he is.' Jasmina's racquet clattered to the floor as she pulled Kanoski's bare arm to her, clinging as if to a comfort blanket, the way she had done with Akbar. 'Shahjahan? Alex Cadman.'

'Hello, sir. Are you well?'

'It's an emergency, Shahjahan. The Rector is hurt, trapped. We need to locate his mobile phone. Can you do that?'

'In cases of national emergency, yes, of course.'

'There's been a bomb. Akbar's trapped somewhere, he called me. He said fourth floor.'

'There has been no bomb in Bangladesh.'

'But he's hurt and trapped somewhere.'

'It was not a bomb. You should see a television. The building collapsed.'

They rushed up to the bar. Beverley and other club members were there, gathered around the old set, watching as the scene unfolded. A commentator gabbled away in Bangla. Grey dust billowed towards the cameras. Gigantic lumps and slices of concrete floors stacked precariously one above the other resembled an immense colourless lasagne. Spikes of rusty steel reinforcement protruded, bent and twisted. Women covered in a thick layer of dirt looked pathetically into the camera. Three arms and a sandal clad foot protruded here and there from the heavy mass, lifeless. Men ran up and down, calling and waving.

'Shhh!' Jasmina shouted to the group, holding up a hand. 'Let me listen.'

Cadman slid to the back of the crowd and whispered into the phone, 'What's happened, Shahjahan?'

'A clothing factory has collapsed.'

'Not a bomb?'

'No, sir. A collapse.'

'But the Rector was on his way home. He shouldn't have been in a clothing factory. Please can you try to locate his phone for us. For Jasmina, Shahjahan.'

'I think he was in the building, sir.'

'Why?'

'I saw him leave today. He told me he was going to buy a sari for his daughter.'

Jasmina was translating aloud: 'Eight storeys. It's called Mirpur Plaza. Savar district. One hundred people.' She spoke in urgent staccato, as if translating a telegram. 'Engineers from Dhaka University inspected cracks yesterday. Advised that the building was unsafe. The owner ordered workers to go back in.' She turned towards Kanoski, who stood expressionless at the back of the growing group. 'But Abu? Why would he be there? I don't think he was inside a clothing factory.'

'I think he was, Mina,' Cadman said, forcing his phone into his pocket.

'Has Shahjahan found him?'

'No. Akbar was buying a sari.'

'A sari? That's ridiculous.'

'For me. He was buying it for me. It was for… my wife.'

'Oh, Alex, no! No! Please say no.' She put her fists up to her face and fell in to Cadman's chest. Kanoski slid his arm between them and pulled her into a hug. Her oversized visor scuttled to the ground. 'But he's alive!' she shouted. 'He's alive! We know he is, we've spoken to him.' She pushed Kanoski away. 'Alex! We can find him! We can get NSI to trace the telephone and we can dig him out.'

'Sorry, Mina. NSI can't help.'

'He's the Rector of the Police Staff College. They must help.'

'They can't pinpoint his location. The best they could do is say that his phone is in the building.'

'What if he's not there?' Kanoski asked. 'Two things can happen at once.'

'Yes, Alex. Two things can happen at once. He might not be there. They should locate his phone.'

'He's there, Jasmina. He said he was on the fourth floor. He told Shahjahan he was going to buy a sari. He told me he would buy the sari for me. We heard the trapped women. He's there.'

'It wouldn't do any harm to check,' Kanoski said.

'No, Alex. It wouldn't do any harm.'

'It wouldn't do any good either. He's there. The best we can do is to go to the scene and dig. We can try calling his phone when we're there. We need water. Tools. Torches. Who'll be in charge of the search? Can you get us in on the rescue operation?'

'This is Bangladesh. Everyone will be helping. There will be no one to stop us. Maybe in a day or two…'

'And specialists? Search teams, X-ray, infrared, heat-seeking? Dogs?'

'The military has such things. But for now, we must just dig, Alex. We cannot wait.'

'OK. When we get there we can assess the scene.'

'Will we be safe?' Kanoski asked.

'Well, no, Samuel,' Jasmina said. 'Digging people from a collapsed building is not safe.'

'No, I meant politics-wise.'

'Politics?' Cadman demanded. 'Bloody politics?'

'It might not be safe for foreigners. Western multi-nationals are the cause of this. Their drive for bigger and bigger profit margins.'

Cadman grabbed the front of Kanoski's orange vest and twisted it in his fist. He thrust his face into the Australian's and Kanoski shrunk backwards towards Jasmina. Cadman opened his mouth. But then, saying nothing, he let go.

'What about the course?' Kanoski whined. 'The students will be back in class tomorrow.'

Cadman's phone rang and Jasmina jumped. She looked at Cadman in scared anticipation.

'It's a blocked number,' Cadman reported, turning his back.

'Guv? It's Joe. Our target has found his cause: some collapsed building in Dhaka? He says only violent jihad will avenge the deaths of the innocents.'

*

The TV images had not prepared them for the reality. The floors could be seen as collapsed layers, the roof and the levels beneath it dangling precariously, almost vertically. The whole front section of the factory complex had fallen forwards and sideways and seemed to be hanging from the back section of the building. It reminded Cadman of one of those little toy puppet men that maintain their integrity by the tautness of the strings and when you push the button in the base you slacken the strings and the man collapses; remove your finger and the strings tighten and the man stands up again. The building looked as if it could be hauled back up into shape if you could just attach strings to all the right places. The buildings either side were largely intact, as if a spiteful earthquake had targeted Mirpur Plaza, though the fall had dragged parts of its neighbours with it. Sections of concrete stairs protruded at ridiculous angles, leading nowhere, swaying.

It was immense; clearly there would have been more than one hundred girls working there. Furthermore, it had not been reduced to a pile of dust and rubble; it would not be as simple as digging. It would be more like descending into a cave halfway up a mountain that could be submerged in an avalanche at any second. First they would have to climb, or indeed descend, the mountain, for the rear section of the roof was intact and there were already hundreds of people up there, trying to clamber down to those trapped below them.

A huge pile of rubble – bricks, lumps of concrete and dust – lay in the road covering the entire width of the building: foothills before the mountain. There would be girls and parts of girls amongst this pile but it would have to be clambered over to reach the mountain itself. Perhaps the biggest danger was the fact that the collapse had not yet finished. Every now and then, with a terrific wrenching and grinding sound, a massive piece of concrete would drop, causing the whole lot to shift with gravity, churning up those inside and destroying those helpers unfortunate enough to be in the wrong place.

And there were thousands of people trying to help, with thousands more standing gawping. About fifty people were zigzagging up and down the sloping front of the mass, inexpert Sherpas leading the way for amateur rescue teams.

The heat was as intense as ever. Any survivors would need water quickly. And there were many, many survivors, a fact that was horribly apparent from the noise. There was no eerie silence here; the building itself seemed to be injured and it wept from every pore. Feminine cries of pain, tears of anguish, moans of despair seeped out through the rubble. They were childlike, girlish – whimpers and sobs.

Cadman stood for ten minutes without moving or speaking, taking it in. Jasmina was no different; despite her desperation to get on and do something to help the women and find Akbar, it simply took that long to absorb all the information. Eventually, it was the sight of a dusty young woman being pulled from the low pile of rubble, alive, that spurred them into action. They had to start somewhere. They ran together to the edge and clambered onto it. As soon as they were high enough for a body to be concealed they began to dig. They had a shovel, but you risked thrusting it through a girl's arm or head if you used it, so they crouched on their haunches and pulled and scraped with their bare hands. When a piece was too big, they worked together, heaving at it until they had managed to pull it aside. Cadman did not speak, but Jasmina spoke unceasingly in Bangla, talking to the bricks, encouraging those beneath to stay alive. Every few seconds he recognised the word, 'Abu'.

Even as he worked, Cadman knew that he would never forget the sound of the crying building. He would never overcome the sense of injustice at young women trying to drag themselves out of poverty being crushed by their workplace. Here were the severed hands that did the sewing, the broken feet that worked the treddles. And those that had not died were trapped inside and their weeping was all around him. And he knew that, somewhere, a young man calling himself Higher Ground felt the same sense of injustice and it had made him a terrorist.

CHAPTER
EIGHTEEN

Cadman's head wobbled on his chest and his neck instinctively whipped it upright. The rickshaw was swinging through a corner and his eyes flickered open enough to see the headlamps of the traffic that sailed past. The bolt of material slid with the motion of the vehicle and he pulled it more securely across his lap. His eyes rolled as the lids drooped over them and once again his head flopped down onto his chest.

'Please, mister.'

Cadman forced his eyes to open. The rickshaw puller's drawn face, silver-brown skin stretched across a small skull, was close to his own. The long stained teeth were exposed by a cautious smile. They had stopped.

'Please, mister. Club.'

Cadman tumbled onto his feet and found his wallet. He thrust five or six notes into the puller's hand and, clutching the heavy fabric, walked through the flow of pedestrians towards the painted reinforced steel door sunk into the non-descript concrete wall, a fading and mouldy cream colour. He pushed it confidently, but it jarred against him.

'Closed?' Cadman called out. An elderly man crouching

against the wall, a small oil lamp illuminating the six packets of Marlboro that he had arranged neatly on the floor in front of him, looked up hopefully at the sound. Cadman thrust a note into his hand, refusing the cigarettes that were offered in return. 'Closed?'

A heavy metallic bolt slid on the inside of the door, which swung out towards him. Cadman blew out through pursed lips, swayed back to allow the door to clear him and then began to enter, but instead walked straight into Beverley coming out.

'Hi, Alex, it's closed, honey. Look at the state of you!'

'I need a beer.'

'The club's closed. I was the last one – just made my call home.'

'He's dead. Four nights. I can't go back there again.'

'Oh, Alex, honey! That's just awful. I guess you've found him then?'

'Four nights.'

'Let's get you to your hotel and get you a beer. My car's just here.'

'No. I can't go to my hotel. It's… it's too…'

'Too far? I can drive you there. It's no problem, honey.'

'No, not too far! Too luxurious. I can't stand it!'

'I don't know what you're talking about. You're not quite with us, are you? Come back to my apartment. You can take a shower and I'll get you a beer and a snack and you can tell me all about it. I just picked up some Buds from the commissary today. You can drink them all if you want.'

*

Cadman stepped from the shower, dried himself and pulled the sarong around him.

'I'm sorry,' Beverley said, 'but I don't have anything that would fit you up top. It shouldn't take long for the T-shirt to dry though, if I ever get that dust out of it.' The Budweiser hissed as she opened it. She pushed it into his hand and he lifted it and drank. The second can hissed into life before he'd finished guzzling.

'My, you were thirsty, weren't you, honey?'

'Not thirsty, desperate for a drink. It's not the same thing. I've not slept for four nights.'

'You've been at the site for five solid days?'

'No. But I wish I had been.'

'Tell me all about it, honey.' Beverley cradled a gin and tonic and patted the sofa cushion next to her. His third Budweiser in his hand, Cadman fell into the seat and then his drinking hand rested comfortably on the top of the curve of his bare belly.

'When we left the club, we went to Jasmina's *thana* and collected what equipment we could. Ezaz – that's Akbar's driver, he's a good man – went off and filled the car with water. He did a good job. You can't imagine what it was like. I've been to bomb scenes – London and Belfast, awful, truly awful – but everyone's dead by the time I get there. Not this time; some were dead. Many were dead, of course. But more were alive. Trapped, in this heat. And you could hear their moans. Some didn't moan. They were fine, they'd survived. People were there to help. But it's too hot. The bloody country's too hot. They died anyway. They went from alive to dead. No water. Mina climbed all over looking for her dad. It was chaos. Hell. Hot as hell. People tried to help but they also wanted to find their own people. Wailing. Women were wailing, so were the men. Groans from inside and wailing outside. Then it would all move and there were screams. Grinding of people in hot concrete. Then more wailing and less groaning. We had a spade. What for? We weren't digging a bloody garden. We needed cranes. We needed the bloody Royal Engineers. The place must have been as big as Selfridges before. It was like a multi-storey car park that had just slid to the ground. People were bashed on their heads with giant lumps of concrete. Walls and ceilings and floors of concrete smashing and grinding you in the heat. And then you lived. You were in a hole and you lived. But your mouth's already full of concrete dust. You can't wait for a drink. You need it now. So you die. You lived and then you die in burning heat with your hands trapped and your mouth full of cement dust.'

Cadman opened his mouth wide and the tips of his fingers and thumb of his free hand came together and hovered shakily over the hole. Then he shrugged his shoulders and his head fell into the hand, the fingers opening into a heavy palm that ran across his forehead, over the top of his head and down across his neck behind the ear. He left it there, his elbow raised and pointing forward. His fingers gripped and pummelled the back of his neck. His eyes were closed.

'Akbar was in there. He made two calls. One the next day and one after that. He didn't say anything. Mina just got these calls from him. Looking for her dad and her phone rings and it says "Dad" on it. Abu. What's that? Torture? And so he sleeps there, in that rubble. Two nights at least he spends there. Boiling. And we can't find him. Two nights in hell. Nothing to drink, just a mouthful of concrete. We drank a car full of water, three of us. Us, not them. They were trapped and we drank the water. Then we stood down. I went back to the hotel and I was so tired and hot and it felt great to have a shower. It felt great! Can you believe what a selfish fucking pig I am? I had a fucking shower and a fucking club sandwich and a fucking cup of fucking tea. And Akbar's there still. And then I went to bed. I went to bed. What's the fucking point? You don't want to hear all this.'

The carbon dioxide escaped with another sharp hiss and Beverley plucked the warm can from his hand and pushed a full cold one in its place. She stroked his chest like a mother soothing a child, her fingers catching on the long grey hair.

'It was how I knew how bad it was for them. When I had enough I came home. I showered, I shaved, I ate, I slept – no I didn't sleep. But it felt good for a second, showering and washing that filth out of your hair, and you feel that you're doing a good job and you just need to rest and then you'll get back there and do a bit more. It's fucking ridiculous. Akbar's still in there. He's still in there now. He's dead at last. Thank Christ. Thank Mohammed, God Rest His Soul. Where's that sari?'

'Is that what it is? Don't worry, I've just put it by the washing machine. You can decide what to do with it later. It's really dirty, honey.'

'Four nights. Four nights I came back to the hotel and washed and drank and ate and Akbar still in hell. On the third day, Mina's phone rings and up it comes: "Abu". And he doesn't say anything. But when we called the phone, we heard it. We were close. Mina calls out for silence and there is a bit of silence and she calls the phone again. But so is everyone else. They're all calling their people's phones. So we hear his phone ringing and we start to crawl up to it and everyone else hears the phone ringing and they all crawl up as well. Who knows if it's Akbar? I don't. It's someone's mum or daughter or brother, so they all crawl up then the whole thing moves again. Some boy crawling up for his mum loses both legs. Ground off. He rolls down with his legs left behind inside with his mum, and his stumps squirting blood. And then in the slide there are people churned out as if they've fallen into a cement mixer. It all slides and people are produced and bits of people. And then Mina calls out, "There!" And there is a man. A dusty, skinny man in some sort of uniform and it does look like Akbar and he's sliding out with a slice of concrete and then he's being sucked in again and ground up and maybe he sees us. There was a look. An open eye. A dead eye. I don't know. A living eye, covered in grey dust. And a hand and the sari. The bloody sari comes out of the mixer in Akbar's hand. A hand that might have been Akbar's. A hand that might have been alive. And it threw out that sari. Ezaz puts it in the car. He says it was Akbar. But then he was taken in again. The slide stopped and we couldn't find him and we can't hear his phone and we don't hear it ever again and he's still in there. Now he's dead. They're all dead. They've stopped looking. It got better after that. More organised. Better equipment. Two more days. Two more nights of showers and sandwiches and white hotel sheets. The army took over. They've stopped looking for survivors now. They've got proper cranes and they're taking it all apart and counting the bodies. Four hundred. Four hundred dead people. It's like 9/11. And they don't count the bodies properly. The burning bus – never counted. He's still in there though. I couldn't bear to go back to the hotel without getting drunk. Too luxurious. So I left Mina and Ezaz and took a rickshaw to the club.' He looked around the smart living room for the first time and then his eyes came to rest on Beverley, perched neatly on the edge of the sofa, looking at him. 'And here I am.'

'Here you are, honey.' Beverley got up and walked into an adjoining room. He heard a fridge open and close and a beer being opened. Beverley handed him the cold can and sat back down close to him; her leg and shoulder were comforting where they touched his. 'You certainly didn't hold all that inside like an English guy, did you, Alex?'

'It's been driving me mad. I couldn't go back to my hotel room again tonight. I know he's dead now, but, well, he'd become my friend and I can't stand the thought of him in there while I'm tucked up between crisp white hotel sheets. I don't know how Mina's coping. She has colleagues and friends, I guess, but going back to the flat that she shared with Akbar all alone…'

'What did they do? For a job, I mean?'

'They were… are… police.'

'I didn't know. I've never spoken to them. I thought they worked at the club until that night you said hello.'

'Akbar was the Rector of the police college. Quite a senior position.'

'How terrible for her to lose her father. And you a friend. Did she love him?'

'Yes, very much. And she needs him.'

'Just as Thomas needs you.' She rubbed his upper arm with her hand; her fingers curved around his biceps.

'And Alexander. I've got two. But Akbar was more involved with Mina than I am with mine.'

'This would be a good time to call them, honey. They're going to be worried about you. It's all over the BBC.'

Cadman upended the empty can. 'I did call Thomas before. I was going to tell you. I'm seeing him when I get back. Especially now. Two years it's been.'

'I am glad. What made you decide?'

'You, I think, Lee. Lee is right, isn't it?'

'That's what my friends call me. And as you're half naked, in my apartment, drinking my Budweiser, telling me your troubles, I guess we're friends.'

Cadman looked down at himself. 'I am a bit exposed, aren't I? I don't think I was with it when you took me in. You don't want to be looking at my fat belly.' He stood with some difficulty: a mixture of the soft sofa, several beers, fatigue and the confining tube of the sarong. 'You don't want me here, I'd best get back to the hotel.'

'You're not fat, Alex'. She ran the end of her fingernail across his navel, just above the level of the sarong. 'And I do want you here. You can sit here and talk it through and drink my beer as long as you need.'

Cadman collapsed next to her. 'Well, since you're offering, I'll have another Bud, thanks, Lee.'

*

'Wow, Alex. You're quite a guy,' Lee said afterwards, as they lay, legs entwined on top of the crisp white sheets.

Cadman had been dozing. 'Me? You're kidding, right?'

'I never knew a guy could be so sensitive. Not that I make a habit of this, honey.'

'I don't know how to answer, Lee. I'm used to keeping it all inside, as you know.'

She ran her slender foot along his thigh. 'Well, don't, Alex. You're a great guy.'

It was the sense of touch that had so astonished Cadman. He had not known he'd been missing it. He had forgotten it, imagined that his lust was inspired by the sight of nakedness, not the feel of it.

'You're the first woman since my wife left. I always thought I'd be nervous.'

'She should have stayed around, honey, she should have stayed around.'

*

At last Cadman slept. It was only a few hours, but he slept dreamlessly and even peacefully. When he awoke, the sky was just showing grey. It was approaching five o'clock. He had to get back to the site and meet Jasmina. He unwrapped himself from Lee's gorgeous smooth limbs and kissed her softly on the forehead. He remembered Akbar's crushed body in its concrete grave and felt guilty, but kissed Lee once more nevertheless.

From the kitchen he found a utility room in which hung his clean T-shirt and underpants and his dusty jeans.

Besides the washing machine was the grubby bolt of cloth that would have been a sari. He slipped it under his arm and silently left the apartment.

He had no recollection of where the apartment building was situated, indeed had no idea of the journey they had taken from the club. He had hoped he could pick up a taxi or a rickshaw and make his way to his hotel. However, once he got outside, he recognised the road; it was just a short walk to Road 11 and he began to pick his way through the potholes, rubbish heaps and street sellers. The morning was not yet hot and it reminded him of the previous weekend when he and Kanoski had set off for Akbar and Jasmina's village. It seemed a year ago. Akbar was alive and kind. Jasmina had a father to guide her. And Lee was an American woman at the club.

The porter greeted him without any sign of surprise at the hour of his return. Wearily, he stumbled into the lift. He thought of Lee constantly. What would he do next time they met? Should he kiss her like a wife? Was their relationship secret? Did they have a relationship? The lift rocked clumsily to a halt and the bell pinged to announce its arrival on the fifth floor. Cadman fumbled to extract his key card from his wallet and dropped the heavy sari just as the sleek steel doors slid open. He stooped to pick it up and, as he stood upright, he saw Jasmina quietly pull Kanoski's door to and scurry away down the stairs.

PART 2

CHAPTER ONE

DCI Cadman shuffled in through the revolving doors and into the lift with the others. There were a few murmurs of recognition, but otherwise they travelled to the fifteenth floor of the Tower Block at New Scotland Yard in silence. London was grey, but it was beautiful. It was tidy and orderly and clean, and Cadman admired the view over the London Eye and the Thames more every day.

It had been a month since he had returned from Bangladesh. People were interested in his tale of his search for the body of the Rector of the Police Staff College of Bangladesh and he told it often but their attention span was limited to the policing elements. They asked him about command and control: how did the various agencies work together to respond to the incident? They wanted to know how prepared Dhaka Metropolitan Police had been, what the temporary mortuary facilities were like, whether DNA samples were obtained from the bodies, how the family liaison officer system was implemented. Their questions reflected their ordered English police lives. London was orderly and beautiful, Dhaka was chaotic, ugly – and affecting. London was dispassionate, Dhaka was emotive. It was touchy where London was stiff. For all those who were interested in process, Cadman had an answer. No one asked him what Dhaka had done to his emotions, and he had no answers. But there were days when London seemed as dead as his dear friend Akbar – a city in which no policeman could ever wear a sarong, even off duty.

'How are you getting on with that anti-globalisation bloke, Alex?' Dave Thorogood wandered in from the corridor and was speaking before he'd come into view. Now he stood in shirt sleeves, leaning on Cadman's desk with his arms outstretched and his fingers extended, the tips pressing into the teak veneer like those of a snooker player supporting a difficult long pot. His striped tie dangled against the desktop.

'You're a coward, you know that, Dave? I've been meaning to tell you since I got back.'

'What do you mean, coward? That's not a very nice thing to say about your boss.'

'Dumping those crappy nominals on me when I was in Dhaka.'

'Oh that. No that wasn't cowardice. That was prudence. Not telling you would have been cowardice.'

'You didn't tell me. You got a DC to do it for you.'

'Oh that. Yes, now that was cowardice. So how you getting on with the investigation?'

'OK. Well, of the forty, one really stands out, though I was struggling with him at first, to be honest.'

'Why?'

'I couldn't see the threat. He's not really Islamist and he's not Irish related. It's a bit like dealing with an eco-warrior or a hacker or something. But we're in his chat room with him. Calls himself Higher Ground.'

'Higher Ground? Sounds a bit apocalyptic, doesn't it? A bit Noah. He was at your collapsed building, wasn't he?'

'No, but he's been posting about it. He's sworn he'll avenge the deaths. And the world's response is hypocritical – makes him even angrier; foreigners sending money only reinforces their stake in Bangladesh. He's a bloody idiot, but he's a threat alright. He's working himself up to something.'

'Have we identified him yet?'

'No. And it's worrying me. We've got his photo from the G8 in Belfast, but we can't tie it to a real name – just Higher Ground. He's really careful how he logs on. He likes to spout off, but he doesn't want to be caught.'

Thorogood paused at the doorway as he was about to leave Cadman's office. 'Talking of Bangladesh, you're seeing your Bengali bird tonight, aren't you?'

'She's not my Bengali bird. She's the daughter of the copper who died. She's a friend, that's all. I've not seen her since the funeral. It'll be nice to catch up.'

He had not heard from Lee. Indeed he had not seen her since the night he had left her bed. The following evening they had found Akbar's body and he had not gone to the club.

The Rector had been dug up by a tractor. Five days clawing at the concrete with his fingers and they had dragged him out with a lump of masonry in the huge yellow bucket of a tractor within about five minutes of it arriving. They should have been there the first day. His head slumped out of the bucket and the cement dust poured out of his dry mouth as the machine backed away and dumped him close to Jasmina's feet. She looked masculine in her dark blue uniform, her hair scraped back into a practical bun, the fatigue trousers shapeless and unflattering. But when Akbar tumbled out in front of her, she was just a girl looking at her dead father. She slumped to her knees at his side, her mouth fell open and she wailed the wail that Cadman had first heard at the burning bus and which had become the soundtrack for his days spent at the site. Sometimes Bangla words tumbled out with the tears and the screech of the wail and, though Cadman could not understand them linguistically, he knew their meaning. She had lost her father, her friend, her housemate, her boss, her guide. Cadman stood dumb, his arms by his sides, as she wiped his dusty face and kissed his forehead and found his broken fingers and clasped them. Jasmina looked like a cop, but she cried like a lost little girl.

The next day had been the funeral, a dismal, semi-formal affair during which Cadman, Kanoski and Sutherland were at once treated as guests of honour whilst at the same time being segregated as non-Muslims. They stood back with the women as the men lowered the body, so recently dug up, into the grave and shovelled the red earth over him. There was no coffin for protection, just a shroud, and Cadman thought of his friend's mouth once more filling with dust. Jasmina clung to Kanoski and sobbed. By the time Cadman approached the grave, Akbar was just a mound of red earth, baking dry under a burning sun. Grey dust to red dust. Cadman said goodbye and looked up to the sky and prayed silently for rain.

Then he had come home. On schedule, on the flight that he had always intended to catch. He had not had time to go back to the club and he didn't know Lee's telephone number. On the way to the airport, he recognised her apartment building and for a second he thought to ask Ezaz to stop. It wouldn't have been too difficult, they were crawling anyway. But instead he pulled the dusty sari closer and stared blankly out as Dhaka slipped past him.

CHAPTER TWO

He was waiting in the Prince Albert, sipping an orange juice. The sari looked fantastic now that he'd had it cleaned. It sparkled and shimmered and he was delighted with Akbar's choice. He knew and loved his daughter and she would love this gift. Akbar would have wanted her to have it. The big pub was just a stone's throw from New Scotland Yard and was all shining brass and dark wood. A massive building with bars on several floors, it was such a classic London pub that the open-top busses slowed down to allow tourists to photograph it. However, the large bar that opened onto Victoria Street was nearly empty on this warm May evening and Cadman was beginning to wonder if Jasmina was waiting in another part of the building. He took another sip and, for a moment, he was back in the club, waiting for her to finish playing tennis.

'Hello? Alex Cadman?' A young Muslim man spoke to him through an immature but well-trimmed beard. His serious face was topped by a pristine white *topi*.

'Yes? Where's Jasmina? Is she OK?'

'Yes, of course, Alex. Assalamu Alaikum. It's wonderful to meet you. I am Tofo. Jasmina's cousin.' He spoke with an educated Londoner's accent, with just a hint of South Asian. 'Please. She is waiting outside.'

Leaving his orange juice and the sari in its dry-cleaning bag on the high table to which he'd pulled up his stool, Cadman followed the young man's flowing white shirt towards the exit. He wore sandals and ankle-length cotton trousers. On the pavement, her arms flying out to meet him and with a huge smile, was Jasmina.

'Oh, Alex! It is so wonderful to see you at last. Oh, I wish Abu could be here.' She spoke over his shoulder, close to his ear, as she hugged him close. Silky material brushed his face and he realised that she was wearing a beautiful coral pink head scarf that coordinated with a cream *shalwar kameez*.

'Mina, Mina, Mina. It's great to have you here. What we went through together…' He paused. 'Never mind that. Welcome to my village!' He gestured towards the door of the Prince Albert. 'Come on in!'

Jasmina hovered a moment and looked fleetingly at Tofo. 'I'm not sure. It's a bar, isn't it? It's not really appropriate.'

'Oh. Of course. OK. We'll go somewhere else. It was just a place to meet.' He pushed the door open and said, 'Just let me get my things.' He came out carrying the bag with the sari. 'I just wanted to show you my village. That's all. This pub's pretty much a part of it.'

'I know. But Tofo – and I – thought that it's best not to go to a place that sells alcohol. It's not very Islamic, is it?'

'Not really appropriate,' smiled Tofo. 'Let's go and get a coffee, shall we?'

'Good idea. There's a Costa just here.'

'No, I know a better place. London's full of great little independent coffee houses.' Tofo led the way across Victoria Street and into the narrow and bustling Strutton Ground.

'Come on. It's up here. Looking forward to hearing what you thought about Bangladesh, Alex.'

They bustled energetically into a cosy Turkish café. In the window overlooking the narrow walkway, with the best views, there were red leatherette bucket seats on chrome stands, resembling tulips or wine glasses that had been sliced in half, and a couple of seating contraptions that hung from the ceiling. Cadman had no idea how he would fit into one of these and avoid spilling hot coffee and so was relieved when Tofo headed towards some red leatherette booths with beige formica tables. Jasmina shuffled in with Tofo next to her and Cadman sat opposite. Credence Clearwater Revival fizzed from small car speakers set in the walls. As the waiter approached, Tofo gestured towards his own head and Jasmina pulled her scarf a little towards the front.

'I like this place,' Jasmina smiled. 'We've been here before, haven't we?'

'Limehouse you're from, aren't you, Tofo?' Cadman asked.

'Yes, I live with Mum and Dad there. Bangladesh is home though.'

'Will you eat with us later, Alex?' asked Jasmina. 'You are most welcome to. Or we could go to a restaurant somewhere?'

Before he could answer Tofo said, 'So you are the hero of the hour, I think, Alex?'

'Hero? I don't think so! Why?'

'Jasmina says that you never gave up looking with her to find Uncle Akbar.'

'I had known him such a short time, but we understood each other. We spoke about life and fatherhood. He had some good advice about that.'

'He was a good father,' said Jasmina.

'And a good friend. And he made me feel very wanted at the college. Not everyone did.'

'You're talking about your disagreement with Samuel!' Jasmina laughed.

'The elephant in the room!'

'Who is Samuel?' asked Tofo. 'You haven't told me that name, Jasmina.'

'Samuel is…' Jasmina hesitated.

'A teacher,' said Cadman. 'Of terrorism. He's a proper pain in the neck but he does know his stuff.'

'Terrorism? Is that what you were learning?'

'Well, counter-terrorism really,' Cadman said, 'but Sam, he'd definitely say you had to know about terrorists before you could know how to counter them. Wouldn't he, Jasmina?'

The waiter arrived with drinks and Jasmina pulled her scarf around her face as he approached.

'You look fabulous, as ever, Jasmina,' Cadman said. 'Is the scarf for mourning?'

'Here it's more important to express my identity as a Muslim woman.'

'Why?'

Jasmina looked at Tofo and then towards Cadman. 'The Bangladeshi community is more conservative in London. This is how I'm expected to dress here.'

'But London is one of the most liberal cities in the world. You should wear what you want. I wore a sarong in your village.'

'The Bangladeshi community in London does not know how to deal with such liberalism, Alex,' Tofo explained. 'We do not necessarily agree with everything that a liberal society brings.'

'Anyway,' Cadman cut across him, 'while we're on the subject of clothes, there's something I want to give you, Jasmina. I hope this doesn't upset you. Do you remember the sari?'

'How can I forget the sari, Alex? The last thing my father did was to throw it away.'

'Throw it away? I never thought of it like that,' he pondered.

'You have it in that bag, don't you? Why did you bring your wife's sari here? It killed my father!' Her cheeks blazed red under the gentle pink and she and Tofo were both looking intently at him.

'Yes, I've got it in the bag. And if I've got this horribly wrong, I'm ever so sorry. I didn't see it that way. A sari can't kill someone.'

'He wouldn't have died if you hadn't sent him to get it. Why did you bring it here?'

'The sari was for you, Jasmina. Your father picked it for you. It was a gift from me for everything you did to make my stay so wonderful: the boat, the dinners, the village tour. Akbar knew where to buy it. He went and got it for me. It was for you, Mina. Not my wife. I just said that to... I don't know why, to make it sound better.'

Jasmina looked at Tofo. 'I can't wear a sari, Alex!'

'Why would you buy a Muslim girl a sari?' Tofo demanded. 'They are not proper dress. They are indecent. It's as if I bought your wife a bikini.'

'Mina is not your wife and she looks wonderful in a sari.'

'Don't make it worse, Alex,' Jasmina said quickly.

'Women in saris expose their belly. Their whole arms. Worse sometimes.' Tofo's coffee slopped from his small cup as he put it down. He pulled the side of Jasmina's scarf further around her face.

'But… I discussed it with your father, Jasmina. You're making it indecent. It's not like that. It was to wear at the course closing ceremony – a formal thing.'

'I don't wear saris anymore, Alex! They are not appropriate.'

*

'How did your date go, Alex?' Thorogood was grinning as he filled his coffee cup.

'It wasn't a date. I'm a father figure. And it couldn't have gone any worse.' Cadman was alongside his boss as they edged their way towards the cash desk. 'What's the matter with this bloody machine? I wanted cappuccino.'

'A father figure? You? When was the last time you saw your own kids?'

'I know, Dave. I know. But her father died, remember?'

'So how did it go so wrong?' By the time they sat together, Thorogood's voice had lost some of the sarcastic edge that it had carried at first.

'She went all Muslim on me.'

Thorogood looked quickly around the room then pulled his suit jacket around him and straightened his tie. 'Keep your voice down, Alex, for Christ's sake! You'll get us both sacked talking like that.'

'You can talk about it, you know. I've been to Bangladesh. I made good friends there. We talked about everything.'

'Well, you can't talk about it in the canteen at New Scotland Yard.'

'And she brought her bloody cousin with her.'

'That shouldn't matter if you're just a father figure, mate!' Thorogood looked around the room again and moved his head in closer to Cadman's. 'What do you mean, anyway, went all Muslim on you? She is a Muslim, isn't she?'

'Well, yes, of course. But in Dhaka she was just a Bangladeshi girl. Religion didn't matter one bit. What I mean is, it never came up in my relationship with Akbar or Jasmina. It was something I knew and they knew that didn't need discussing. I went to their house and we ate together and we were friends. But here, in London, I didn't seem to be able to open my mouth without somehow trampling all over Islam.'

'What was the cousin like?' Thorogood bit into a thick cheese roll.

'The same. All Islamic in an unnecessary way. I spent three weeks in Dhaka living and working with Muslim police officers. Every day they prayed at lunchtime. It was relaxed. They were friends. You know what? Not one of the men wore *topis* and *shalwar kameez*. The only chap who dressed like that in Bangladesh was the imam who opened and closed the course with prayers. It was beautiful, too.'

'But the cousin wore them?'

'That's right, he did. Nothing wrong with it. I don't care. But somehow, he cared. And he was influencing Jasmina too. Dragged us out of the pub and constantly making her pull her headscarf round her face. I feel robbed, Dave.'

'Robbed? What of?' He stubbed his fingers at bread crumbs on his plate and touched them to the tip of his tongue.

'She showed me her village. I was going to show her mine. Not his bloody village. She's not seeing London, she's seeing a carefully controlled version of it. We weren't even allowed to go in Costa Coffee. Had to drink that thin stuff in the fake Turkish place in Strutton Ground. I'm sure it's Nescafé.'

'They're Afghans in there, aren't they? You going to see her again?'

'I don't know, Dave. I'd like to. She gave me her uncle's number. I'll probably call her in a couple of days. I can't really see her without her cousin though, can I?'

'So how's your eco-jihadist investigation going anyway? Change the subject a bit.'

'To terrorism? That should lighten the mood a little!'

CHAPTER THREE

Cadman picked up the transcript and flicked his eyes across it, turning the pages rapidly.

'Terrorist attack planning?' he asked without looking up.

'Yes, guv.' Pritchard said it with a distinct air of smugness in his voice.

Cadman put down his coffee mug and looked from the paper to Pritchard's face. 'As straightforward as that? Are you sure?'

'Yes. I assess that they're in the early stages.'

'Show me, Joe.'

Pritchard leant across the desk and looked at the paper. 'Here on page two.'

Cadman read the passage.

HIGHER GROUND: 500 dead. It keeps going up.

MARX15: So many innocents. We should do something. In Bangladesh even. The American Embassy.

HIGHER GROUND: It's time to send a message. Like those who fight for the brothers in Syria.

MARX15: ISIS?! LOL!!

HIGHER GROUND: Why LOL? Don't Muslims have the right to equality?

MARX15: They're terrorists!!

HIGHER GROUND: They're doing what they believe in.

MARX15: This is a Marxist forum. Time you went somewhere else.

HIGHER GROUND: We're not terrorists. You're the one talking about terror. There's nothing we can do at the embassy. We're raising money for the injured. Aid. Only we want to deliver aid that will make a difference. Daina's the man on the ground. He can make it count.

'What do you think, guv?' Pritchard asked, watching as Cadman's finger moved across the words.

'There's no more?'

'No, guv. MARX15 takes the conversation back to the G8.'

'And you think that they're attack planning?'

'Early stages.'

'It's a bit of a stretch. I agree that he's sympathising with terrorists, but…'

'It's the way he says it's time to send a message, like those who fight in Syria. That's not aid he's talking about.'

A knock on Cadman's door was immediately followed by a head popping into view and the young detective made an embarrassed scrabble to clear his sensitive papers. 'Sorry to interrupt, sir. There's a visitor for you in reception.'

The head disappeared again. 'OK,' Cadman said. 'Keep talking in there. But I need to be sure that it's real. I don't want us to put words in his mouth. Just keep it nice and passive as you've been doing. And let me know immediately if there's any indication of time, date or place.'

'Will do, guv.' The young man was halfway out of the door.

'Still no idea who he is, I suppose?' Cadman asked.

'No, guv. Still unidentified male 17 from the G8 photos. He's using public networks and public computers – Internet cafés – so we've not tracked him yet.' Pritchard carefully scooped up the transcript and slotted it into a cardboard folder.

'This is good work, Joe. You keeping the Service in the loop?'

'Doing it now, guv.' Pritchard was up on his feet and backing out of the door. 'Cheers, guv.'

Cadman swigged down his lukewarm coffee as he opened another email and then remembered his visitor. He shrugged on his suit jacket and bustled off down the corridor. Thorogood was in the lift ahead of him.

'Hi, Alex. Glad I bumped into you. You're just the man I was thinking of.'

'At six o'clock on a Friday? If you want something done ask a busy man? What?'

'What, *sir.*'

'Oh, it's something shit, is it, sir? Another forty cyber terrorists need watching?'

'Not at all actually, Alex. I've just opened a letter from some RCMP bloke seconded to the UNODC. François Sutherland? Do you know him? He wants to run another course in Dhaka. Fancy going?' The lift stopped and Thorogood disappeared up the corridor. 'Another drink you owe me,' he called back. 'And try to keep the Police Staff College people alive this time, will you, mate? Good weekend...'

The lift doors jerked shut and Cadman was alone. Who the bloody hell wanted him this time of night? As if he had time to go swanning off to Bangladesh again. He'd not even caught up on his work from last time. And this bloody Higher Ground wouldn't leave him alone. And anyway his friend was dead and his daughter had gone all weird. And he had 400 emails to deal with. He hurtled through the revolving doors and there in the lobby, standing with the low spring sunshine streaming in from behind her, was his caller. The usual handful of visitors sat on the low furniture waiting to be met, looking uncomfortable and bemused, fingering their guest badges. The brightness of the sun through the plate glass made her into a mere silhouette.

'Lee?' He blinked and shaded his eyes.

As he stood in disbelief, she pulled out a sarong, threw it around his shoulders and tugged him towards her open mouth.

CHAPTER FOUR

In the Prince Albert Cadman ordered a pint of Budweiser and a gin and tonic and they took up stools on the same table at which he had waited for Jasmina. Lee held Cadman's large pink hand in her slender brown one and stroked his fingers with hers. 'Your hands are so damaged, Alex. You should put cream on them.'

'They are still a bit sore.'

'Perhaps that's why you were so sensitive that night,' she oozed, and kissed his lips, lingering slightly.

Cadman studied her exquisite features and grinned. 'Is this real?' he asked her. 'Are you real? What are you doing in London?'

'I came to find you, Alex honey. I was making my call to my daughter and I was telling her I'd met this guy, this handsome cop, this English gentleman, this super guy who cared about his dying friend and was emotional and great in bed.'

'You didn't tell her that!'

She ran her hand over the backs of both of his and kissed his cheek. 'Yes, I did, Alex. And then I thought, "You know what, Lee? You need to go and get your man." And then, right then, that Canadian guy walked in. The one who plays tennis with the handsome Australian guy?'

'Handsome?! Don't say that, Lee, please!'

'Now don't get jealous, honey. He's not my type. He looks a little frigid, don't you think?' She laughed and wrapped both hands around Cadman's arm, squeezing him and pushing her face against his shirt sleeve. 'Aren't you pleased I'm here, Alex?'

'Pleased? Pleased?! Oh, Lee. I've missed you so much. That sounds like Hollywood.'

'It is like Hollywood, Alex.'

'We don't need to do anything silly, do we? Just enjoy each other. Just let it happen. Slowly, or fast, if that's how it is. Only...'

'Only what, Alex? You don't have someone else, do you?'

'No, nothing like that. The opposite. We don't have to do anything fast – only I do have to sleep with you pretty quickly, if that's OK?!' He held her chin lightly and kissed her lips. He felt them begin to shape themselves into words even as he kissed her.

'It was great, wasn't it? Anyway, the Canadian guy tells me you're a London cop and he tells me you're Counter-Terrorism Command – how cool is that? – but that's all he'd tell me. And I thought and thought about calling, but it didn't seem right. I couldn't bear a kind of polite conversation. So I figured I'd get myself here and case the joint. Is that what you say, case the joint?'

'In Hollywood, maybe.'

'I know. Isn't it Hollywood? So I'm staying in the hotel opposite. It's a good one. Butlers with top hats and tails, Alex! I have a great room. And I've already stacked the fridge with Buds. And there's a bottle of champagne on ice...'

'But I might have said no.'

'That's why I brought the sarong, honey. I thought I might need to get you back into role.' She flourished the gold tartan cotton and then said, 'Stand up! Come on, let me see my Dhakan guy.'

He did as he was told and she wrapped the sarong around his waist. She was holding it there as Thorogood tripped through the door with a group of young detectives.

'Alex? What the f...?'

'It's a sarong, Dave.'

'I can see it's a sarong. But who is this beautiful woman?' He shook Lee's hand and was looking at her admiringly as Cadman replied.

'She's a friend from Bangladesh.'

'We're lovers,' Lee put in, helpfully.

'How many more are coming to see you?'

Lee let the sarong drop from one hand and it hung from the other, dangling on the pub floor. 'More?'

'Nice one, Dave,' Cadman said.

*

'Have you ever been to London before, Lee?' Cadman stood with his back to the bed, wearing just the sarong. 'Do you take sugar and milk? How strange not to know that but to be standing here like this!'

'Just black please, Alex. Do you prefer Al?'

'You can call me Al, if you like.'

'Like the song.'

'Good song. Good video – Chevy Chase?'

'Yes. That'll be our song: "You Can Call Me Al" by Chevy Chase.'

'I'd like to show you around London this weekend. If you want me to.'

'I'd love to. But I'd rather meet Thomas and Daniela. And the baby. Did she have the baby?'

'A boy. I haven't seen him yet.'

'Haven't seen him? You said you'd called Thomas. Why on earth not?'

'I don't know. Work. It's been two years, more, since I saw them. Akbar died and I met you. I feel awkward.'

'Well, I won't. A boy. It'll be like having a grandson. I haven't got a grandson. Take me to meet them? Please?'

'It's a bit soon.'

'For what? You just said you haven't seen them for two years.'

'A bit soon for… for us.'

'Not in Hollywood.'

'But we're not in Hollywood.'

'Only if you don't want us to be. Who makes the rules? Come on, Al. Call them and tell them you met a girl in Bangladesh and she's great and beautiful and everything you've ever dreamed of.'

'You are those things,' Cadman said quietly, sliding onto the bed next to her.

'Don't spill coffee on that sarong, honey.'

He sipped his coffee and did not reply.

'Call them and tell them that the baby and me are great reasons to get together.' She scooped his smartphone from the bedside cabinet and handed it to him. 'Go on.

Call them. We'll go down there today. We've only got one weekend. What's the baby's name?'

'Samuel.'

'That's a beautiful name. Very traditional. Sounds very English.'

'It's the name of the handsome Australian guy.'

'You don't like that man much, do you, Al!'

*

'Dad! Alex, it's Dad!' Thomas emerged at the side of the newly built semi-detached house carrying Samuel – it had to be Samuel – high up on his chest. The baby had his eyes wide open and stared at the stranger. 'Look, Sam, it's Granddad.'

Tears streamed down Cadman's face as he tried to say something meaningful. Instead, he fell into a clumsy hug that was more like a rugby maul. He buried his tears in his son's neck and kissed him there. A tiny hand found its way into his lips and he kissed that too. They were in danger of toppling over when they were propped up by Alexander, who came running from the garden to the narrow side entrance where they were gathered.

'Dad!' he shouted. 'You're actually here.' The elder son's strong arms engulfed the group and the three generations squashed together and celebrated. Cadman was just beginning to feel self-conscious when Alexander said, 'He's crying! Dad, you're crying.'

Cadman managed to disengage himself and look his eldest son in the face. 'Yes, yes. I'm crying. I missed you. I'm stupid, I know, but I missed you and it's made me cry.'

Thomas jiggled Samuel in the crook of his arm. 'Look at Granddad crying,' he said, 'he's a bigger baby than you.'

'I didn't know you were so sensitive, Dad,' Alexander said, slapping Cadman on the back so hard that he nearly cried out with pain.

'Oh yes, he's sensitive alright,' Lee broke in, 'he wears a sarong.'

It was a warm May afternoon in England and the family group squeezed into the neat patio area of the suburban house and the sausages spat on the barbecue. Cadman looked at his boys' smiles and listened to their boisterous laughter and admired their pretty wives and cooed over his new grandson. More tears welled and could easily have sprang out, but instead he felt a broad grin emanate from deep inside his chest and spread itself warmly and involuntarily across his stupid face. How stupid he'd been. He searched for Lee with his eyes. She sat quietly on the back door step as the young men ribbed their father and they told their police stories and enjoyed their reunion. She looked up from her drink and Cadman caught her eye. 'Thank you,' he mouthed silently.

His phone rang and he instinctively stood and walked inside the house, away from prying ears. As he did so, he saw Alexander look sideways at his brother, tilt his head towards their father and roll his eyes. He thought, for just a split second, about delaying the call, explaining that he understood the meaning of his sons' silent exchange, that he loved his boys more than his job, but Pritchard's voice drew him in and away.

'Sorry to disturb your weekend, guv.'

'You're not disturbing me, Joe.'

'Just a quick one. We haven't got time or date, but we have the place alright.'

'Go on…'

'Bangladesh.'

CHAPTER FIVE

The Commissioner stood in front of the revolving three-dimensional triangle. He looked cool and relaxed even though he wore his tunic and hat in the heat of the afternoon sun. He smiled reassuringly as he answered the reporter's question, looking her straight in the face, seemingly unaware of the soundwoman holding the long furry microphone under his chin and the cameraman crouching to get both the man and the New Scotland Yard sign in the shot.

'The boss is on the news tonight then,' Pritchard said.

'So it seems,' Thorogood replied, without showing any signs of interest or curiosity.

'Only if he slips up,' Cadman said. There would not be much of a story in the carefully scripted and rehearsed lines reassuring Londoners that all was well, even in the wake of the news that three British Asian girls had gone to be jihadi brides in Syria. Cadman struggled to understand why the story was news at all, given what was going on everywhere else in the world. Hundreds of innocent teenage girls had died at Mirpur Plaza and yet their stories were less newsworthy than the fates of three would-be terrorists who had chosen their own path.

They crossed Victoria Street and into Strutton Ground. Cadman couldn't resist scanning the coffee shop as they walked past but Jasmina was not there. Beyond the bustle of the little street with its cafés, bars and shops, they entered into the altogether more sedate, vehicular and business-like Horseferry Road.

Ten minutes later they were climbing the grey stone steps of Thames House, under the shade of the magnificent entrance arch. The three black doors offered no clue as to what lay beyond them. Though they all led to the same foyer, the doors always instilled in Cadman a sense that the choice was important, that the outcome of the meeting ahead would differ depending on which door one entered. They were set into a polished stone art deco façade, above which could be seen the unadorned coarse stonework and barred windows of what looked like a dark prison, but which was actually the headquarters of MI5. Today he chose the left, whilst Thorogood and Pritchard went through the centre.

'Hi, guys. I'm Spencer.' He took a swig from a bottle of water in place of a handshake and around his neck hung an identity pass, in place of a tie. His open-necked shirt was dark purple and his crinkly chinos were beige. In spite of the fact that he was well under thirty, his ginger hair was thin and wispy and Cadman took much satisfaction from the thought that he'd soon be bald.

'Hi, Spencer,' Pritchard said. 'Good to see you. This is Detective Superintendent Thorogood and Detective Chief Inspector Cadman.'

'Hi, guys. Come on up.'

They were issued with security passes and then entered via claustrophobic security gateways – shower-cubicle-sized see-through tubes rising out of the floor. Spencer led them to a small meeting room with a table that was already laid with a plate of biscuits and flasks with tea and coffee. Sitting at the head of the table, he took another swig from his plastic bottle and said, 'So, updates on Higher Ground.'

'He's planning an attack in Bangladesh,' Pritchard said in a matter-of-fact tone whilst pulling some papers from a rucksack.

'Are you sure?' Spencer asked.

Cadman looked towards Pritchard and received a faint nod. 'Yes, we're sure,' Cadman said.

Pritchard slid a sheet of paper onto the tabletop. 'This conversation took place yesterday afternoon:

HIGHER GROUND: I'm coming out. I've applied for a visa.

DAINA: That's good news. Come through Dubai or Abu Dhabi, not Turkey.

HIGHER GROUND: I'll draft you a list. You're the man on the ground. You'll need to get some things.

DAINA: When?

HIGHER GROUND: Tonight.

DAINA: I'll pick it up tomorrow. Already late here.

HIGHER GROUND: Are we going to do this?

DAINA: Yes, if you think it's the only way.'

'What do you make of this "list", Joe?' Thorogood asked.

'Not sure, guv. I think they're using a shared email address. Create a draft but don't send it. Then the other one reads it and deletes it. I think "tonight" means that

Higher Ground will create the list tonight, not that there's going to be an attack tonight. There's not been an attack anyway.'

'Anyone disagree with Joe's assessment?' Cadman asked.

Spencer drank from his bottle whilst Pritchard studied the transcript without looking up.

'So in terms of response…' Thorogood began.

'I'll take the lead from here on in,' Spencer said into his bottle, his puckered moving lips visible through the clear plastic.

'I'm not so sure about that,' Cadman said quickly.

'Come on, Alex,' Thorogood said. 'You know the Service has the lead.'

'So, just keep on doing what you're doing, don't take any action without checking in with me and I'll get hold of SIS – make sure the Bangladesh office is all over this.' Spencer plonked his empty bottle on the table and stood up. The bottle fell over and rolled onto the floor beside Cadman's feet. He crushed it under his sole. Spencer showed them out of the meeting room and back to the foyer. 'Good work, Dave,' he said to Thorogood, patting him on the back as the three of them exited.

'That went well, guys,' Thorogood said as they descended the steps. 'He took no convincing that this is a pucker job and he's happy to take the lead.'

'As long as we do all the work,' Cadman grunted. 'Facetious little bastard.'

*

'So this is "the Tube" eh?' Lee shouted as the train rattled out of St James Park station.

'We're just going one stop – to Westminster – then we're changing lines. It's about an hour from Westminster to Heathrow.'

'I can't imagine a bomb on here, Al.'

'Don't then. I thought I'd never use it again. But I live in London. You have to in the end.'

'Will I get to see your apartment?'

'Apartment! Makes it sound so fancy. Yes, of course you will – next time you come. Come on, we change here.'

She clung to his arm as they navigated their way to the Jubilee line. Cadman pulled her luggage along and enjoyed her awe at the magnificent feat of engineering, the grey concrete buttresses and huge silver tubes, the gleaming escalators of Westminster Underground Station. Once they were seated side by side on the Heathrow train, she slid her arm into his and pulled him close.

'What's your apartment like? Is it all masculine – dirty clothes and bits of motorcycle engines?'

'Flat. I call it a flat. Apartment is far too grand a word. It's the downstairs of a converted Victorian house. It's rather nice, actually. Two bedrooms and a garden where I hang all my sarongs.'

'And a great big bed?'

'No. But it's not a single bed, either. I couldn't bring myself to buy one of those. I always hoped I had some sort of future, I just didn't know what it was. It's a nice enough bedroom, but not a patch on your hotel room! I've never lived so close to work!'

'It was a nice hotel room, wasn't it? It's been fabulous, Al, just fabulous. I am so glad that I chased you.'

'Me too, Lee. I don't remember ever feeling like this. I loved my wife, but I don't think it was ever this intense.'

'Do you love me, Al? Don't answer that,' she said instantly. 'You don't need to. I don't care. Let's just be happy in Hollywood. When will I see you again?'

'Well…'

'I know – a cop's salary's not gonna get you to Dhaka every other weekend. You'll break my heart, honey.'

'That's not what I was going to say. I'm coming back out to Dhaka in two weeks' time! I'm teaching on another course. Me and the handsome Australian – the one my bloody grandson's named after!'

'Oh, Al! That's great news. You can stay at my apartment. You will won't you?'

'Only if you've got a sarong that's capable of holding this guy down.'

'You won't need to be held down, honey.'

For a while they rattled on in happy silence, she studying the map and the people and he studying her.

'Are you going to see Jasmina, honey? In London I mean?'

'Well, I feel as if I ought to, but I feel a bit awkward after what happened last time.'

'You felt a bit awkward about seeing your sons. Promise me you'll see her. Akbar would have liked you to.'

'But that cousin…'

'Promise me, Al.'

'Alright. I know you're right. I promise I'll see her before I come to Dhaka.'

'Call her now. Why not?'

'Because there's no phone signal down here, that's why not. I promise I'll call her.'

Then they were at her departure gate and he was kissing her. They kissed like lovers, like Hollywood lovers, Cadman thought. She hung from his neck and her willowy body clung to his as if she were naked. Her thin blouse moved against his shirt and her breasts seemed to want to unbutton it and clamber in with his plump hairy chest. Her legs touched his from thigh to ankle and he clasped her narrow back and they kissed like teenagers. Not like a teenage Cadman, who had never kissed like it before, but like a Hollywood teenager.

'Call me,' he said to her as she finally slid away from him.

'You can call me, Al.' She beamed victoriously, and she was away and through the gate.

'You've been practising that!' he called out.

CHAPTER SIX

'Jasmina's already returned to Bangladesh.' Tofo's voice was irritatingly dispassionate.

'Already gone back? Why?'

'She has gone to take up her new role.'

'What new role? Don't talk in riddles please, Tofo.'

'I'm sorry, Alex. I didn't mean to talk in riddles. You mean so much to my cousin. My family can never repay you for the way you helped to find Uncle Akbar. My father says that we owe you a great debt. Please can we meet at our favourite coffee house?'

*

Tofo was waiting in one of the booths when Cadman walked into the café.

'Hi, Alex. Thank you so much for coming.' He stood and offered Cadman his hand and shook it vigorously, then smoothed his long shirt under his backside and sat down. 'I am so embarrassed by my conduct last time. When I reflected on it I realised that I had not been a friend.' The young man smiled in the gentle way that Akbar had done.

'No problem, Tofo. It's a pleasure to meet you again. I don't have long, I'm afraid.'

'I was a bit over the top with Islam, wasn't I? I can be like that sometimes. I'm just enthusiastic about my religion. My father says I'm a fundamentalist, whatever that is.'

'You were fine,' Cadman lied.

'I was just anxious to protect my cousin. I didn't know you. But I should have trusted Uncle Akbar's judgement. This is what my father has told me. Please forgive me for being a little over-zealous. Now, what can I get you?'

'Cappuccino, please. Don't think more about it, Tofo. Tell me about Jasmina.'

The waiter took their order and Tofo continued. 'There is no problem. She just left hurriedly. She has been seconded to the Police Staff College. I believe you know the place?'

'That's great news! I'll see her next week.'

'Yes. She said that.'

'But why didn't she say before she left?'

'Who knows the mind of women, Alex?' He spoke as if sharing the wisdom of a like-minded man.

'Well, I've been busy too. She probably tried to call.'

The coffee arriving came as something of a relief. Now that he knew why Jasmina had gone back he could think of nothing to say to the young man who sat silently and confidently opposite him. His mind raked through possible subject matters as he stirred the chocolate sprinkles and froth. He came close to asking Tofo whether he had any pets before opting to return lazily to the subject of Jasmina. 'How is she coping?' he asked. A stupid question. Her beloved father had just died – her mentor, her rock.

'Well. Considering what she has been through, I mean. Her new role will be good for her, though everyone will compare her to her father. She is also angry.'

'Angry?'

'The poor girl looks for someone to blame for her father's death.' Tofo's sentence seemed practised and trite; it reminded him of Joe Pritchard's use of standard phraseology. 'And for the deaths of all those poor workers. What a terrible situation this global economy has created.'

'She's angry with me, because of the sari. I'm angry too. But who with? Myself? The stupid consumer who takes no care as to how his clothes are made (which is also me)? There's no logic in blaming myself. Akbar's death was just one of many. They weren't all there because of me.' Cadman could hear the self-pity in his own voice.

'No one is blaming you, Alex.'

'Jasmina does. Because of the sari. I wish I'd bought her a bloody fridge magnet.'

'It has nothing to do with the sari *per se*, Alex'. Tofo leaned back slightly and touched the tips of his index fingers together to form the sides of a triangle. His hands were soft and well manicured, almost feminine. 'Though I think saris will not remain acceptable dress in Bangladesh in the future. Too revealing for modern Islamic taste.'

'I think they're beautiful, a part of your culture to be proud of.'

'But to get back to the point. It is the greedy West which is to blame for Akbar's death, Alex. Not you, nor the sari.' His fingertips parted and he used them like batons to mark the beat of his words. 'Huge profit margins for a few Western shareholders lie at the bottom of this problem, while the cost is felt by the poor workers in my country. In Bangladesh it is profit margins in the clothing industry that drive globalisation, because that is what Bangladesh is good at. This is why I wear these simple clothes.'

'A sari's not a product for the evil West.'

'No, but it was made using slave labour, just the same. Greedy owners cramming their staff into dangerously over-crowded factories. Whether these businesses were churning out cheap clothing for the East or for the West, it's the principle that matters. The exploitation of the poor by the rich.'

'Is it that simple, Tofo? I was there in the filth and heat. I feel anger too. But it's difficult to blame a shareholder in England for the failings of a building contractor in Dhaka. It seems to me that's where the money should have been spent – on putting up a decent building.'

Tofo pushed his coffee cup aside as if clearing the table for a briefing. 'Let me explain, Alex.' Cadman folded his arms across his chest as Tofo said this. 'My anger is not about Mirpur Plaza. Mirpur Plaza represents an example, that's all. Mirpur Plaza shouldn't have happened. Mirpur Plaza wouldn't have happened if the West hadn't interfered with Bangladesh's economy. We were a rural country.'

'I've been to your village. It's beautiful.'

'People were happy on the land and the land was indeed beautiful. Then arrive the big multinationals. They promise people a better way of life – money. The concept of cheap labour is an exploitative Western one. Fat Westerners won't work for peanuts, so we'll get the Bangladeshis to do it.

They won't mind. Life is cheap there anyway. Banks and telephone companies setting up call centres in Dhaka for English people. It's ludicrous – proud Bangladeshi men with MBAs from Dhaka University earning a pittance so that the globals can increase profit margins. Clothing companies set up factories with impossibly high productivity expectations – pure greed. The women leave their villages and cram into these factories and then they die. Just so that a handful of fat foreigners can get rich. They're the ones. They're the bad guys. Wherever they are, they're the enemy.'

'Jasmina says that the women need the jobs for their independence.'

'Well, there's the problem. In a proper Muslim society, women don't yearn for independence. Their men provide for them.'

'Is that why you don't want Jasmina to wear a sari? Because it demonstrates her independence?'

'Jasmina chose not to wear a sari in London. I did not influence her.'

'Akbar liked her wearing a sari.'

'Uncle Akbar was not looking forward, he looked backwards. Modern Islam will not tolerate uncovered women. Even in Bangladesh. You can see it here in London. It will come to Bangladesh.'

'Your ideology seems twisted.'

'How?'

'You want equality, but not independence for women. Everyone is equal, but men are more equal than women?' Cadman's voice had slowly been getting louder and this last question came out as an angry accusation.

Tofo stared at Cadman in silence. His dark eyes squinted like a TV presenter trying to read an autocue that lay somewhere beyond Cadman's head, and his fingers, which had again come together into a triangle, were shaking. But his stare was unmoving and Cadman was forced to look down and stab his spoon at the messy brown stain of froth in the empty cup. He did not look up until Tofo spoke. 'Let's not argue, Alex. We're friends.' His voice bubbled in the back of his throat as if the words were coming with difficulty. 'We're friends because of Jasmina and Akbar.'

Cadman dropped the spoon and it rattled against the cheap china. 'You're right, Tofo. I didn't intend to argue. I'm just trying to understand. Sam says I'm just a thick copper. Perhaps he's right.'

'I would like to meet Samuel. Jasmina tells me that he has a good understanding of the root causes of other issues – such as terrorism. He seems like a very bright guy. I would enjoy discussing things with him. I like to debate with those who have a similar mind to my own.'

'Look, I should be at work. I'll see you about.' Cadman stood and was about to leave when he noticed Tofo's extended hand. He took it and shook it. 'I'll see you about, Tofo. Look after yourself.'

'Goodbye, Alex. Thanks for everything that you've done for my family. I won't forget it.'

CHAPTER SEVEN

Cadman sat in the sweltering heat of the roof terrace. The rain fell heavily about him and ran in unbroken arcs from the corners of the green umbrellas. The noise of running water and the drumming of raindrops on the canvas was cacophonous but it provided some insulation against the gabbling, revving, hooting hubbub of Dhaka. A damp, tenty aroma seeped from the umbrellas, and the warm water on the tiled floors and gutters of the club exuded a smell of old limescale. The few patrons who had ventured out were downstairs eating at the gingham-covered tables and he was alone with the Bangladeshi barman. In the evening gloom the lights of the bar shone, making it feel homely. The television puttered away in the background and the barman had his back to Cadman, watching a local news programme. Even after all these weeks there was an article about developments at Mirpur Plaza and Cadman looked away when his eyes accidentally focused on old footage showing the day of the collapse. He was instantly reminded of club sandwiches and pristine white sheets and took great comfort from his decision to stay at Lee's apartment during this course.

'Alex. I thought I might find you here. Couldn't find you at the hotel. How are you, mate?' Kanoski stood grinning in the rain.

'Hello, Sam.' Cadman shifted his seat to allow room for Kanoski. 'Come under here! You're getting soaked. How are you?' The barman scurried over as Kanoski settled and he stood waiting, his shirt rapidly becoming transparent.

'Two beers,' Cadman shouted. 'Don't stand there getting wet!'

'Two Fosters?' the barman asked, not budging.

'Yes. Fosters will do,' Cadman said and shooed the man out of the rain.

'You cool about this, Alex?' Kanoski asked. He scrutinised Cadman's face. He looked uncomfortable.

'About you and me working together, you mean? Yes. I'm OK with that. What's your point?'

'The last time we were here you had a handful of my shirt. Just downstairs. I thought you were going to punch my lights out, mate.'

'Things were hardly normal, were they, Sam? I'm an easy-going bloke. We'll be fine together.'

'That's great, Alex. I've got some great ideas for this course. I've spoken to Frank…'

'Just don't undermine me in class. OK? If you have a problem with what I'm saying, you wait and then you talk to me on a one-to-one basis. Alright? The quickest way for you to get your lights punched out is to undermine me in front of the students.'

'Got it. No problemo.'

'I'll give you your due though, Sam…'

'What's that?'

'I'm glad you came straight out with it and cleared the air.'

The waiter arrived with the beers, trying to apologise in his imperfect English for not opening the cans in order to avoid them filling with rain water. Cadman planted one in Kanoski's hand and held out his own. 'Here's to the second UNODC Advanced Counter-Terrorism Course, Sam.'

'Cheers, Alex. Good to be working with you again.'

'Oh! Here's one you'll like. I finally caught up with my sons.'

'The ones you hadn't seen?'

'Well, I've caught up with them now. And she's had the baby... a boy... and called him... Samuel!'

'Shit, mate. That's a bummer. I told her not to name him after me!'

'You don't help yourself much, do you, Sam?'

'Cheers, mate!'

They bashed their cans together too hard and a squirt of beer shot from each one, so that they both jumped clear. In doing so, Kanoski stumbled and Cadman supported him, his arm around his friend's shoulders. They huddled down under the umbrella and talked. The air felt thick and low in oxygen and had to be gulped down like a tepid lumpy soup. Cadman thought wistfully for a moment about the fresh heat of the May weather in London, then his boys and the barbecue and Lee's clarity of vision that had reunited him with his children.

'Have you seen Jasmina yet, Sam?'

'No. I thought she was in London.'

'Well, she's not. She was. I saw her there, but she's now working at the PSC! She'll be there tomorrow. What's the matter?' Kanoski's face was that of a mortuary corpse:

colourless, lifeless, a Kanoski-shaped mask. He stared blankly, his eyes seeing nothing. Finally, his head slumped and his shoulders slid forward, his arms hanging limply, fingers scraping the damp floor.

'Are you alright, Sam?'

Kanoski shook his bowed head and a faint airless whine fell from his slack mouth.

'Are you alright?' Cadman asked again, resting his hand on the back of the Australian's neck.

Kanoski straightened, sipped his beer and said, 'It's bloody hot, isn't it? I thought the rain was supposed to clear the air.' He looked up and there was silence. Cadman studied him as he surveyed the starless night sky.

'You said you had some good ideas for the course?'

Kanoski looked down through heavy lids. He didn't speak for a second or two. 'Yes. You remember the business about the IRA?'

'How can I forget? It was my first taste of humiliation.'

'But it worked out fine. They enjoyed the comparison between Irish and Indian terrorism. Anyway, you said something about the victims that stuck in my mind.'

'What was that?'

'You said I didn't care about the victims, I was only interested in the methodology and the causes. Something like that anyway. When I got home, I did some research on Pritilata. They've just unveiled a statue of her where she died. They're teaching about her in Bangladeshi schools now; it took about eighty years for her to move from colonial terrorist to Bangladeshi freedom fighter.'

'And the victims?'

'That's what's now interesting me, thanks to you. She killed an elderly woman. A civilian, a Mrs Sullivan. Bangladeshis don't discuss this; they focus on the heroism, of course. Her struggle was heroic, but let's not talk about the fact she killed an unarmed woman. A classic terrorism victim, completely random. Just happened to be in the club at the time. The target was the club, because of what it stood for and because of the dogs and Indians sign. Poor old Mrs Sullivan wasn't a target as such, she was just in the wrong place at the wrong time.'

'Who was she?'

'That's what I'd like our students to research. Why was she there? I can't answer those questions. I'm writing a paper on it. A comparative case study of the two IRAs: how they influenced each other, their motivation and the impact. Including something about the victims, of course.'

'You're the academic. Sounds a bit inflammatory to me. But if you think you can get them talking about the victims without causing a diplomatic incident, then go for it. Sounds interesting.'

'I'm calling my paper "Dogs and Indians Not Allowed". Good title, eh?'

'Yes, it's good. How did the course go without me, by the way?'

'Much more smoothly, mate.'

'You do want your lights punched out, do you?'

'No, the students missed you. They're coppers. They like what I say, but they look to you to endorse it.'

'So I could humiliate you in class?'

'I would've done if I was you! Got any good cases on the go?'

'I can't talk about those, Sam. Not to an unvetted, lefty, foreign upstart. Though there is one that would interest you. From a motivational point of view. A bullied Muslim anti-globalisation activist who is inspired by AQ. There are some root causes in there, aren't there?!'

'It sounds as if he's polarised and looking for an identity,' Kanoski said seriously.

'Believe it or not, Sam, I've found myself thinking something very similar.'

'I can believe it, Alex. You learnt at the hands of a very wise and widely respected Australian academic.'

'With no social skills.'

'And no beer. Fancy another, mate?'

'Yes, why not? Is François coming this evening, do you know?'

'Yes, I do know. He's not coming. He called me earlier and said he'll meet us at the PSC. He's sending a car to pick us up. I think he has to pay for one this time, now that Akbar's dead.'

'I wonder if Jasmina kept Ezaz on?'

'Who's Ezaz?'

'He was our driver. Akbar's driver.'

'I never knew his name.'

'You never bothered to ask him. He's a good man. Next to no English, but we communicated somehow.'

The barman arrived with two open cans of Fosters and two glasses and they realised that the rain had eased to a fine spray. In a few minutes the sounds of surface water drained away and the smells and clamour of Dhaka began to drift over the club walls. The barman walked around the tables sweeping surface water into the gulleys.

'There's something I need to tell you, Sam. But I need you to keep it to yourself.'

Kanoski had been watching the clouds break up. Now he pulled his chair in and his face was close to Cadman's. 'You can trust me, Alex. I wouldn't betray a secret.'

'Like when I told you I'd shit the bed, you mean? You kept that to yourself. And Jasmina. And Akbar. And Ezaz.'

'Who's Ezaz?'

'The driver. We just spoke about him.'

'Sorry. These names don't stick in my mind.'

'And Shahjahan, come to think of it. Oh, and the bloke who serves the teas and the lunch!'

'Shahjahan's speaking on the course, by the way. François told me. He's coming to give an input on National Security Intelligence.'

'That's good. He's a good bloke.'

'Your secret, Alex?'

'Not a secret exactly. It's just that I won't be staying at the hotel some nights. I'll meet you there in the morning before the car comes.'

'Where are you staying then?'

'I met a woman last time I was here. An American woman. Beverley. She came to see me in London and we're now… how do you say it these days? I've never heard myself say it before?'

'Shagging each other?'

'I was going to say we're a couple, or we're going out. Like I say, you don't help yourself, do you?!'

CHAPTER EIGHT

Cadman and Kanoski stood shoulder to shoulder at the front of the class. Twenty-odd pairs of suspicious dark eyes stared back at them.

'Assalamu Alaikum,' Cadman said, loudly, his voice cracking slightly.

'Wa Alaikumus Salaam,' the class replied in respectful unison.

'Good morning, all. Assalamu Alaikum. I'm Samuel Kanoski. Please call me Sam. This is Detective Chief Inspector Alex Cadman from London's Counter-Terrorism Command. You'd best call him sir.'

'You can call me Alex.' He nearly said it. He nearly said, 'You can call me Al'. He smiled inwardly, and outwardly, as he continued. 'Or sir or whatever you feel most comfortable with. We thought we'd start the course with a case study, get you straight into the subject. Can anyone tell me what happened in London on 7th July 2005?'

Kanoski retreated to the back of the class and listened as Cadman began his analysis of the impact of the bombs that killed fifty-six innocent people on London's transport system. From time to time he took notes. Just before coffee break, he stood and hooked his finger over his top lip.

'Do you want to come in, Sam?' Cadman asked.

Kanoski paused, finger still hooked on lip. 'No, thanks, Alex. It can wait until after coffee.'

*

'Tea.' A cup of tea in a delicate china cup marked with the blue, gold and red emblem of the Police Staff College was thrust into Cadman's hand, the cup wobbling on the saucer. The small chunk of lime bobbed in the storm.

'Hello, my friend.' Cadman shook the powerful hand of the white-coated man who beamed back at him. 'What *is* your name?'

The face fell. 'Coffee?' he thundered.

'No. Tea.' Cadman lifted the cup to his lips and took an exaggerated swig before smiling happily and the host tripped away satisfied.

'Hell-o!' Jasmina sang the welcome from across the cavernous chamber. She wore the same dark blue uniform as she had worn during their search for her father. Her hair was pulled back into a neat, dark bun the way it had been then.

'Hell-o!' Cadman sang back, his cup and saucer rattling as he placed it down. Her arms outstretched, she smiled pallidly as she walked slowly across to Cadman. Her eyes were heavy and tired, her skin pale. She embraced him, raising herself on her toes to reach his neck.

'Oh, Alex. Welcome back. It's wonderful to see you. I'm so glad that you came back.' There was an absence of enthusiasm in her voice.

'Jasmina.' She felt plump and young as she briefly cuddled into him. 'How are you? You sound tired?'

'I am well – a little tired, yes. Thank you.' A wisp of grey hair freed itself from behind her ear. 'I miss my father. That's normal, of course.' She gestured around the hall with her arm and said, 'But now I am here, in his place, close to him. The police service has looked after me and I have many friends.'

'I met Tofo. In that same coffee shop. He told me you had been posted here.'

'Yes. He has told me. I didn't say goodbye, did I?' Her voice was thin and airy, as if she spoke from a distance. 'I don't know why. I wanted to see you more in London. I had not planned it the way it was. I had hoped…' Her voice trailed to nothing as if she were distracted. 'There he is,' she said quietly, not quite to Cadman.

Kanoski was juggling a bottle of water as he bustled out of class. 'Alex…'

'Welcome back to the Police Staff College,' Jasmina said towards him, without moving.

Kanoski's brows hung over his eyes and he looked out from under them. He said to the space next to Cadman, 'Hello, Jasmina. Alex told me you were here. I knew we would meet.'

'You are an international trainer and I am one of the managers at the Police Staff College. Of course we would meet.'

'Veg-et-a-ble,' hollered the white-coated man, thrusting plates containing two samosas in front of the three of them. Jasmina and Cadman each took a plate, Kanoski, the bottle to his lips, refused by lifting his hand.

'You do not accept the hospitality we offer. Even in our village,' Jasmina stated. 'Alex does.'

'Look what it did to his guts.'

'My father was right to be cautious of you. He said I should also be cautious. I should have listened. I know that now.'

Kanoski pursed his lips and crunched the empty plastic bottle in his fist. Cadman was glad to have a mouthful of samosa.

'I have a lesson to plan. Excuse me, Jasmina.' Kanoski turned and went back into the classroom.

'You can tell me if you like, Jasmina,' Cadman said.

'There is nothing to tell, Alex. I believe Mr Kanoski would have preferred there to have been an elephant in the room. I prefer to remove it.'

'It feels as if it's still here.'

'Mr Kanoski is not one of us, Alex. He does not share our profession, our sense of duty, nor our friendship.'

'Well. I'll eat my samosas then.'

'Enjoy your break, Alex. I'll see you later.' Cadman watched her until she turned into her office.

'All alone, Alex?' François Sutherland swung in from the heat and clipped across the smooth marble floor. He looked dapper with his slim waistline, red tie and white shirt and smart grey trousers.

'Hi, Frank. Good to see you again. You're just in time for tea.'

'Sam about? Have you seen Jasmina yet?

'Sam's in class. He's on next. Jasmina's in her office.'

'What did you do with Jasmina in London?' Sutherland asked, as a coffee arrived in one hand and a plate with a samosa on it in the other.

'Just one? He gave me two.'

'He knows what I like. See? Black coffee, not tea.'

'What's his name?'

'I don't know.'

'Anyway, what should I have done with Jasmina in London?'

'Did she look alright to you? After the funeral, she came in every day for coffee at my office. She was fine, all things considered, though I think she's fallen out with Sam over something.'

'Tell me about it. They just met for the first time since the last course. Two minutes ago.'

'Frosty?'

'Worse.'

'So I saw her for coffee. We even made some arrangements to play tennis at the club when she got back. To be honest, I was surprised she came. I was pleased, but surprised. I thought she'd have plenty of local friends to turn to.'

'I think she's got local friends. She was popular with the other students on the course. I suspect she's just being hospitable, like Akbar would have wanted her to be.'

'Well, she came for coffee and we talked about Akbar and her future. She said then that she was interested in training. She was doing OK, a bit tearful here and there. Then she went to London to see Akbar's brother's family, and you. She got back a week or so ago and she looks ill – such a deterioration. I've been working with her getting this course ready, so I've been seeing her every day again.'

'Just normal, isn't it? Grieving's a strange old business.'

'Oh, I'm sure you're right. But the poor lady does look rough now. I think she's suffering.' He put down his empty plate and sipped his coffee. 'Got everything you need for the course?' he asked.

CHAPTER NINE

'How was your first day, honey? Do you need to meet Sam tonight?' Lee had been out when Cadman had let himself into the apartment. Now he was showering and Lee was bustling about, arranging clothes and rearranging toiletries.

Cadman stepped from the shower. 'It was a good first day,' he called out as Lee re-entered the bathroom. 'Lee, I'm naked!'

'Why do you think I came back in here? I thought you were going to take forever, with me pottering about trying to look busy. Come on, kiss me.'

'You'll get soaked. Let me dry first.'

'Shall we just stay in and watch TV? I've got some shrimp to grill.'

'That sounds just perfect, Lee. Just perfect.'

'You don't have to see Sam? How was the first day? Are you wearing pants or a sarong?'

'Pants. Trousers, I think, Lee. Not every night can be a sarong night. Can it?'

'Can't see why not. Pants is fine by me. You look swell in pants.'

'You are real, aren't you? I'm Alex Cadman – the fat English copper.'

'You're not fat, Al. You could lose a little weight, but you're not fat. I love you as you are, honey.'

Cadman pulled on the trousers muttering 'Hollywood' to himself.

'How was your first day? Can I get you a beer? It's great having you around.'

'My day was good, thanks. Tell me about yours.'

Lee was in the kitchen and called out to him as he searched about for his T-shirt. 'A normal day at an NGO. Politics. Frustration.' Her conversation was punctuated by the sound of vegetables being chopped. 'Another farming community disappearing without a choice. Work for the men, but no work for the women.'

'How do you cope?' Cadman kissed the side of her neck then set off to find his shoes.

'The same way you cope, honey. You do what you have to do. I try not to get too emotionally attached, but I don't want to get too blasé either. Shrimps are good for Bangladesh, I'm sure. But these women have never known anything other than rice farming. Their husbands will retrain, but the ladies will end up working in sweatshops.'

'Have you seen my flip-flops?' he called out from the bedroom, where the case he'd left full this morning was now empty.

'Not since you stepped out of the shower, honey! I can't see them through those pants! How was your day?'

'What are you talking about, Lee? Are you being rude?' He was opening wardrobe doors randomly.

'A little, honey. But I have no idea what flip-flops are.'

'Oh, Americans. What do you call them? Thongs?'

'In the dressing room. Shoe drawers are on the bottom left.'

'Dressing room? There's a dressing room? Ah!' He flapped across the tiled floors back to the kitchen. 'This is a great apartment,' he said, kissing her neck again. 'I'm like a kid. I'm happy like a kid.' He pointed to his feet. 'These are flip-flops.'

'Thongs. So now will you tell me how your day went?'

'My day was good. They're a good group of students again. Perhaps not quite as good English speakers. Something's gone on with Mina and Sam, though.'

'How do you mean, Al? Put the TV on, honey'.

He searched around for a remote control. 'They used to be great friends. Tennis and that. She used to faun over him a bit, to be honest.'

'Sounds like you were jealous, Al.'

'Maybe I was. I felt old and fat compared with him. Like you say, he's a handsome guy.' He pointed the gadget at the TV and it pipped into life.

'With frigid flip-flops?'

'Don't be rude, Lee.'

He heard her giggle to herself in the kitchen. 'So today they weren't great friends?'

'No, they could barely talk to each other. Didn't shake hands even. They would've hugged a few weeks ago. She told me he couldn't be trusted.'

'Sounds like they've been more than just good friends to me, Al.'

'He wouldn't be that stupid, would he? François and I both warned him.' He was flicking through television channels as he spoke.

'François?'

'The Canadian guy. These local news channels are full of Mirpur Plaza again! Can't they leave it alone?'

'Four hundred and seventy dead, Al.'

'CBS. Come and look at this, Lee. There's been a development by the look of things. CBS is running with it even.' She joined him and stood with her arm around the small of his back as they read the 'Breaking News' tape that reeled across the bottom of the screen.

'"Charged the building owner with culpable homicide. Now faces death penalty",' Cadman read, unnecessarily. 'I never really thought about that. It doesn't mean much to an American, I suppose. I wonder how they carry it out here?'

'Hanging,' read Lee, again unnecessarily.

'Bloody hell. Will they really hang him?'

'You don't love her, do you, Al?'

Cadman looked up from the TV, the remote in his hand. 'Love her?'

'She came to London to see you. A man and a woman would grow close if they went through that. Jack…'

'Don't be silly, Lee. Jack what?' He dropped the remote on the sofa and took her hands, one of which still held the knife. 'Jack what?'

'I lost Jack before he died. A woman going through the same as he was. I don't want to lose you, Al.'

CHAPTER TEN

'We've called you here this evening because we have been asked to brief you on one of our investigations.'

Cadman looked around the narrow office and decided that it wasn't a sixth form common room that it reminded him of; it was the prefects' room at school. He hadn't been a prefect himself so had never been inside but he used to get glimpses as he passed. Untidy: sports bags thrown here and there, piles of exercise books and papers, ring binders and coffee mugs and raucous, clever boys swaggering about in their prefects' ties. There was no 'we' as far as he could tell; he and the charmless MI6 officer whom he had previously met were the only occupants. 'You'll need to come into the secure room.'

He beckoned Cadman into the tiny carpet-lined box and pulled the thick door closed with a quiet swish. It was like a padded cell; you could bash your head against the wall for hours. The prefect's small face was square-jawed. His straight black hair, which had needed cutting last time Cadman saw him, hung in a preposterous, perfectly deliberate fringe over his eyes. He flicked his neck from time to time and the mass of hair swung backwards into place as neatly as if it had been combed that way.

'We would like you to read this before we start the conference call.' He handed Cadman a sheaf of nine or ten pages in a typed, rather small, pale grey font. Each page was topped and bottomed with classification marks and handling instructions, so that, once he'd got the hang of the layout, Cadman only had to read a paragraph or two squashed into the centre of each page. 'We'll need you to sign to say that we've shared this with you.' He flicked his hair back into place.

Cadman read Pritchard's transcript of the chat room. It was the first time he had seen it all in one document.

'Any questions?'

'No. I've seen it before, of course.'

The young officer's lips quivered and his hair hung between the two of them for rather longer than normal.

'How can you have seen it before?'

'You don't remember me? It's my investigation. This is intelligence from my team. I don't know where you got it from…'

'We are not at liberty to divulge the source.' He flicked his head twice. 'This is a joint investigation with the Security Service. We have taken the lead, as it's clearly an overseas operation.'

'Righto,' Cadman said. 'Where do I sign?'

He was just finishing his tenth signature when the phone rang and his host answered. He spoke for a few moments and then, with a flick of the head, switched it to loudspeaker.

'Hi, Alex. Spencer here. Joe's with me.'

'Hello, guv,' came Pritchard's shouted yet quiet voice. He was clearly sitting some distance from the phone.

'Have you briefed Alex, Julian?'

'Yes. He's now up to date,' Julian replied. He stooped over the desktop phone and his fringe hung like a veil obscuring his eyes from Cadman's view.

'Then let's move straight into the new information. What have you got, Joe?'

'I told you,' Cadman said quietly, but Julian did not reply and Pritchard began to speak.

'A new guy has joined the chat room.' Pritchard's voice was raised uncomfortably like that of a weather reporter. 'Calls himself LEFTrights. He has a long chat with MARX15 about G8. It seems they were both there. They worked out that they know each other. Anyway, then Higher Ground and Daina join the chat. I'll just read the pertinent bit.'

'Go ahead, Joe,' Cadman said. Julian looked up from the phone at Cadman and flicked his hair out of his eyes. He was about to speak when Pritchard continued:

'So Daina says, "Good news. The owner has been charged. He'll probably be executed."'

'I saw that on the news myself,' Cadman put in.

Pritchard continued: 'MARX15 says, "Harsh treatment. Do we want that in a utopian society?" Higher Ground says, "It's not harsh. It's the right thing. But he's just a fall guy. In a socialist utopia there wouldn't be greed." Daina says, "We can deal with the greed. Hurry up and get here." Higher Ground says, "Did you do the shopping?" Daina says, "No, I haven't started." Higher Ground replies, "Did you pick up the list?" Daina says, "Yes." Higher Ground says, "Then you can do the shopping. This is the right thing. The only message that will be understood." Then LEFTrights comes in: "What are you talking about? What message?" Higher Ground says, "Mind your own business. It's private." MARX15 says, "Send an email if it's private. This is a Marxist chat room." LEFTrights says, "What message?" And Higher Ground says, "Daina knows. He was there. He saw the suffering." LEFTrights says, "I can get the shopping if you want?" But Higher Ground and Daina don't reply. That's it. MARX15 stays in there and so does LEFTrights, but Higher Ground and Daina haven't been in there since.'

'Read it again,' Cadman ordered, but Julian stepped in.

'No need. The transcript will be more useful. That's it. Thanks, guys.'

'Thanks,' Pritchard shouted and Julian ended the call before Spencer said anything.

'Thanks for coming in,' he said to Cadman as he unlocked the door to the cell and they entered the prefects' room.

'What now? What about LEFTrights?'

Julian put his finger to his lips and rolled his eyes around the room. 'Not out here, please,' he snapped.

'But we haven't decided our next steps,' Cadman said.

'The next steps don't concern you, we're very sorry to say, Alex.' There was no hint of any sorrow in his tone of voice, just a sort of nonchalant efficiency. Cadman assumed from the 'we' that he was apologising on behalf of his organisation. They passed through the bank vault door and Julian fished Cadman's phone from its little wooden box and dropped it into his hand.

'Then why did you brief me?'

'Because we were told to.'

They reached the bottom of the stairs and sailed quickly past the large crest in the waiting area. Julian opened the door for Cadman, but instead of returning inside, he walked out with him. Halfway between the door and the perimeter gate he stopped and held Cadman by the forearm.

'You are friendly with an NSI agent called Shahjahan, we believe.'

'Well, not exactly friendly. He's a nice guy. He was on the last course I ran here.'

'We think you should be careful of him. He's something of an amateur.' He flicked his hair expertly.

'What do you mean?'

'He's a transferee to the agency. We're not sure of his credentials. His background is not in intelligence. He was a policeman. Goodnight.' He held out his hand and Cadman shook it incredulously before the anger had time to burst from him.

He had just reached the perimeter gate when Julian reappeared out of the darkness. 'One last thing, Alex,' he said. 'No need to worry about LEFTrights. You should let Constable Pritchard know that.' He tapped the side of his nose with a slender finger, winked, flicked his hair back and was gone.

CHAPTER ELEVEN

The rain fell half-heartedly from a restless, shifting grey sky that would neither commit itself to a downpour nor to sunshine. It pattered between the street vendors and the rickshaws that slowed hopefully when they saw the two white men standing on the kerbside of Road 11. It spilt onto the hot cement and tarmac in dark patches that shrank and faded instantaneously. A familiar, ageless lady, beshawled and carrying a naked baby, grinned at Cadman and he slipped her a note from the wad he now kept in his shirt pocket for just such circumstances.

'Still doing it?'

'More since Mirpur Plaza.'

'It used to be good squeezing in with Akbar and Mina…' Kanoski stopped himself mid-sentence and rubbed his toe over an evaporating damp shadow on the pavement. 'When's Shahjahan talking to the course?'

'What's gone on with you and Jasmina?'

'Nothing.'

'Nothing? It used to be tennis and flirting, now she says you can't be trusted.'

'Her father died. You know what François said about her. She's a mess. She doesn't know how to react to me, that's all. I think she was falling in love with me before.'

'God knows why.'

'I'm a handsome guy, Alex. You have to give me that, mate.'

'And a pain in the bloody neck. You've not hurt her?'

'No. Of course not.'

'She looked hurt.'

'What is this? A bloody police interrogation? I haven't done anything to her, alright?'

'Here's Ezaz.' The Toyota scuffed up against the high kerb and two hotel porters quickly stepped forward to open the doors. Ezaz popped open the boot and they dropped their bags inside.

'I'm meeting Jasmina tonight,' Cadman said as they pulled into the throng. 'Just for a chat, perhaps we'll have dinner somewhere. You're more than welcome to come – you could sort it out with her.'

'No, mate. I'm working on my paper this evening.'

'Well, the thing is, Ezaz was going to take us. I was thinking Jasmina could come in the car with us after class. Drop you off and we'll find somewhere round here.'

'Don't worry about me, mate. I'll be fine. I'll grab a taxi. I might suggest to Frank that we have a game of tennis.'

'I thought you were working on your paper?'

'Not all night!'

*

It was late afternoon and there was no electricity. The generator had kicked in so that there was light and power for the computer, but no air conditioning. A large rotary fan whirred noisily over the closing stages of Kanoski's Role of Ideology in Terrorism. Cadman's eyes were feeling heavy; one of the students, a man about Cadman's age and stature, was suffering too. His eyelids fluttered slowly closed and his chin sank into his chest as if he'd been drugged. A colleague rubbed him on the shoulder and he jerked his head upright, the whites of his eyes showing as his eyeballs rolled back into place. Cadman looked ostentatiously at his watch before he stepped out of class.

Even the sombre lounge area, usually a cool haven from the heat, was stifling. Cadman stretched his back and arms and wandered over to Jasmina's office, where he tapped and popped his head in. She sat at her desk, reading through handwritten notes that Cadman recognised as being her jottings from the previous course.

'You were a very conscientious student. What are you reading up on there?'

'Alex!' She closed the notebook and laid it on top of a pile of papers on her desk. 'Are you still taking me to dinner this evening?' She fumbled with a pin holding her hair bun in place.

'Well, I skipped lunch today. What time?'

'I can't go in uniform, so give me half an hour when class finishes. OK?'

'Looking forward to it.'

He climbed slowly up the stairs towards the toilets and, as he reached the top, he heard the classroom door open and the students waft out, their end-of-day chatter subdued by the heat. By the time he came down again, a few stood around but there was no sign of Kanoski. Cadman wandered into the dank classroom and began to shut down his computer and tidy his papers. The room smelt of body odour. His laptop flickered out; he closed it and slipped it into his rucksack beside the heavy roll of material.

There was a sudden breath of flowers and Jasmina was standing in the doorway. She wore the same sari that he had first seen across the river as she stood in the blazing sun with her parasol. The turquoise and black patterns sang out from the shocking pink material, her hair swam in heavy waves to rest on her shoulders and her bangles played a tiny tune as she raised her arms in question.

'What? You've never seen a beautiful Bangladeshi girl in a sari before?'

'What can I say, Jasmina?'

'You can say I look beautiful.'

'You look beautiful. More than beautiful. I don't know a word for very beautiful.'

'Very and beautiful are good words. They go well together. Take me to dinner would you please, Alex?'

A student ran ahead of them to open the main door as they walked arm in arm across the polished tiles and out under the portico. Ezaz drew up and grinned at them, then jumped out, took Cadman's bag and helped them into the back seats.

'Should I ask?'

'I will tell you before you ask. My good English friend likes to see me in a sari. I am a free woman. I make my own choices. Tonight I choose to wear a sari for my good English friend.'

'And a fine choice it is too. Where are we going?'

'My favourite is a restaurant that specialises in kebabs. Bangladesh is well known for its kebabs. It's in Road 11. Dad used to like it there. It is very popular, so there is always a good atmosphere.'

'Let's try there then.'

The kitchens were highly visible from the outside. Sweating chefs were grilling meat on open flames as part of a performance to draw in customers. A mouth-watering mix of aromas was pumped out into the darkening Dhaka evening: charring meat, frying onions and fragrant, heady spice. Every table appeared to be full and eight or ten Bangladeshi men and women waited outside the door. 'What a pity,' Cadman said. 'It's full up. Should we try elsewhere?'

'No. I have reserved us a table here.'

'You've reserved a table? Excellent.'

They walked through the crowd and were quickly pounced upon by three young waiters who beamed as they escorted their charges through the crowded ground floor. Well-dressed, affluent-looking young Bangladeshis occupied the tables: family groups, couples and parties of students, both boys and girls. Some scoured the menu enthusiastically, whilst others were enjoying succulent-looking grilled meats and rice. 'Mmm. It really does smell good.'

'Yes. Good fresh meat here. No tummy problems.'

They were shown to a table upstairs, in the window overlooking the crowded main road. Tea lights on the table and on ornate wooden shelving behind her flickered in the zephyr of her sari. As she sat, he glimpsed the tender brown skin of her midriff.

'You can give your bag to the waiters, Alex, if it's in your way.'

'No, that's OK. My laptop's inside. I'd best keep it.'

The waiter brought fresh plum juice in big stemmed glasses. 'To my good English friend Alex.'

'To my beautiful Bangladeshi friend Jasmina.'

They sucked on their straws for a moment and then Jasmina said, 'To my father, who would have loved to have been here with us.'

'Yes. To Akbar.' They touched their glasses and Jasmina looked directly at Cadman. Her black eyes glistened and the creases around them gave her a wisdom that he had not seen there before. The black dot in her forehead flashed as it caught the moving candlelight. The tiny crevices of her lips were moist and her smooth cheeks glistened. Lee writhed naked through his mind.

'Very beautiful,' he said. 'I know why Tofo didn't trust me to be alone with you.'

'We have been through a great deal together, Alex. Only you and I, perhaps Ezaz, know what we experienced at Mirpur Plaza. Of course we are close.' Reaching to the back of her head, she pulled her hair together in the palm of her hand and pulled the thick dark rope of hair over her shoulder, so that it splayed out on her lap. She groomed it a few times with her fingers then pushed it back in place behind her.

'If we could only turn back time,' Cadman mused.

'Then we wouldn't be so close.'

'I think I meant if I could just make myself twenty years younger, Mina.'

'You are beautiful inside, Alex. Like my father. That does not age. It's why you do simple things like accept hospitality and exchange smiles with people from my village. Not like…'

A waiter hovered.

'You pick please, Jasmina. I'm hungry, by the way.' He watched her whilst she discussed the menu in Bangla.

'It's a beautiful language,' he said when she looked up at him.

'Bangladeshi people are proud of their language. We even have a special day, Mother Language Day, to celebrate it. The struggle for the right to speak our own language lies at the heart of our struggle for independence.' She combed her hair with her painted fingernails as she spoke. 'In 1952 students protesting for the right to speak Bangla were murdered by the regime. Expelling the foreign invaders became an imperative from that time.'

'I can't imagine being forbidden to speak English.'

'Well, the English were usually the invaders, so nobody was making you speak another tongue.'

'I suppose you're right. I'm glad the Empire is in the past and you and I can meet as equals, aren't you?'

'Of course, Alex. It was different that time. Though there is still a need to banish the foreigners, of course.'

'You mean Sam?'

'No. Not Sam. Why would you think I meant Sam? I meant the multinationals. The foreign occupation of Bangladesh by the big globals.'

'Mirpur Plaza?'

'Yes. Colonial occupation of Bangladesh is just as oppressive as it ever was. Nearly 500 women died at Mirpur Plaza alone.'

'But you said the women need those jobs for the sake of their independence? If you banish the multi-nationals…'

'Yes, but not colonial jobs.'

'Colonial jobs? Bangladesh isn't being colonised. Governments colonise. Foreign states. Companies don't colonise. They just place orders.'

'No. They don't just place orders. They move in and take over production. They use cheap labour to produce goods for themselves. They do colonise. It's just the same as the British invasion of India the first time.'

'I don't see that. The British invasion, or colonisation or whatever it was, of India was by the British government, the army. Not a British company.'

'But it started with a company, Alex. Don't you see?'

'A company?'

'The East India Company.'

Cadman noisily sucked up the remains of his juice as he pondered.

'And the East India Company had an army and the army enforced the company's globalisation policy. India's First War of Independence, you call it the Mutiny, was an uprising against the company's troops.'

'But there's no army enforcing globalisation this time.'

'No. It's being done in much more subtle ways.'

'What ways?'

'Anything that interferes with globalisation is now called terrorism. The Americans and you, the British, I mean, the Australians, you tell us that time and time again.'

'But we haven't sent in an army.'

'Not in Bangladesh. You tried it in Iraq and Afghanistan and Libya, but it caused so much damage there that you've stopped doing that. Now you send police officers to teach us to counter terrorism ourselves.'

'Oh, Mina. I'm not here to support globalisation. Look at me. I'm your friend. I'm here for the victims. Your dad was too.'

'First you make sure we get the message that violence against multinational companies is terrorism, then you teach us how to fight it. We're doing your work for you.'

'But you're talking so… I don't know, theoretically about me, Jasmina. Your dad and me. We're not politicians. We're policemen. Akbar told me about the bomb in the park on Bengali New Year. The bodies and the suffering. I've seen that too. I work in counter-terrorism to try to stop the killing of innocents. That's all.'

'I know that, Alex. You're different. My father was different. But who killed my father? Who killed the innocent women of Mirpur Plaza? Terrorists or capitalists? It's starting all over again.' She pulled her hair back over her shoulder, separating hairs with her nails and examining them. 'What can I do, Alex? What can I do?'

'Can we do anything? We need governments to do something.'

'It's the government's responsibility, but the young people of Bangladesh won't wait forever. You've seen the *hartals*. Bangladeshis are people of action. When they stopped us from speaking our own language we began the liberation movement. The young will free themselves from the threat of globalisation before it leads to Bengal becoming a repressed colony again. And if the government doesn't do something in the face of the deaths of all those women, take some action to curb foreign investors, the *hartals* will become more demanding.'

'Well, we'll fight the cause together then, shall we?'

The waiter reappeared and placed a white plate of brightly coloured relishes in the centre of the table. Then he cleared some space near Cadman and began to arrange more plates close to him. 'These are lamb kebabs from Pakistan, very spicy,' he said in fine English. 'These chicken ones from Afghanistan. Not too spicy.' He laid the skewers out on the table and Cadman was momentarily reminded of the sticks of dung he'd seen on his way to Jasmina's village.

'Nothing from Bangladesh?' he asked.

'Yes, sir. These beef kebabs are special from Bangladesh. I hope you enjoy them.'

'They look very good. Thank you.'

'More drinks, sir?'

'I think we'd like more of that very good plum juice.'

'Yes, sir.' The waiter walked away beaming.

'I really think you could fight it with me, Alex. You understand Bangladeshis.'

'I don't know about that. I think I understood Akbar, Shahjahan maybe. But I don't understand you, Mina.'

'Why not?'

'You wear a sari just for me, you bring me to this romantic corner, you feed me delicious food and then you…'

'I accuse you of being an agent of a capitalist plot against Bangladesh.'

'Something like that, yes.'

'Perhaps my father warned you about me?'

'No. If he did, he'd have been wrong. Now, Sam on the other hand…'

'He didn't really warn me about Sam. I made that up to hurt him. I warned myself. But I didn't listen.'

'Did he hurt you?'

'No. Nothing happened'. She said it quickly as she pulled a cube of chicken from a skewer with delicate, manicured fingers. 'Perhaps I misunderstood him. I felt humiliated and silly.'

'Why?'

'I thought he was genuinely offering me a scholarship to study in Australia. I told people about it. I told my father. Then he said that there were no places left. That's all. Now I think he said it just to…'

'It must be awkward working with him. Do you think you can somehow sort it out?'

'Oh yes. I'm sure I can lead that elephant out of the room.'

'Can I reintroduce one?' Cadman reached under the table. 'This is the sari your father was buying for you when he died. He chose it for you and he wanted you to have it. It was my idea, a gift from me, but he went to get it for me. He wasn't throwing it away, Jasmina. He was throwing it to you.'

He handed the heavy bolt across the table and it sagged close to the food.

'Careful, Alex, you'll spoil it.'

'You care then.'

'Yes, I care.' She stood and draped the material over her arm. A magnificent swathe of pale lemon cascaded towards the floor, the gold pinstripe sparkling in the ambient light of the restaurant.

'Oh, Alex. It's beautiful.' She spoke without looking away from the sari. In the pause during which Cadman imagined she was studying the pattern, three big tears plopped together onto the new garment and glistened for a moment before being absorbed.

'It's jasmine,' he said, standing.

She looked up, her eyes liquid, her cheeks stained, her nose beginning to run. She smiled widely, her white teeth pristine behind the red lips and brown skin. 'I know what colour it is, Alex,' she groaned, as she fell on him.

Cadman felt the moisture at his neck and then through his shirt on his chest as she sank back down on her flat feet. The new sari sat awkwardly on the crook of her arm and began to fall as they embraced. He reached to stop it and his fingertips instead fell on the hot bare skin of her abdomen.

'Alex,' she whimpered into his collar. 'Thank you, Alex. It's beautiful. Abu…' She cried into his chest and kissed his neck and the rolled sari teetered awkwardly between them like a barrier waiting to be lifted. Cadman said nothing and while she cried, his hand rested self-consciously on her naked skin.

CHAPTER TWELVE

From their position under the portico of the Police Staff College, the two trainers had a good view along the driveway and out over the lake. Cadman's eye was drawn to a swarm of large winged insects, like daddy-long-legs, hovering in a concentrated mass just above the water's surface. Small circular ripples interrupted the otherwise serene smoothness of the lake each time that one of them broke the hypnotic zigzagging flight pattern and flitted onto the water. As he watched, a large black snake, more than a metre long, appeared far out in the dark green water, its head clearly visible, its thick submerged body writhing as it swam towards the flies. Then it was amongst them, quietly devouring those that came within range, whilst the swarm continued oblivious.

'Did you get much work done on your paper last night?'

'Yes, I did, thanks, mate. I read some interesting stuff. I'm thinking of going down there at the weekend.'

'Down where?'

'Pahartali. I'd like to see the European Club for myself. And the statue of Pritilata. Fancy coming?'

'What, terror tourism?'

'Yes, I suppose. A busman's holiday. I'm going to try and find out a bit more about Mrs Sullivan too, if I can. Perhaps find the European cemetery.'

'I think Lee has other plans. She wants to take me to Chittagong for some reason.'

'We'll go together then.'

'What?'

'I'm only joking, mate. I don't want to get in the way of you two. But Pahartali's a suburb of Chittagong as far as I can make out. We're going to the same place.'

'We can travel together. Why not? I think Lee would like to meet you.'

'Is this him?'

A dark Honda with blacked-out windows drew up under the portico and Shahjahan, wearing a smart, slim-fitting black suit and a thin navy tie, emerged from the back. He put on sunglasses as he approached them, grinning.

'Looking good, Shahjahan!' Kanoski held out his arms to the slight Bangladeshi and they came together in a brief hug.

Cadman held out his hand. 'Good to see you again, my friend.'

'It is good to see you again, sir, and Mr Kanoski too. It is very kind of you to allow time for a presentation by the NSI.'

'Your role is definitely something the students should know about,' Kanoski said as he led the way into the building.

'How is Jasmina?' Shahjahan asked.

'Oh, she's OK I think, Shahjahan. Missing her father, of course. I had dinner with her last night and she finally accepted the sari from me.'

'I have only seen her once since her return from London. She was very angry.'

'Angry?' Kanoski asked.

'With me and with you, Mr Kanoski. She thinks I should have done more to locate him that time. She had a very false expectation of our capability. I told her that we only have limited capacity to monitor telephones. It's the truth. But she was very emotional. She had no rationality. Before his death, even afterwards, it seemed we would be friends, she and I. I'm worried about her, sir. She is not the same as before.'

'Why was she angry with me?' Kanoski asked.

'Because you could have done more to locate him too. I told her that you're an academic, Mr Kanoski, not law enforcement or intelligence services. Your responsibility was to ensure that the training continued.'

'That's bloody right, mate.'

They paused outside the classroom where there was suddenly a loud shout: 'Tea!' The white-coated man's hair stood up proudly and he smiled affectionately as he held out the tray.

'You're speaking in Bangla, aren't you, Shahjahan?'

'Yes, sir.'

'In that case, Sam and I will leave you to it. The students are waiting for you. We'll come in after about forty minutes to help you to wrap up.'

The dapper young intelligence officer swished confidently into the classroom and the door rattled closed behind him. Before Cadman and Kanoski had a chance to sip their tea, Shahjahan poked his head around the door.

'Sir, when I have a chance I must speak to you alone. Sorry, Mr Kanoski, operational work. Law enforcement eyes only. I'm sure you understand.' He disappeared again.

'I wonder what that's all about.'

'I'd love to know what he's telling them,' Kanoski said. 'I bet he's warning them about us.'

'Why would he do that?'

'That's what they do, isn't it? National security comes first.'

'We're allies, Sam. We're not a threat to Bangladesh.'

'She said I was.'

'Alex! Sam!' Jasmina appeared from her office and clipped purposefully across the expanse of tiled floor. She wore uniform shirt and trousers and fiddled with the bun in her hair as she walked. She waved a piece of paper. 'You'll need an escort back to Road 11 tonight. The opposition has just called another *hartal*. Mirpur can be dangerous in the evenings. I will make the arrangements now. Don't leave the PSC until you've heard back from me.'

'Yes, ma'am. What's the *hartal* about?'

'The owner of Mirpur Plaza has been released without charge.'

'But why?'

She called back to them without looking back. 'Money. Why else?'

'She's bad-mannered,' Kanoski muttered, sinking into one of the black faux-leather armchairs that occupied the lounge area outside the class.

'Bad-mannered? Jasmina?'

'Just walking away like that, talking out of her arse at us.'

'What do you expect, Sam?'

'I expect common decency. That's what I expect.'

'Did you show her any?'

'What are you talking about, mate? Of course I did.'

'It's just that Frank and Shahjahan both say they're worried about her.'

'Look, wind your neck in, alright? You're bloody interrogating me again. That's why your wife left, mate. You can't stop being a bloody copper.' Kanoski stood and began to walk towards the stairs.

'I'm sorry, Sam. I didn't mean to interrogate you. We call it interviewing these days, anyway.'

Kanoski walked back towards Cadman. 'Well, don't interview me, alright?'

'Lee needs to make a call home tonight, so we're going to the club. No signal at her place. Fancy teaching me how to play tennis? I can't stand listening to her when she schmoozes all over her grandchildren!'

'How's mini-me, by the way?'

'Sam? He's great. A real darling. Wide blue eyes, beautiful smile and he has this way of crawling that makes me sure he's going to be an early walker.'

'You're doing it now, mate.'

'What?'

'Schmoozing about your grandson. It's boring. Don't do it, mate.'

CHAPTER THIRTEEN

They sat in the car under the portico until the escort vehicle pulled up alongside them and motioned for Ezaz to follow. It was the same type of canvas-topped, open-backed lorry that had safeguarded them previously, with four armed officers wearing an assortment of uniforms. As before, their faces were deadpan and they perched two on each bench, facing each other without acknowledging their charges. Slowly the two vehicles moved off in convoy towards the front gates, which were locked with a fat rusty chain and padlock. His ancient rifle hanging from his shoulder, the guard came from his hut holding up a large key rather theatrically. Unlocking the padlock, he threaded out the chain and swung open first one gate then the other. Then he came to attention, saluted them and they pulled into the traffic. Cadman looked back to see him pulling the gates closed behind them.

'Well, that's nearly the end of week two,' Kanoski said, placing his arm on Ezaz's headrest and craning his neck backwards to see Cadman. 'Tomorrow morning, a weekend in Chittagong, then we're into the final week.'

'And I can go home and forget all about you.'

'I'm looking forward to thrashing you at tennis this evening.'

'Cantonment, Ezaz?' Cadman asked.

219

'Sir?'

'We go cantonment?'

'Yes, sir. Cantonment.'

The main road outside the college was busy but moving. The escort truck eased carefully over a high speed hump and then switched on its blue lights and siren and hurtled forward. Ezaz was slow to react and by the time he had managed to manoeuvre the much lower Toyota over the hump, there were seven or eight vehicles between them. They reached the first major junction and were held by traffic lights. The cantonment was just a few minutes along the dual carriageway towards the right. Straight on there was another main road that appeared to lead to a commercial area. Between the two, emptying out onto the junction like a widening funnel, was the snake-like lane that led past the bed and iron mesh factories.

As usual, the market on the corner showed no signs of any recognition of a strike. The sacks of rice and spices and piles of vegetables lined the roadside and a happy ethnic mix of multicoloured clothing hung at head height. A few customers milled about amongst the crouching tradesmen whilst a dozen or so rickshaw pullers lazed in their empty vehicles, some fast asleep in impossible positions.

'What's that noise?' Kanoski asked.

'A train?'

A low roaring sound, a deep booming overlaid with a treble of white noise, had gradually become apparent. It was indistinct but rapidly increasing in volume.

'We're nowhere near the railway line yet. I don't think it's a train – we'd have heard it before.'

'Roadblock, sir.'

'Ezaz?'

'Roadblock.'

A solitary rickshaw puller had broken away from the dozing pack and had parked his vehicle in the middle of the road, attempting to block both lanes of the major road. The skinny man was leaping from carriageway to carriageway, waving his arms in futile fashion as vehicles squeezed past him on either side. Horns began to sound even more regularly and harshly than usual. The escort vehicle was somewhere ahead.

'Go round him,' Kanoski ordered. Ezaz did not reply. He looked at Kanoski as if trying to find the words, but sat steadfastly.

It was now apparent what the noise was. Many male voices were chanting and shouting. It was like the electrifying rumble of football fans from outside a stadium. The rickshaw driver was still hopping from lane to lane, though most vehicles were coming from behind them and simply steering around him and his tricycle. Now, as the stadium crowd noise peaked ever louder, other rickshaw pullers were waking up and dragging their vehicles into the road, to reinforce the block.

'Go, Ezaz!' Cadman shook the driver's shoulder and Kanoski released the handbrake.

At last Ezaz turned the wheel and, taking the opportunity as the man darted sideways, began to edge around the rickshaw.

'We're the last car through!' Cadman called, looking back. The other rickshaw pullers had acted and had formed an unbroken chain of men and tricycles behind the Toyota, stopping any further traffic from beating the blockade.

'Go. Go, Ezaz.' Cadman waved his hand forward, but the first rickshaw puller had seen them and he darted forward and slung himself across their bonnet, his feet planted, his skinny legs in front of the radiator grille. He was shouting at the screen and holding up the palms of his hands. Horns blasted behind them. The escort truck with its armed guards was nowhere to be seen.

'Go!' Kanoski shouted.

'No, sir. Mr Akbar say no.'

It was too late. The voices were upon them; a wide and dense file of marchers swung into view from the snake lane and cut across the front of them towards the cantonment. The main road was instantly blocked. Hundreds of men were in the front ranks alone and the procession just kept on spilling out. The small white Toyota was isolated – stranded in the no-man's-land between the marchers and the roadblock behind them. They waved banners and shouted in unison. Most wore white *topis* and long white shirts. All of them wore beards. The banners were in Bangla, alien red scrawl. But some were in English too. 'Justice for Mirpur Plaza Dead!' 'Stop Foreign Invasion!' 'Islam Against Global Trade!' Their anger was universal and clear. They swept around the Toyota. They clamoured for justice. They shouted and waved their banners and sticks. The roar for revenge was deafening. They slammed their fists on the car roof as they swarmed past and the Toyota rocked.

'Where's the bloody escort?' Kanoski screamed.

'Jasmina!' Cadman was shouting into his mobile phone.

'Tell the escort to come back. We've lost it. We're at the first major junction after the PSC and before the cantonment. There's going to be a riot!'

'Well done!' Kanoski called.

'We'll just sit it out.'

More and more of the column squeezed out onto the main road. Now they clambered over the bonnet of the Toyota and the car rocked violently. Furious chants filled their ears. They were heading towards the cantonment but the body of protesters behind them continued to swell out of the side road, so that the foreigners were constantly exposed to more angry eyes. The clamour thundered all around them.

'What's he doing?' Kanoski pointed. His voice was thin.

The rickshaw puller was amongst the marchers. He tugged at the white sleeve of one of the men and pointed towards the Toyota. All around them were white cotton legs and arms, clambering over the car.

Ezaz opened his hands and began to pray.

'Bloody hell! It's no good praying. You should have…'

A thud and a smash, and the screen in front of Ezaz's praying hands was a sagging cobweb of shattered laminated glass, the end of a cricket bat embedded in the centre. It swung back again. Smash! The car rocked with the force. The window gave way. A clear circle of open hot air. Ezaz cowered and prayed. His lap was full of shards of glass.

The roar was louder. Unceasing, deafening. Jeers and taunts. Faces at the windows, pressed to the glass. Hands pulling at the locked doors. A crash and the roof bowed inwards between the two men. A foot kicked through the windscreen. The whole screen toppled in on Ezaz and Kanoski.

Kanoski squirming through the narrow gap between dented roof and headrest to reach the back seat. Ezaz hauled through the screen. Hands grapple at the driver's door, fumbling with the lock. Terrible noise: shouting, babbling, crashing of sticks on metal and glass. A petrol can in the crowd, moving from madman to madman. Cadman's door flies open and hands are on him. Everywhere. He clings to the headrest. Brown fingers pull at his. Kanoski in the same position, fingers trying to prise him free of the headrest. A splashing sound and a stink of petrol. A stream gurgling through the windscreen onto Ezaz's seat. Wet dollops of petrol on Cadman's hands and sleeves.

'Get out!'

He releases his grip and they shoot in opposite directions out of the car. Sirens. An immense burst of heat. The car wrapped in orange flames. The hard road surface in Cadman's face. A gunshot. Cadman rolls away from the car. White legs, shirts and hats running, leaping. A familiar face. Running with the crowd. A familiar face. A man Cadman knows.

A pair of blue trousers and black boots were beside Cadman's face. A gentle Bangla voice. Someone helping him up. The policeman in blue camouflage.

The roar continued and the march snaked on, out of the side road and towards the cantonment. Cadman was heaved up onto the escort truck. Kanoski and Ezaz were side by side opposite him, Ezaz praying, Kanoski silent and still, his face black with smoke, running with sweat, his eyes staring.

A tarpaulin swung down at the back of the truck and Kanoski's and Ezaz's faces disappeared. They sat in darkness and Ezaz prayed in soft Arabic. The noise of the crowd was diminishing; the tail of the column of marchers had passed them.

In the gloom of the lorry, Cadman's mind raced, scraping and digging until it found what was bothering him. The face in the crowd. It was Tofo.

CHAPTER
FOURTEEN

'Alex! You're alive!' Jasmina was still in uniform when she came running up the stairs and into the club bar. She clung to him, almost spilling his beer. 'It must have been awful. Ezaz should have stuck with the escort.'

'Yes. It was awful. Sam's OK too.'

'Yes. Good. Of course.'

'He's here somewhere. We were going to play tennis.'

Cadman's mobile phone rang before he could finish his sentence.

'Excuse me, Mina. Hi, Joe.'

'Hello, guv. I got the message you called. Sorry I wasn't in touch yesterday. I was tucked up and there was nothing to report on Higher Ground. Are you OK, guv?'

'Yes, I'm alright. A bit shaken up, like anyone would be, but I'll be fine.'

'Were you injured?'

'No. Not injured. But my laptop was destroyed in the fire. Let Mr Thorogood know, will you?'

'Yes, guv.'

'So you got my message.'

'You mean the chat room? No, nothing. Not for a couple of days now. Not from the main two.'

'The other two?'

'Yes, both chatting away. LEFTrights keeps asking the other one where they are. I think he's in it with them, guv. Or wants to be.'

Cadman could see Lee sitting at her usual table, talking to her daughter. She looked towards him and he smiled back.

'Thanks, Joe. That's all it was.'

'OK, guv. No problem. Speak soon.'

'Joe…'

'Guv?'

'Send his photo out to me, will you? We snapped him at the G8, I think?'

'Yes, guv. Or at least a bloke purporting to be him. I'll send it to the lads at the High Commission. Is that OK, guv?'

'That's great. Thanks, Joe. See you.'

Jasmina was waiting for the call to finish. 'Alex, I won't stay. I have work to do. There are extra plans for your safety. You'll go in a police truck tomorrow. The *hartal* is twelve hours so we'll review it over the weekend. Probably just get a new car. I just wanted to see you, Alex. To check for myself.' She pulled away from him to go, then returned and squeezed him again before disappearing down the stairs.

'Fuck me, that was a close call.' Kanoski appeared from nowhere.

'Certainly was. Thank Christ that escort got back to us when it did.'

'No, I meant just now. With Mina. I nearly bumped into her.'

'It must have been some argument you two had. You've got to sort it out, Sam.'

'I will, Alex. I will. Who's this? Lee?'

She carried a gin and tonic in one hand and her tablet in the other. 'Hi, honey. So I finally get to meet the handsome Australian guy. I'm Beverley. Pleased to meet you, Sam.'

'Beverley. I thought it was Lee.'

'Friends call me Lee. You can call me Lee, Sam.'

She offered her hand to Kanoski and he held it. 'I will, Lee. I will. You didn't tell me she was this beautiful, Alex.'

'Oh, I like this guy, honey. Handsome and charming too.'

'Don't take your eyes off him.'

'You two OK?' she asked. 'You look a bit, I don't know, dishevelled.'

'Sam and I have had quite a day.'

'They're all like that in Dhaka.'

'No. Sam and I were…'

'Attacked by a mob and set fire to,' Kanoski said, thrusting his fingers into his trouser pockets, the thumbs hooked outside, like a teenager.

*

'He seems a nice guy.'

'Handsome Sam?' Cadman said listlessly as he flicked through Bangladeshi television channels. They were slumped on the sofa, Lee nestling against Cadman, her hair brushing his chin.

'Now, now, honey. Don't be jealous. You've got nothing to be jealous of.'

'No. I know, Lee. I think Sam is the one to be jealous of us, don't you? There's next to no coverage of my heroic escape.'

'You don't need to see yourself on TV.'

'No. Something strange though. I'm sure I saw Jasmina's cousin in the crowd.'

'She may well have skeletons in the cupboard. Most of us do. I saw her at the club tonight, didn't I?'

'This cousin lives in London. He's English.'

'That is strange, honey. Why didn't you introduce us? I'd love to meet her. Did you ask her about her cousin?'

'No. She left quite quickly. There's nothing on TV. Shall we go to bed?'

'Why didn't you introduce us?'

'You were on the phone.'

'I would have finished the call to meet her. She'd have waited, I'm sure.'

'She had to get back to work. To arrange my protection for tomorrow.'

'I'm sure she's good at that. Did you give her the sari?'

'Yes, last night. I didn't get a chance to tell you. She loved it. It's the most gorgeous jasmine colour now that I've had it cleaned.'

'I remember it that night. Just a dusty old lump by the washing machine.'

'Jasmina's been through so much.'

'What does she think about you meeting me in the middle of all this?'

'No, there's nothing on. Shall we go to bed?'

'Alex?' Lee slid forward and perched on the edge of the sofa, looking into Cadman's eyes.

'She's had a rougher time than you think. Something's gone on between her and Sam.'

'You haven't told her about me, have you?'

'I've told Sam.'

'Oh, Alex! How could you not tell her? Don't I mean anything to you?'

'I told Sam.'

'You went to dinner with her last night. Just the two of you. You could've told her then!'

'Lee. It's been a crap day. Let's go to bed.'

'No. We're not going to bed. You can sleep at the hotel. How could you not tell her?'

'Now you're jealous.'

'Of course I'm jealous, Alex. She's beautiful. Young. You spend all your time with her. You never stop talking about her.'

'I never stop talking about you either.'

'Not to her.'

'I'm sorry, Lee. I'll tell her.'

'You can still sleep at the hotel.'

'But we're going to Chittagong tomorrow, aren't we?'

'Tomorrow's different. Of course we'll sleep together tomorrow. It's meant to be romantic. But tonight you've hurt my feelings. You can sleep at the hotel.'

CHAPTER FIFTEEN

The platform of Biman Bandar railway station was full. No embankments, cuttings or boundaries prevented the city from spreading, and so it did. Like a growing puddle, it seeped over and between and under the ancient colonial arteries of transportation. Travellers who couldn't fit spilled onto the lines and mingled with the slum dwellers, those whose villages offered no opportunity and who had come to Dhaka in search of employment as rickshaw pullers and machinists. Now they were the 'floating' people, drifting from street to street, begging, waiting for something to come up. Their slums were built alongside the track, corrugated iron and wooden hutches that, at best, provided shelter from the rain but offered little more in the way of comfort. There was nothing to divide the lines from their environs.

Lee sought and held Cadman's hand as a child would and he half expected Kanoski to grasp the other.

'This is certainly getting straight back into the saddle,' Cadman said and the grip between their hands tightened perceptibly.

'What do you mean, honey?'

'Yesterday we were attacked by a mob, today we're straight back into it.'

A circle of people had quickly formed around the three foreigners. The watchers stood, two or three deep, looking intently, up and down their bodies, into their faces.

'Everyone's looking at us,' Kanoski said. 'You're a copper, Alex. Does it feel safe to you?'

Cadman had already scanned the mass of people several times. 'There are plenty of escape routes. In that respect it feels safer than the London Underground.'

'The Tube,' Lee said.

'These people are too close,' Kanoski said. 'I don't like it, Alex. Let's go back to the hotel.'

A train rumbled slowly into the station. The huge blue diesel engine was encrusted with passengers, clinging like molluscs to any exposed iron. Beneath them, the form of the locomotive could just be made out; far from the sleek glass-fronted bullets of London's locomotives, this looked as if it had just emerged from the steam era. The driver's plate was situated behind the immense engine, which boasted a small cattle catcher, huge round buffers and wouldn't have looked out of place in a cowboy film. Five young men sat side by side on the forward-most part of the train, perched on top of their luggage, on a narrow iron inspection shelf above the buffer discs. They looked happy and comfortable, though there was nothing obvious for them to hold on to. Behind them, another narrow iron shelf ran the length of the engine. Six or seven smiling men stood on it, casually leaning against a safety rail, looking as if they felt they had the best spot on the train. Above them, partially obscured from view by the corrugated iron roof shelter that ran for most of the length of the platform, a batch of dangling legs indicated that people were sitting on top of the engine. Even before it had stopped, the train was besieged by more external passengers, clambering over those already there to find their own spaces. There was a cooperative atmosphere; people threw their baggage up to complete strangers who caught it before offering a hand to haul their new travelling companions aboard.

As the engine drew past them and the train came to a stop, Cadman saw that there were people on top of every carriage. Not children or joyriders, but long-haul passengers, travelling earnestly to their destination. He watched as a large family group of three generations – men, women and children – organised themselves. The children scrabbled atop first, then the baggage was thrown up to them: huge linen bundles tied neatly with blue nylon rope, cardboard boxes wrapped with tape, boxes that once contained TVs and computers and which had been discarded only to be eagerly reclaimed as roof luggage. Then came the elderly women; people inside the train slid the windows down so that they were fully open, to provide the ladies with a foothold. The adults heaved their haunches from behind, people inside helped arms and legs on their way and children pulled at wrists and arms from above until the ladies were in position. Next came the fitter adults – men and women – who clambered up amongst nattering advisors keen to assist, until all were settled on the roof. Sandals were lost and found and thrown back to their owners; concerned frowns turned into satisfied, toothy smiles. Though Cadman had previously seen these train roof people from a distance, it was a humbling experience to see them at close quarters; it was neither a game nor a choice – it was their means of travel back to their villages or wherever it was they were heading. Meanwhile, other travellers opted for more conventional, interior accommodation, rushing along the platform looking for opportunities, cramming into the doorways, families desperate to stay together, single people, couples, all looking for any gap to be exploited.

With the serious business of train boarding to be considered, the group of spectators around them had dissolved away but, as the train panted slowly out of the station, a new group began to assemble.

'Come on,' Cadman suggested, 'let's move down the platform a bit.'

The heat under the iron roof was punishing. His shirt stuck to his chest and even his trouser legs began to show patches of wet. They shuffled through the crowd for 100 metres or so and stopped again. Cadman looked for somewhere to get a drink; there were two or three little kiosks dotted along this section of the platform, but it was too hot to bother. Lee still held his hand whilst Kanoski stood close behind them, breathing over his shoulder. Another circle of onlookers began to gather. They stood without shame, facing the three of them and examining them.

'Tell them to piss off,' Kanoski hissed.

'Hell-o,' Cadman sang mechanically to the man nearest to him, managing to conjure up a positive note in spite of the oven-like temperature. The man smiled with dirty teeth and nodded to the man next to him.

'Hell-o,' Cadman said to the next man.

'Where are you guys headed?'

Kanoski flinched noticeably. The voice came from another watcher: a young Bangladeshi wearing a white *topi* and sporting a curly beard with no moustache. He had a slight American lilt to his accent.

Cadman held out his hand to the young man, who shook it with gusto. 'We're going to Chittagong. Your English is excellent. Where did you learn it?'

'Thank you. Here at school in Bangladesh. I guess the Internet and TV too. Can I get you guys a drink? You look so hot. This is Tanvir.' He said it as if he was introducing a third person, yet he laid the palm of his hand on his own chest.

'Can you make them go away?' Kanoski asked.

'I could, but they won't harm you. Bangladeshis are friendly people. You were right to say hello to them. They are just unaccustomed to seeing you here.'

'Tanvir, I'm Alex. This is my…'

'Girlfriend, Lee.' She shook Tanvir's hand warmly.

'And my colleague Sam. We're a bit nervous, Tanvir. We were caught up in the *hartal* yesterday.'

'At Mirpur? Guys, I'm so sorry. I heard some foreigners were harmed. You're not the ones from the burnt car? Let me get those drinks. We can get Coke or Pepsi and 7-Up here for good prices. Don't worry, I'll pay.' He disappeared into the mass of people and the circle of onlookers closed in again.

'Hell-o,' Cadman said to another young face in the crowd, a boy of about fourteen sporting a garish rucksack.

'Hello,' he retorted instantly. 'How are you?'

'I'm fine, thank you. How are you?'

'I'm fine, thank you. This is Ali. Who is your favourite cricket player?'

Kanoski chirped up, 'He's English, don't ask him. Mine's Shane Warne. A proper cricketer. Finest bowler in the game. Yours?'

'Malinga. Shane Warne's OK.'

Tanvir returned as Kanoski was about to reply. 'There you go, guys, drinks. I got one of each.' Their bottles hissed open simultaneously and Cadman guzzled his down. An announcement crackled over the public address system. 'Your train is next,' Tanvir said. 'Do you have tickets?'

'Yes. First class. Will people take any notice though?'

'Of tickets? Yes, of course. If someone is in your seat they will move instantly if you show them your ticket. This is your train now.'

The five of them, Kanoski still engaged in sporting rapport with the young Ali, edged towards the track. An engine, caked with people, trundled alongside the low platform, which was no more than a single step up from the level of the track. Seeing the height of the train from this perspective increased Cadman's admiration for those who had to climb onto its roof. He knew that he couldn't do it, though Kanoski and Lee probably both could. 'Are you going to Chittagong, Tanvir?'

'Yes, but on top. I'll show you where your seats are. Show me your ticket.'

'But it's nine hours to Chittagong!' Lee exclaimed.

'Yes – this is our train. It's called Mahanagar Godhuli – Metropolitan Afternoon or something like that. And you're on bogie number 7, seat 26. Not this one… here it is. *Saat.*'

'Tanvir! It's nine hours.'

'Here. This door.'

An elderly man with dyed orange hair was clinging to the handrail alongside the open door. Using his back as a shield, he ushered a woman of his own age and two teenage boys in front of him. He was about to join them when Tanvir called out to him in Bangla, indicating the three foreigners.

The orange-haired man smiled broadly. 'Oh. This is also your bogie?' he asked. 'Please, come. Follow my grandsons. I will show you your seats.'

Kanoski squeezed quickly past him, followed by Lee and Cadman. They stepped over luggage and people who were crouching in the cramped boarding space at the end of the coach. Others were trying to find room amongst them. They thrust their way through a further door and they were into the carriage itself. Every conceivable space was full; people stood or sat in the aisle, children were squashed four to a seat, women perched with toddlers or immense packages on their laps, or both. The orange-haired gentleman edged his way past his own family to the front of the trio and guided them to two empty seats in the middle of the carriage. Kanoski flopped into an aisle seat next to an immaculately made-up young girl with startlingly clear skin and neat features. The corresponding aisle seat was empty, but a scruffy middle-aged man occupied the window position. Their guide spoke to him curtly and he instantly rose.

'Oh, sorry, sorry,' he smiled as he shuffled clear.

Lee settled on the newly vacated window seat, her eyes glued to the window. Legs and feet were disappearing upwards and out of view. 'Ooh look, honey, there's Tanvir.

He really is going on the roof. And Ali! He's just a boy.' Cadman sank down beside her, across the aisle from Kanoski. The orange-haired man, clearly satisfied that he'd done his duty, made his way through the standing passengers back towards his own seat.

'What makes him think it was a good idea to dye his hair orange?' Kanoski chuntered.

'It's a sign of piety.' Lee leant across Cadman. 'When South Asian men have done the *hajj* they wear it that way. Anyway, he's a nice man. He helped us – can't you think of something nice to say?'

'She doesn't hold back, does she, mate?' he mumbled to Cadman.

'I heard that, honey.'

'It makes me realise how unlucky we were yesterday,' Cadman sighed, rubbing his eyelids with his fingertips. 'All these lovely people and we happened to be at that junction at that time to meet a few bad ones. It's what I tried to say to Jasmina that night she ran out of the club on me. Why would she mix with us lot when there's this lot she could be with?'

'Terrorism victims,' Kanoski put in. 'Random. Wrong place, wrong time.'

'This is OK, isn't it? We've got a bit of room here.'

'It's hardly first class, is it?' Kanoski whined. 'How much did we pay for these tickets?'

'Think of all these poor people standing,' Lee said. 'And of poor Tanvir and Ali on the roof. It's air conditioned and we're sitting down. What more do you want?'

'A cup of tea would be nice,' Cadman winked at Kanoski.

The train eased forward. A child of about three sat on the adjoining rail, his chin resting on the palm of his hand, his elbow on his slim bare knee. He looked in at Lee and Cadman with bored disinterest until his attention was distracted by a cricket ball that looped for six over a nearby wall and rolled neatly to his feet. He scooped it up, turned his back and ran, scaled the wall by means of a series of boxes placed there just for the purpose, skipped a metre or so along the top and then threw the ball to an unseen wicket keeper. Close to where he'd been sitting, a set of children's clothes – T-shirt and shorts – was laid out on the sleepers, weighted down by stones and drying in the sun.

A terrace of slum shacks backed onto the line just outside the station. Behind each one were immense piles of rubbish, mainly plastic bags, as high or higher than the shacks themselves. Two sheep and a yellow-brown cow nibbled away at the edges of one whilst a bearded, bedraggled and shirtless tramp, his hair hanging in filthy dreadlocks, munched mournfully and with exaggerated ruminations on a fruit that he held in his grubby fist. A tricycle selling ice creams trundled along amongst them. Then there was the usual system of side-lines, points and shunting areas seen outside any metropolitan railway station in the world. Between the lines, a group of boys were playing cricket, on a wicket that looked remarkably flat and green. Lee dozed off as they began to leave the suburbs, moving into country similar to that which Cadman had seen before. An upturned canoe in the centre of a dry paddy field suggested that the monsoon rains had not yet come.

'It reminds me of much happier times,' Kanoski said.

'You read my mind – you mean our journey to Akbar and Jasmina's house?'

'I was happier then. I did have something going with Mina, you know, mate. But, you know, there's Lisa and our plans and, then there's the whole Muslim thing.'

'Muslim thing?'

'Well, cultural thing. Look at this place. Mina belongs here. It's just too weird for me. Look at yesterday. Bloody ripped from our car and nearly set alight. At the end of the day I might just have to settle for wearing Bangladeshi-made tennis shirts. It's about as close to the culture as I'll get, I reckon.'

'Did you think that before?'

'Before what?'

'Before you had your fling with Mina?'

'Fling? What kind of word's that, mate?'

'What word would you use?'

'I don't know. Something cruder, I guess. Like, in my country, you can just sleep with a girl. She looks after herself. A bloke don't have to.'

'Did you sleep with Jasmina?'

'Are you interviewing me again, Alex?'

'Perhaps. Come on, now's a good time. Tell me what went on.'

'Nothing went on. It was just tennis and big talk. You know me by now.'

Cadman didn't reply; he sensed that this was the time. The train wasn't an ideal interview room, but there were advantages. There were no obstructions between the interviewer and interviewee and Kanoski had nowhere to escape to. He waited for Kanoski to say more, but he didn't speak. Kanoski, seemingly unsettled by the absence of a response, looked at Cadman in puzzlement. Cadman looked back at Kanoski, into his eyes. In his head, Cadman counted slowly to ten.

Slowly.

One.

Two.

Three.

Four. Still looking into Kanoski's eyes.

Five.

Six.

Seven. Kanoski smiled weakly.

Eight.

Nine.

Ten.

'I saw her coming out of your hotel room,' Cadman said at last.

Kanoski was silent for a long time. He looked away and out, past the young girl next to him, through the window. 'It was just flirting,' he said, turning back to Cadman as he did so.

Cadman waited and Kanoski said nothing more. Two women bustled noisily between them.

Cadman leaned across the aisle and looked directly into Kanoski's eyes and counted. Their faces were close. Cadman waited. If Kanoski had not been hemmed in by the girl next to him, Cadman knew he would have backed away.

Slowly.

One.

Two.

Three.

Four.

Five.

Six.

Seven. Nothing. Kanoski just looked straight back at Cadman, indolent.

Eight.

Nine.

Ten.

'It was four o'clock in the morning, Sam.'

'Jesus Christ. What were you doing, spying on my room all night?'

Cadman did not reply. He waited. He counted. Slowly.

One.

Two.

Three.

Four.

Five.

Six.

'She wanted company,' Kanoski blurted. He folded his arms high across his chest and turned his head away.

Again Cadman waited. Kanoski didn't speak. He fixed his eyes on the window, whilst Cadman waited and watched the back of his head. The pause stretched on; Kanoski didn't answer and Cadman counted.

Slowly.

One.

Two.

Three.

Four.

Five. Cadman still looked at the back of Kanoski's head.

Six.

Seven.

Eight.

Nine.

Ten.

Kanoski did not turn back.

'It was before they'd even found Akbar's body.' Cadman's voice was flat, emotionless, deliberate.

This time he did turn. He looked into Cadman's face. Cadman remained silent. Kanoski stared at the police officer. There was something like hatred in his eyes, but not only hatred. Cadman waited. Kanoski turned away. Cadman was counting silently in his head.

Slowly.

One.

Two.

Three.

Four.

Five.

Six.

Seven. Kanoski dipped his head and shoulders, still looking out beyond the girl.

Eight.

Nine.

Ten.

'When she was at her most vulnerable,' Cadman stated.

'What the fuck? What's it got to do with you anyway? I gave her one. OK? Satisfied? I f…' He squirmed in his seat and glanced sideways at the girl next to him, who was glued to the window.

The counting was over. Cadman backed off. 'Tell me about it, Sam.'

'It's a long story.'

'It's a long journey. Tell me about it.'

'You going to fingerprint and photograph me now?'

'No, I'm going to try a bit of water-boarding on you first.'

'Better than that silent shit. Where did you learn that?'

'I investigate terrorism, Sam, remember? I don't study it.'

'Yeah. Very clever, Cadman, you bastard. It's not how you think though. We fell in love, you know. I loved her. Not at first. At first she was an interesting conquest. Something a bit different. But, you know her. She's charming, mate. I always get flattered when a girl falls for me. Always – I can't help it. It makes me feel good.'

'Go on.'

'Early on, I think you were going to come to tennis, but you didn't. Well, it was just me and Mina at the club, so I pretended to have a bad shoulder and we had a drink instead and, well, we got on really well. It started then. We liked each other. I made her laugh. "Sam-u-el – your sense of humour!" Later, I don't know when, I told her I could get her a scholarship at the university. A masters – to study terrorism and security. She really fell for me then. But it kind of started that night at her house. Well, morning really. You and Akbar were up early in the garden. I walked up to her room and…'

'You bastard. Don't tell me, Sam. I don't want to know. Under Akbar's roof?'

'Mina's roof too. Don't make me out all bad. Akbar wasn't dead. I didn't know that was going to happen. You asked him to get the fucking sari, not me.'

'You're a piece of shit.'

'Alex, we've got to work together, mate. Anyway – don't hate me, because I fell in love with her. It was honourable. I only kissed her at Akbar's. We just kissed and stuff. No sex. Her dad was downstairs, don't forget.'

'You? Honourable? Convince me.'

'Then nothing happened until Akbar died. There wasn't the chance.'

'But when he died you found time, did you?'

'Each day when the search ended, she came to my room. We talked. And then, I don't know, on the third night…'

'You took advantage of her.'

'You talk like a bloody Victorian colonialist sometimes. You know that? It's the twenty-first century, for Christ's sake. Men don't take advantage of women anymore. Listen. After the course finished, I didn't go home.'

'What?'

'I didn't go home. I told Lisa I had some research to do. It was true: Pritilata, Mrs Sullivan, the IRA. I didn't go home until Mina went to London. It turns out the UN's not paying as much for our hotel as we thought. It didn't cost me much. She came to the hotel every night until she went to London. That's when we fell in love, during that time. So you see, I didn't mistreat her.'

'So what is she so upset about? Why doesn't she trust you? Because there was no scholarship?'

'No. There was a scholarship. She could have taken it.'

'What's the problem then?'

'I didn't tell her about Lisa. She thought I was single. I kind of didn't prevent her from thinking otherwise.'

'By which you mean?'

'I told her I wasn't married.'

'When did you tell her?'

'When she rang me from London to tell me she thought she was pregnant.'

'Oh Christ. No.'

'She wanted to have the baby, talked about bringing him up in Australia. I told her, I can't. I'm married.'

'Is she pregnant?'

'She thinks she is. That's for sure.'

'Oh, no.'

'And her family in London wouldn't support her if she was, apparently.'

'No, I've met one of them. He's a traditionalist alright. I warned you about this from the start.'

'Yes, well, you were right. She says she doesn't know what they'll do to her if they find out. Excommunicate her at best, she thinks. They might even harm her.'

'You know what, Sam?'

'What?'

'You're a bastard.'

'But she's an adult too. It takes two.'

'But you let her fall in love with you.'

'And I fell in love with her. I'm not the evil so-and-so you make me out to be.'

'Yes, but you didn't tell her about Lisa, did you?'

'What's going on here? Can you believe this? Look at that bloke.'

The train had not stopped and the crowds had not thinned out in the slightest; people were still wedged onto seats and propped up in the aisle, hanging listlessly from any handhold they could find. Yet, impossibly, a white-coated steward was picking his way carefully through the maelstrom with an oversized tray on which teetered about twenty dainty china cups of tea, complete with saucers.

Cadman bought three and gently woke Lee. She came to slowly and settled comfortably against Cadman's arm, the small cup in her hand. She sighed happily as they watched Bangladesh go by. The hot, sweet, milky tea was soothing.

They were travelling alongside a network of ponds amongst which a few tiny hamlets were interconnected by a network of narrow bamboo and wooden walkways above the water. The surface of the ponds was completely obscured by a mass of big shiny green leaves sprouting exquisite purple blossom: water hyacinths. A tiny girl, about seven years old, dressed in a shocking pink Western-style party dress, tip-toed daintily, barefoot, across one of the bridges towards an arbour that overlooked the vast landscape. A slim little boy trotted behind her, wearing only a tiny pair of shorts of the same hue. His young brown back and legs shone healthily in the late afternoon sunshine. He walked cautiously, as if in procession, and he held in both hands a magnificent purple bouquet.

'Did you tell Jasmina about me today, Alex?' Lee asked.

CHAPTER SIXTEEN

Somewhere in the darkness, not far away, a small wave rippled across the sand. Though he could see nothing, Cadman could picture the tiny breakers foaming up the beach, slowly being absorbed and disappearing in little frothy bubbles. Behind him the lights around the shack illuminated no more than a metre beyond its wooden walls, creating a luminescent cocoon against the rest of Bangladesh. Lee, in cut-off denim shorts and a faded vest, emerged from it carrying a bowl of salad.

'So what's Sam doing in Chittagong?' she asked, looking out towards the sea.

'He's visiting a place called Pahartali. It's where the colonial railway was based.'

'I thought he had a chip on his shoulder about the empire?'

'So he does. A Bengali suicide terrorist, a woman, died there carrying out an attack against the empire.'

'Why's he interested in that old business?'

'A student on our last course told us about it. She'd be one of the first female suicide terrorists, I guess. He's interested in what would make a woman do such a thing.'

'Did she kill anyone? Apart from herself, I mean?'

'Another woman. A European, but not a symbol of

power, just an anonymous woman. No one even knows who she was.'

'Not even her name?'

'Mrs Sullivan.'

Mrs Sullivan? No first name? Why was she there? A railroad wife?'

'That's what Sam hopes to find out.'

Cadman could see nothing beyond the narrow circle of light that the small battery lantern generated. He held the skewer up to the bulb.

'How do I know when these prawns are done?'

'When I say they're done. Another Budweiser, honey?'

He picked up the almost empty can beside the low barbecue and finished it off. 'Yes please, Lee. I'd love one. These sarongs are great for squatting in, you know. They've no seams to split. They've got plenty of give – just what a man of my age needs.' She sank down, cross-legged, into the sand beside him, the ice tinkling in her gin.

'And they're easy access too!' She plucked a beer from the cool box and ran the ice cold can along the inside of Cadman's thigh.

'Ooh, too cold, Lee, too cold.'

'They're not done yet then, are they, honey? Just a little more cooking.'

'So there's a beach out there somewhere, is there?' He rearranged the skewers as he spoke. They were beginning to smell good. 'Nearly done, I think. They don't take long, do they? Sausages take ages.'

'Cox's Bazaar. The longest sandy beach in the world, honey. Nothing but the best for you.'

'Who'd have thought, eh?'

'I'd say they're done – let's eat. Inside or outside?' She stood in one easy motion, drink in hand, and turned towards the shack.

'How do you do that? Outside. You don't get many chances to in London. Or in Dhaka come to that. Shall I put some music on?' He lifted the skewers onto a plate and walked towards the wooden picnic table under the shack's awning.

He heard the pop of a bottle of sparkling wine. She emerged carrying the bottle with two glasses and a portable CD player. 'This can plug in here, by the look of things. Do you have any music? I've only got my pad.'

Cadman skipped up the six steps and pounded across the boards. 'Close your eyes,' he said, as he returned, 'it's special.' He pushed the CD into her slim fingers. 'OK, open up.'

'What's this? *Graceland*, Paul Simon? I haven't heard that in years. It was a good album, wasn't it? Why's it special?'

'I bought it in Oxford Street. I made a right fool of myself. There was this young girl and an older bloke about my age. The girl looked a bit frightening, so I asked the old guy, "Have you got 'You Can Call Me Al' by Chevy Chase?" I should have asked the girl, she was too young to know. The guy burst out laughing. Right in my face.'

'Why, Alex? Isn't our song a cool one?'

'I don't know, but it's not by Chevy Chase. It's by Paul Simon. "Chevy Chase was just in the video, pal." So there you are, honey – you can call me Al.'

'Well, put it on then, Al.' She poured their drinks while Cadman fiddled with the CD player in the half-light.

'Is that champagne? How did you get champagne?' A fanfare of synthetic trumpets blasted out of the little machine and he jerked backwards; bubbles sloshed over the side of his glass. 'Oh! Too loud.' He moved to find the volume control but, as the infectious rhythm and African bass guitar burst into the night, Lee was on her feet, glass in hands.

'No. Leave it, Al. Let's dance.'

Cadman looked ruefully at the barbecued prawns as he struggled up from the rickety bench, his own glass in his hand. Lee was moving well with sexy, perfect timing. 'You dance well.'

'I forgot how good it is! What a great song.'

Paul Simon was singing, his characteristic lyrics crystal clear, asking himself why he was soft in the middle.

'That's me!' Cadman shrieked. 'I'm soft in the middle!' And he rubbed his free hand across his paunch.

Lee crooned along, slightly unsure. Then, more confidently, joyfully poking Cadman with her long finger she danced around him. 'Beer belly! It *is* about you, Al!'

Cadman sang back that he wasn't amused anymore, feigning hurt.

Simon launched into the chorus.

'Be my bodyguard, Al. Please,' Lee begged and then sang, 'I'll be your long lost friend.'

Then, in unison, they sang, 'Call me Al', Cadman pointing ostentatiously to his chest.

'Oh, this is great! Dancing on the beach! Who'd have thought?' He wiggled in the sarong and rotated, his elbows rocking, as the synthesisers again blasted out their big brass

251

sound. They were less sure about the second verse and Simon started it alone, lamenting the absence of his wife and family during his long nights.

'I'll fill your nights, Al.' Lee swam into him and kissed his moving cheek as he jiggled up and down.

Cadman warbled to the sky, his head back. He took a swig of champagne and then it was his turn to poke Lee and she danced quickly around the table to avoid him as he taunted her.

'You're the roly-poly one,' she giggled.

Simon sang of a being a stranger in a foreign land filled with incident.

'What is this? Cadman laughed. 'The story of my time in Bangladesh?'

'It really is our song, Al. It really is all about you!'

Cadman had exhausted his knowledge of the lyrics and his wine. He stooped over the table and poured himself more. Lee jigged over and held out her own glass.

Cadman plonked his wine on the table and Lee gave hers up as he took the glass. He laced his arms around her slim waist and pulled her close to him.

'I see angels,' he sang to her, then stifled her attempts to sing back at him with a long kiss. Then they were dancing and singing raucously again.

'Call me Al,' they sang together.

CHAPTER
SEVENTEEN

Cadman awoke to the sound of Lee humming along to *Graceland* in the kitchen. He slipped naked from the bed, tied on his sarong and padded out to join her. She had her back to him, and wore the same shorts and vest. Her short, straight hair was tousled. She was adding boiling water from a kettle to two mugs, steam rising and condensing on the beach scene glimpsed through the glass. Toast popped up from a chrome machine beside Cadman.

'Good morning, Hollywood!' Cadman called to her, making her jump. He handed her the toast. 'Aren't you supposed to be wearing one of my shirts and frying eggs?'

'Morning, Al. That stinky thing? Have you any idea how much you sweated on that train?' She kissed his lips carefully as she pushed his coffee into his hand. 'You need a shave.'

Cadman rubbed his chin. 'Well, if I'm going to be your bodyguard, shouldn't I be a bit more rugged?'

'No, honey. There's no reason a bodyguard can't be clean-shaven. Besides, it's almost white, Al.'

'You know how to hurt a man.'

'And how to love a man. Isn't that true?' She rubbed his naked hairy belly lovingly with the palm of her hand.

'Beer belly,' he said. 'What a great night! I haven't danced like that for years. I've never danced like that, come to think of it. On the beach.'

'Come and see the beach this morning – it's fabulous. Coffee and toast for breakfast. Is that OK?'

'Perfect, Lee. Just perfect.' He followed her down the steps onto the sand, shading his eyes as he emerged. 'Wow! How fantastic. I had no idea the sea was that close. I mean I could hear it, but…'

The sea was calm, breaking, as he had imagined the night before, in small rippling waves that were not even knee high. A line of crispy seaweed showed that the water had come almost to the barbecue at some point in the recent past. He stooped and placed his coffee mug on the beach and wandered down, across the short area of flat wet sand to the sea line. Looking back, he could see that their shack was the middle one of five spread over a distance of about 200 metres. The neighbouring two were closed up and he could not see anyone at all. Left and right the sand went on forever, a massive, barely perceptible curve.

'The Bay of Bengal,' Lee called out.

He took a few steps into the water up to his shins. The bottom of his sarong was dipping into the warm water. He unwrapped it, threw it back onto the damp sand and waded into the water.

'Alexander Cadman! That is no way for a British police officer to act.' She came running down to the water's edge.

'I've never danced on the beach and I've never skinny dipped. Come on!'

'Neither have I.' She angled her way out of her vest and

shorts and splashed in next to him. He enjoyed watching her so much.

'Ooh it's cold. Quick, into the water, before somebody sees,' she giggled.

They waded in and bobbed below the surface. He swam a few metres and found that he could now just about touch the sandy bottom with his head protruding. She swam up to him and clambered onto his body, wrapping herself around him like a limpet.

'Will you be my bodyguard, Al?'

'You don't need a bodyguard, Lee. I've never met a more able woman. In Bangladesh all alone, flying to London to get your man…'

'Did I get him?'

'Yes, you got me.'

'Can I keep him?'

'Would you like to?'

'Yes.'

'Where would we live? My work is in London.'

'Then I'll come to London. We'll live in your apartment.'

'Flat. What about your work?'

'I'll find something, Al. And if I don't, I'll sell the house in Boston.'

'You've thought it through then?'

'I've discussed it with my daughter. She can't wait to bring the kids to visit their grandma in London.'

'You've not seen my flat, Lee.'

'Oh, don't be so practical, honey. You know you're skinny dipping in the Bay of Bengal with a mermaid draped over you at the moment?'

'I know. Great, isn't it?'

'I'll go when you want me to.'

'I have the feeling you wouldn't. But I don't want you to. One thing though?'

'What's that?'

'We keep it Hollywood. We don't lose this. Let's dance and sing. Like we did last night. Don't let me lose you to my work.'

'Agreed. But you have to do your work. It's important. It's part of what I fell in love with.' She kissed his unshaven cheek and looked up at him. 'Can I ask one thing too? Just one?'

'Of course, Lee.'

'Will you tell Jasmina about me? Once she knows, she'll get over you.'

'Oh, Lee. Of course I will. There's no competition between Jasmina and you. It's different. Of course I will.'

'Jack never did tell her. I did. After he died.'

'I love you, Lee.'

'So, *will* you be my bodyguard, Alex?'

CHAPTER
EIGHTEEN

Cadman was on fire. His body was burning. He tried to put himself out, but his hands had lost their fingers and had curved into little burning pyramids, with yellow skin that bubbled. His hair was on fire and he couldn't get out of the bus. He jumped up and his burning sarong fell away and he was naked inside the bus and the other passengers were laughing. He tried to cover himself up but his hands had burnt away. He tried to pull up the car door lock, but his fingers wouldn't grip, and then the plastic knob melted under the heat of his burning fingers. They came to watch him burn. Bearded men. Tanvir was there, laughing, calling people in a slow, deep voice to come and see. Tofo came over on a rickshaw and laughed too. Tofo was looking in. Tofo laughed low and deep and slow as Cadman pushed at the car door. Tofo's face filled the window. It was just Tofo. Tanvir had gone. He was on the roof of the train. Tofo was running away with the crowd, chasing the train. Tofo leapt onto the roof but Cadman couldn't hold it with his burning fingers. Tofo laughed from the roof. Tofo laughed robotically. Loud then soft. Loud then soft. Loud then soft.

Cadman lay in the dark. Lee was breathing deeply next

to him, in time with Tofo's laughing. Gradually his laughing faded and it was just Lee breathing.

*

He caught a rickshaw from Lee's apartment to the hotel. Kanoski was already standing outside waiting for Ezaz.

'You have a good trip, mate?'

'Fantastic, thanks, Sam. I loved the train, but…'

'Glad you flew back? Me too. Look, mate, I'm only saying this once. I'm glad you made me come clean. I'm going to talk to Mina. I don't know what I'm going to say, but I'm going to talk to her.'

'I don't know what you're going to say either, Sam. How did your research go?'

'Fifty percent, I'd say. I found the European Club and the statue. All the old colonial railway buildings are still there. Big red brick places. There's an old turntable for turning the engines, still working by the looks of things. Interesting. The club's still there. Looks like it's barely been used since independence. It's all locked up, but you can see inside it and get round the side a bit. Just like a scout hut.'

'Mrs Sullivan?'

'No. Couldn't find anything. In a way, that's appropriate. Pritilata didn't know who she was either. That's terrorism for you.'

'No luck finding a cemetery?'

'No. It's a chaotic little market area, heaving with people. Overwhelming. The driver had to ask about a hundred people before anyone knew who Pritilata was. I don't think the locals take much notice of the statue. I tried to find a European cemetery, but I kept being told about the Commonwealth war cemetery. It's a bit of a tourist spot for old colonial enthusiasts like you. But it's for soldiers, not the likes of Mrs Sullivan. She was killed in peacetime.'

'The IRA didn't see it as peace.'

'Not in India and not in Ireland. But the British didn't see it as war. One man's terrorist, and all that. I've finished a draft of my paper. Could you do me a favour and have a look at it for me?' Kanoski scrabbled through his bag and produced a bright orange thumb drive. It reminded Cadman of Kanoski's tennis shirt. 'There's only one file on it. I don't want coppers snooping through any of my other stuff. There're photos there too, of Pritilata and the club and stuff.'

'Wasn't your laptop burnt in the fire?'

'What fire?'

'The mob. They torched the car?'

'No, mate. I didn't have my bag with me. Did you?'

'I bloody well did. The job won't let me forget that either. Never mind the risk to me, I'm replaceable, but if you lose a laptop, you're really in it!'

'That's a bummer.'

'I'm just pleased I gave Mina the sari before the fire. That really was irreplaceable.'

Kanoski pushed the thumb drive into Cadman's hand. 'You can use Lee's laptop. I'm really interested in getting your opinion, mate.'

'I'll have a look, Sam, but I don't suppose I've got anything useful to add.'

'That's funny. I'd have said the same thing a few weeks ago.'

A navy blue Honda with blacked-out windows pulled up. 'Is this Shahjahan?'

The driver's door opened and Ezaz jumped out, grinning. 'New car, sir.'

It had even taken the fastidious hotel porters by surprise. Cadman was caught for a split second waiting uselessly for someone to open the car door, as if he'd never opened one himself.

'I might try and meet with Jasmina tonight,' Cadman said as the car pulled away. 'I want to tell her about Lee.'

'Why? You don't think she's got enough on her plate?'

'It's important to Lee.'

'I'll stay away then. Put off my difficult little chat for a bit longer.'

'It needn't be difficult.'

'Look, Alex. You're having trouble telling her about your girlfriend. When this course is over, I'm going back to Australia. To Lisa. That's not what she wants to hear and it won't be easy telling her.'

'Is it the right choice?'

'Don't moralise, mate. I've had enough. I didn't know what I was getting myself into.'

'I did warn you.'

'That doesn't help now, Alex.'

'Alright, Sam. Let's have a beer tomorrow night, shall we? I'll read your paper and we can have a chat about it.'

CHAPTER
NINETEEN

The thick evening heat engulfed Cadman as he stepped out of the High Commission, his mobile phone already to his ear. Ezaz pulled up, but Cadman motioned to him to wait.

'Dave? Alex. Joe's been briefing you, hasn't he?'

'Is it him?'

'Yes, it's him. I'm one hundred percent sure. Joe sent three photos. One shows him in a group with the other protesters, two are close-ups. They're both a bit blurry, obviously taken on a long lens, but it's him alright.'

'Higher Ground.'

'Yes. And he's here.'

'Did you brief the guys in the High Commission?'

'No, I haven't. They're probably listening anyway. I wanted to talk to you first. Perhaps get Spencer's assessment.'

'Do you know where he is?'

'Spencer? No. You don't mean Spencer, do you? He was in the country on Wednesday. That's when our car was attacked.'

'I take it you're alright?'

'No problem. It frightened the shit out of me, but I'm not injured. I've had a great weekend away since with, you know, the girl you met in London?'

'Which one?'

'The American – Lee. She's a real cracker, Dave.'

'What do you think?'

'About Lee? It's pretty serious.'

'No. About the guy in the photo.'

'I think we should spin his house. We've got this other guy he's been talking to – he's unidentified and we don't know how real it all is. If we go overt we'll show our hand – we might frighten them off. If they're only playing at it, it'll bring it to a head. On the other hand, if they are serious, we might scare them into acting more quickly, but at the moment we don't know who he's working with or where they are. I think the risk assessment balances in favour of overt action.'

'What about his cousin? Your other girlfriend?'

'I've thought about that too. My relationship with her is really strong. I assess that she'll speak to me in confidence about him, if we need that. I'd say have a look at his house first, see if that takes us anywhere. Then reassess whether to make an approach to the girl. What do you think?'

'It's sound. Don't do anything yet. I'll brief Spencer now.'

Cadman walked towards the car and Ezaz jumped out to open his door for him. 'Club, sir?'

*

Jasmina was paying a rickshaw puller outside the club as Cadman stepped from the car.

'That was good timing, Jasmina. I thought I might be late.'

She was dressed in silver-grey *shalwar kameez* and wore a matching scarf loosely over her head. 'Hello, Alex, this is kind of you to buy me dinner. Though it's a strange place to bring a Bangladeshi woman.'

'Why strange?'

'You know my feelings about colonial clubs.'

The heavy metal door swung open and they walked in through the dark entrance to emerge into the haven of the club. It was busy; four Western women were playing doubles and, as they passed through the dining room, most of the gingham-covered tables were occupied. He led the way up the stairs to the familiar bar with its green umbrellas. A group of four Western men in tennis gear sipped bottled water. They were obviously waiting for the court to become free. The old television crackled above the bar. Two Western men, their ties loosened, empty beer glasses in front of them, sat in Lee's customary telephone seat, looking as if they were coming to the end of a business meeting.

'Hello, sir. Heineken?'

'Yes please – and an orange juice please.'

'I'm the only Bangladeshi in here, Alex. Apart from the man serving us.' She pulled her scarf further over her head.

'I thought that's why you came here. To be seen to be equal. Didn't you say something like that?'

'Well, I'm tired of making that point now. We should have gone somewhere else.'

'I'm sorry, Mina. I didn't think…'

'No. You don't think. I took you to that nice restaurant and you bring me to this, this…'

'Jasmina…'

The barman arrived with the drinks and Cadman paused. The man turned the can to show Cadman the label before cracking it open and pouring it, showman-like, into the chilled stemmed glass. He placed the glass in front of Cadman on the table and stood. Cadman took a sip and the barman leaned forward, poured the rest of the beer in and returned to the bar with the empty can.

'He's a good barman that one, he always does that. Our little ritual.'

'You talk as if he were a good dog. Englishmen like their dogs. Only not in their clubs, of course. Dogs aren't allowed. Neither are Indians. He's the only dog and I'm the only Indian.'

'Jasmina, why did you come? You should have told me you didn't want to come here.'

She brought her juice to her mouth and closed her lips around the straw but did not drink. She looked at Cadman for a long time and then put the glass back on the table. 'I'm sorry, Alex. I'm taking it all out on you. I shouldn't. You've done me nothing but good. Did you go to Chittagong at the weekend? I didn't get a chance to ask you today. He was around all the time.'

'I wish you'd make it up with him somehow.'

'It can't be made up, Alex. Too much harm has been done. He is everything that is wrong with the West. Everything that I've spoken to you about is summed up in him. He has no respect for Bangladesh.'

'But he came here to help Bangladesh.'

'Do you really believe that, Alex? He came here to help himself.' She pulled the scarf further around her face. 'And he did.'

'Well, he can be a difficult person to like sometimes.'

'He lied to me, Alex. He told me he wasn't married. Did you know that?' Her eyes blazed as she threw the question at him, staring Cadman in the face, then pulling the scarf over her hair and looking away.

Cadman didn't know how to answer. His beer glass was still full and he took a small sip from it.

'If ever there was an example of Western colonial arrogance, it's him.'

'But he hates colonialism. I'm the British one.'

'He talks one way and lives a different way. You're honest. You are a foreign guest, he is a foreign invader. When my father was killed by Western capitalists at Mirpur Plaza, you tried to save him. He continued to teach.'

'Well, he's a teacher. Not police.'

'Continued to preach the message that it is terrorism to want to free one's country from the yoke of globalisation. Five hundred women died, Alex. Five hundred. And he continued to teach Bangladesh how to protect the capitalists, whilst you and I dug with our bare hands.'

'Jasmina…'

'And these clubs are symbols of the foreign invasion. There are no signs these days, but there are no Bangladeshis either. Nothing has changed, Alex. Look at those businessmen discussing their murderous trade. It's a foreign occupation all over again. Dogs and Indians Not Allowed.'

'Jasmina! I'm sorry. This is a place that Akbar brought you to. It must remind you of him. I shouldn't have brought you back here. I'm sorry. It was thoughtless of me. Let's go.'

'Alex, it's not you. It's my father and Samuel and… I'm really sorry. It's been a difficult day. I wanted this evening to be nice. You haven't even drunk your beer.'

'Come on, let's take you home. There are still a few days before the end of the course. Let's try again when you feel less angry about Sam. And I won't bring you here again, I promise.'

She stood quickly and was walking towards the stairs, her back towards him. He swept up the beer and guzzled it down as he watched her flounce away. Her headscarf caught in the breeze and fell down her shoulders. She quickly pulled it back up again, but Cadman had seen. He caught her halfway down the stairs.

'Your hair, Jasmina! What have you done with your hair?'

She looked down, towards the gingham table cloths. 'I've sold it.'

'Sold it? What sort of answer is that? You don't sell hair.'

'Alex, a person who comes to this club knows little about Bangladesh. To the poor, everything has value.'

'But hair?'

'It makes its way to Milan, I believe. There it is turned into very expensive hair extensions for the ultra rich.'

'But I loved your hair.'

'My mother loved my hair. As a girl she would brush it over and over for me. It seemed to last hours. She would tell me how beautiful it looked. She would tell me how I would one day be married and happy with a daughter of my own and I would brush her hair.'

'Oh, Jasmina. Why?' Cadman stepped towards her, to touch her, but she held up her hand and stopped him.

'For a victim of Mirpur Plaza.' She looked directly into his face now.

'You sold your hair?'

'Did I ever tell you how many victims of Mirpur Plaza come from my village, Alex?'

'No. It didn't occur to me that there were any.'

'Seven. Six women died. One lost her legs. She is carried about by her husband like a sack. She has a daughter with long, beautiful hair like... mine was. She brushes her daughter's beautiful hair every day and she tells her about her future. One day she will be able to work in the garment factories and she can brush her own daughter's hair. Her daughter is seven and she was going to school because of her mother's income. Now there is no income. Her husband cannot work so often in the fields because he must tend to his wife. So there is less money. The little girl no longer goes to school. So the mother told me she was going to sell her daughter's beautiful hair. Perhaps this would pay for a month's school – who knows? I told her, "No. Take my hair instead." Last night I cut it off and I have sent it to her.'

'But...'

'But what, Alex?'

'It's futile. She'll have to sell her daughter's hair anyway. A month of school isn't enough. I... I would have...'

'What? Paid? Then you don't understand.'

She ran down the last steps, through the dining room and out through the heavy steel door. Cadman chased her, self-conscious in front of the diners. She stopped on the street outside and turned towards Cadman. The crouching old man selling cigarettes looked up hopefully.

'It's symbolic, Alex,' she sobbed.

Cadman wanted to hold her and comfort her. He wanted to guide her, as Akbar would have done but he did not know how. She held his eyes with her own and he tried to fathom them. The Honda pulled up like an intrusion. Cadman gestured towards it questioningly.

'I'll get a rickshaw,' she snapped and strode off into the darkness.

The driver's door of the car remained closed and Cadman, a droplet of sweat forming on the end of his nose, waited and watched Jasmina in the distance as she climbed into the seat, her scarf wrapped around her head. But Ezaz didn't appear. Instead, the rear window of the car rolled down and a slim brown face wearing sunglasses could be seen.

'Get in, sir,' Shahjahan said. 'I must speak with you.'

'You've been watching too many movies, Shahjahan,' Cadman said as he stooped into the car. 'It's not done like this in reality.'

'I'm sorry, sir. I didn't know. I didn't think you would want anyone to see us meeting in public. How should I have done it?'

Cadman studied the young intelligence officer's honest face. He had removed his sunglasses and the car was now moving slowly in the evening traffic. 'I was only joking,

Shahjahan. You have done a good job. You met me perfectly. Your car is very similar to my new car and I was confused for a moment.'

'Sir, this is a clean car and the driver is an NSI officer. We can speak freely in here.'

'OK, Shahjahan. I will speak freely.'

'Sir, you must be careful.'

'Why?'

'My service has picked up chatter. I think you call it chatter.'

'Chatter. Yes.'

'There is a threat against you.'

'Me?'

'Not you personally, sir. Against foreigners.'

'What sort of chatter?'

'I cannot tell you that, sir.'

'What can you tell me?'

'Sir. You taught us about threat levels. I have used your lesson to assess the threat. We know the terrorists' intention but we don't know their capability.'

'Do you know who they are?'

'No, sir – just chatter. I am working with the British High Commission, sir. We met that time. But I was once a policeman like you, sir. Protect and Serve. I had to warn you to be careful.'

'So what's your assessment of the threat?'

'They intend to hit a Western target, sir. I cannot assess their capability, but their intention is clear. The threat level is imminent, sir.'

'Imminent? The highest level?'

'Yes, sir. You are my friend, sir. I wanted to warn you myself. Please be careful, sir.'

'Can I tell others?'

'Tomorrow, sir. Only of the threat. Not about the chatter. Nor our meeting, sir.'

'Have you told Mr Kanoski?'

'No, sir.'

The driver pulled up outside the club. They had apparently just been around the block, though Cadman hadn't noticed.

'Thank you, Shahjahan. You're a good friend.'

'See you soon, sir. Be careful.'

Cadman stepped from the sleek car and an identical one drew up behind it. Ezaz leapt out and opened his door.

'Hi, Ezaz. Thanks, my friend.'

'Mrs Lee, sir?'

'Yes please, Ezaz. Oh f…. No. Hotel.'

'Not Mrs Lee?'

'No, Ezaz. Hotel.'

CHAPTER TWENTY

'The American Embassy's closed!' Kanoski held out the *Daily Star* for Cadman to see. 'They've withdrawn all their staff. "The French Embassy is also expected to close, following the violent disorder that took place there last month",' he read.

'Bloody hell. The Americans have shut up shop, have they? That'll piss the Bangladeshis off. What about us?'

'Us?'

'The Aussies and the British. Are we still open for business?'

'Hang on. "The Australian High Commission has changed its travel advice for Australian citizens, warning them to avoid coming to the country unless it is essential to do so."'

'Oh! That'll piss the locals off even more.'

'Why? We're just protecting ourselves.'

'You and the Americans have just set the Bangladeshi economy back a year. Tourists will cancel holidays and merchants will cancel business trips. What about us?'

Kanoski scanned the page. '"European embassies, including the British High Commission, have not yet changed their travel advice, but are reviewing the need to do so in light of the USA's closure."'

'See – sterner stuff, us Europeans.'

'You're talking as if you know something.'

'I did pick up something at the High Commission yesterday but very little and I wasn't expecting this response. I wonder what the Americans know?'

'About what?'

'About the threat. Either they've overreacted or they know something that the rest of us don't. Anyway, we should be careful, mate.'

'Why are you here, anyway?'

'I didn't know it was going to be all over the papers today. I came here to warn you.'

'You arrived early.'

'I came last night.'

'To warn me?'

'Yes. Why not?'

'What about Lee?'

'I called her.'

'With no signal at her place?'

'I'll warn her today. Is this a police interrogation? Give it a rest.'

'You didn't tell Mina about her, did you?'

'No. I bloody didn't. Lee told me to sleep at the hotel if I hadn't managed it. I think it was a joke, but…'

'Not very nice, is it, Al?'

'What?'

'Being imperfect, like me. Have you made the right choice?'

'Leave it out, Sam.'

The waiter appeared and lowered a plate in front of Kanoski. 'What are they?'

'Fried eggs, sir.'

'They're not fried eggs, that's an omelette. Every bloody day…'

*

After breakfast, the two men sauntered through the hotel foyer and out onto the street. A pseudo-military police officer in all black uniform stood on the top step. He wore reflective sunglasses and a black beret and carried a black Colt AR15 assault rifle. His face was set and unsmiling, as if it had been trained that way. He did not acknowledge the foreigners, but stepped forward towards the street and lowered his weapon in readiness.

'Bloody hell, that was quick.'

'He's RAB – Rapid Action Battalion. I've heard about them,' Kanoski said. 'We are honoured.'

'They're taking this seriously then.'

'I'll be glad to get out of here, mate.'

'Four days to go yet, Sam.'

'I can't wait. You're on all day today, aren't you?'

'Yes. I'll use this in my lesson.'

*

The gates of the Police Staff College were open wide as they swept in from the main road. The elderly guard was inside his guardhouse and preoccupied with something he was reading. He did not look up as they drove through. His antique weapon lay across the bench beside the hut.

'Oh, no! There she is.' Jasmina was walking to and fro under the portico, speaking on her mobile phone, as Ezaz drew the car to a halt. In uniform, she strode with determination to the edge of the pond, turned and walked back to the steps leading inside, where she turned back towards the pond. Her head was down and she spoke quietly and seriously. The fringe was swept back, the hair on top parted on one side and at the back trimmed close to the nape of her neck. If Kanoski noticed, he didn't say anything and Cadman couldn't bring himself to say anything about it. To have done so would have somehow been unsupportive of such a noble act. He imagined Kanoski scoffing and he didn't want to be the cause.

The two men took their bags from the boot of the car and Ezaz drove on to park the car. Jasmina had turned again at the pond and was now walking alongside Cadman and Kanoski, but she did not look up.

'Yes,' she said, quietly. 'Yes. Yes. *Insha'Allah.*' As they climbed the steps to the college, she turned away again.

'Good morning,' Cadman called to the group of administrators. As usual, they straightened and smiled, but none of them spoke. They found the classroom door locked and looked around for some help.

'No one's opened up today?' Cadman asked. 'Security, do you think?'

'Incompetence more likely.'

'Tea!' The deep voice boomed and its owner beamed as he marched towards them with a tray, his white coat glowing.

'The door's locked,' Kanoski said as he took the cup.

The man's face dropped instantly. 'Coffee?'

Cadman pushed against the door to show him. 'Locked. Can you find someone?'

He thrust Cadman's tea into his hand and ran off, the tray flapping beside him.

'I'm going to miss that chap,' Cadman said.

'No sugar again. He knows I take sugar.'

Half a minute later, the white-coated man appeared with Jasmina. He gestured towards the classroom door and she walked towards them. A bunch of keys jangled in her hand.

'Here it comes,' Kanoski said.

'Good morning, Alex. Good morning, Samuel. I didn't see you come in. I'm so sorry. I'm a little late opening today. It won't take me long.' Kanoski raised his eyebrows at Cadman and began to slope away with his tea. 'Samuel,' she continued as she fiddled with the lock and pushed into the class, 'this has gone on long enough.'

'Mina…' he began.

'Let me finish, Samuel. Come in here.' She flicked on the lights and air conditioning as she spoke. 'I have decided that we must resolve this… this problem of ours.'

'Yes, Mina. I agree.'

'So, what do you suggest?' She had moved to the computer.

'Can we meet tonight? At least let me try to explain.'

'Yes. I would like you to explain. Shall we meet at the club?' She looked at the computer and then towards the wall screen, which began to glow and then flickered into life.

'The club?' Cadman interjected.

'Yes, Alex. I have been wrong to allow the club to intimidate me. My father was not intimidated by it.'

'Good for you, Jasmina. I think it's the best approach.'

'About six, Samuel?' She closed her eyes for a moment and swept the palm of her hand across her head and down to the back of her neck. She slowly exhaled a lungful of air as she pushed her way out of the classroom. She stopped in the doorway. One hand held the door open and with the other she pulled at the short neck hair. 'Alex?' she said, without turning. 'It's important that Samuel and I are alone.'

'Understood, ma'am.'

The door clattered to a close. Kanoski and Cadman looked at each other. Before they could speak, the door swung open again and the white-coated man was grinning at them. 'Coffee!' he shouted, as he held out two more drinks.

CHAPTER
TWENTY-ONE

'Protect,' Cadman started, 'is about reducing the vulnerability to attack. The physical security at borders and at key points of national infrastructure and the guarding of VIPs and other high-profile people.'

'Like closing the American Embassy?' one student asked.

'Yes, exactly. Closing a vulnerable building is one way of protecting its staff. Another example would be the RAB officer who appeared at our hotel this morning, to protect foreigners staying there. Prepare, on the other hand, is about reducing the impact of an attack if it should take place. For example, ensuring that the emergency services are trained to deal with the aftermath and that they have the right equipment to do so.'

'So we need to prepare in case we don't protect properly?' the same young man pointed out.

'Yes. And we'll be looking at both of those concepts in greater detail during the course of today. We'll look at the UK as an example and discuss the roles of the various agencies in Bangladesh. All clear?'

'Clear,' the class answered in unison, as had become the habit on the course.

'Happy?' Cadman asked.

'Happy,' they replied as Cadman's phone jangled in his pocket.

'Take over please, Sam, would you? I was about to put them into groups – discuss what's currently in place for Prepare. I have to get this. Work.' He wandered out of the class and was soon pounding up and down beneath the portico as Thorogood briefed him. He walked the same path as Jasmina had taken in her telephone call at the time they had arrived – to and fro: to the pond, to the steps and back again.

We've searched the house in Limehouse, Al. It's his parents' place. Dad's a great guy.'

'Just like Akbar.'

'He's really worried about his son now, though he's never seen any warning signs. The boy's always been the serious type, perhaps shown a bit more interest in his religion lately, but nothing radical, his dad says. Spends all his time on his computer.'

'In political chat rooms.'

'But he's shown no interest in politics, according to his dad.'

'Where is he now?'

'Bangladesh. That's what his dad's worried about. Did you know the American Embassy's closed?'

'Yes. There's increased security everywhere. What's he worried about?'

'Tofo and the old man are British. He was up early praying – already awake when we got there – and he'd heard on the radio that there's a threat in Bangladesh against Westerners. He's worried for his son! He doesn't speak a word of the language. He's never been there before.'

'Well, he's settled in quickly. He's certainly at home in a riot. Why's he come?'

'You'll like this one. He's fallen in love with his cousin.'

Cadman mimed drop-kicking his phone into the pond. 'Bloody hell. What is it with her? She's got blokes falling for her left, right and centre. Alright, I don't want to hear that bit. Tell me something nasty about him.'

'We've got loads to do on his computer. Could take weeks. The hi-tech guys are at the house now, trying to get as much quick-time as they can. But he's young, Alex. He's computer savvy. He didn't once use his own computer in the chat room.'

'Any literature? Printed downloads? There must be something.'

'There's one book of interest in his room. I wrote it down. *Do and Die: The Chittagong Uprising 1930-34*. The "die" bit got them interested, that's why they told me about it. And because there's nothing else there. He's a clean and tidy boy. It's a history book. About the Raj. I'm not sure there's anything in it.'

'Nothing real?'

'Real?'

'No trace of explosives, or AK47s, or ski-masks? Tanks? Weapons of mass destruction... nothing?'

'Nothing. And there's not likely to be. This is a clean house, Al. I'd drink a cup of tea there. In fact, I did.'

'You've been there yourself?'

'Yes. Nothing too surprising about that, is there?'

'Yes! When was the last time you stepped out of the Yard? Other than to go to the Prince or the Lincoln?'

'If you must know, I did it for my mate.'

'Who?'

'You! I knew you'd have gone if you'd been here. I think the blokes are still in shock now! Quite enjoyed it, as it happens. I could have dined out on it for years.'

'But…'

'But we didn't find anything.'

'Thanks anyway, Dave. I appreciate it. What next? I don't think I should ask Jasmina – the cousin – about him, if there's a risk she's fallen for him too. Do you? Where's he staying, by the way?'

'No. Don't approach her. We don't know where he's staying. Dhaka. That's all. I can't go into detail on this, Alex. But I've briefed Spencer. There should be coverage.'

Cadman barged his way back into the college and into the classroom. Kanoski was nowhere to be seen. The students were still in their discussion groups and were scribbling on flip charts.

Kanoski ambled back into the class, carrying a sheaf of papers. 'Hello, mate. Have you seen…?'

'Where the bloody hell have you been?' Cadman snapped. 'Was it too much to ask to sit in and debrief the class for half an hour?'

'Don't start on me. I've debriefed two groups and given them another task, alright?'

'Well, why weren't you in here?'

Kanoski grabbed Cadman's damp sleeve and led him out of the class. 'Look, Al,' he whispered, 'I've had a shit time lately too, you know. And I've got a shit time tonight. Don't take out your bloody problems on me. Told you to sleep in the hotel again, has she?'

'No. It was work.'

Kanoski waved the papers in Cadman's face. 'Well, this is work too. Your work, as it happens, mate. They've asked me for a copy of your bloody stupid strategy, but I can't find Jasmina to get it copied for me. Alright?'

Cadman looked towards the point on his sleeve that Kanoski still had a hold of. Kanoski let go. 'Don't touch me again, Sam. I'll break your arm next time you do that.'

'You were going to do it in there. I didn't want the students to see you killing me.'

Cadman looked at Kanoski who looked back at him defiantly. More than a second passed while they stared into each other's eyes, like a pair of boxers before a title fight. Then, simultaneously, they started laughing. Cadman giggled then laughed loudly. Kanoski's frown dissipated into a snigger and then he too broke into full-blown laughter. 'You know what?' Cadman tittered. 'The ridiculous thing is that we're actually a good team! We're actually good at this teaching thing. They like us. If only we liked each other!'

'Is that an apology?'

'As close as it gets today.'

'Good. You get in there and teach them how to protect us and I'll get these bloody papers copied. OK?'

'Alright, Sam.' He took a deep breath, went to enter the class and then walked away.

'Where are you going?' Kanoski called from across the cavernous lounge area.

'Toilet.'

CHAPTER
TWENTY-TWO

They were on their way to lunch, walking alongside the pond looking for snakes when Thorogood called again.

'We've got him, Al.'

'Physically?'

'No. Evidentially. We're into his computer. Home-made explosives. He's been studying London 7/7. Peroxide-based HME. Rucksack bombs. No evidence that he's actually tried it, but four or five HME recipes and information about detonators and primers. He's downloaded clips of the 7/7 martyrdom videos too. Sidique Khan. Oh, and loads and loads of stuff on the collapsed building where your mate died. The plaza place. There's nothing for you to do, but I knew you'd want to know.'

'Nothing for me to do?'

'Teach people and look after yourself, that's all. Well done, mate. You've identified your terrorist alright. The, er, High Commission's onto it. I've got to shoot, Alex. There's loads to do.'

'Don't go. What about the other guy? Who's Tofo working with?'

'You're talking too much, Al. We don't know. Haven't identified him yet. We're on it. Everyone's on it. The whole place is flying. The father's been nicked now and so has the other chat room communist. Joe Pritchard is working his nuts off. Our CT liaison officer's on his way to you from Islamabad, by the way. Should arrive tonight, I reckon.'

'It's my bloody investigation. I'm already on the ground.'

'Alright, Alex. What do you want to do? Drive around Dhaka and find him? The only thing you could do is speak to the girl. That's too high a risk. Maybe that'll change. When it does, the liaison officer will arrange for the interview to take place.'

'But I know her.'

'Exactly. When was the last time you allowed a detective to interview his girlfriend? I've got to go. Spencer's calling.'

Thorogood ended the call. 'Well, thanks for nothing, Dave,' Cadman said to the dead phone.

'What was that all about?' Kanoski asked.

'Shit, I forgot you were there.'

'Someone taken one of your investigations?'

*

Cadman was trying to teach 'Prepare' but was struggling to concentrate on the lesson. Tofo's father and MARX15 were in custody at Paddington Green and Tofo was on the loose somewhere in Bangladesh planning an attack. He should be investigating terrorism, not teaching it.

'So let's consider how we'll coordinate the multi-agency response in the event of a major terrorist incident,' he droned, boring himself. 'We've talked about London 7/7 already during the course and the way that the transport companies worked in tandem with the emergency services. The problems they encountered in their relationship make a fascinating case study.' It didn't, and Cadman knew it. Tofo made a fascinating case study. Kanoski seemed to have dozed off at the back of the class and one or two of the students' necks were having trouble supporting their heads.

Three or four of them were tapping away at smartphones or computer pads below the level of their desks.

'So we're going to talk about the gold, silver, bronze command structure, using London 7/7 as an example. Then in groups, we'll work through the way this can apply in Bangladesh.'

One of the students in the back row leaned over and showed something on his small screen to the woman in front of him. She reached into her handbag and took out her own smartphone.

'The Coroner's report of London 7/7 illustrates some intelligence failings, but also some failings in communication. This could be seen to be a failure to prepare – the theme of today's lesson. This short video taken from CCTV cameras shows what the first responders did.'

Cadman turned his back to the class to set up the video clip. When he turned back, every one of the students was looking at a smartphone screen; some had even left their seats and were standing or crouching in groups. Kanoski had woken and was also thumbing a device.

'Oh come on!' Cadman shouted. 'Is it really that dull?'

'Sorry, sir,' one of the students at the front replied, sliding his phone back into his pocket.

But nobody followed his example. 'Is this some sort of joke?' Cadman asked.

'Sir, you must see this. There is a video on YouTube about the threat to Westerners in Bangladesh. It's an English guy.' It was a woman in the second row who spoke.

'Alex, come and look at this.' Kanoski beckoned Cadman with his free arm, not looking up. 'It's a classic martyrdom video. It looks as if you're right to teach these guys to prepare.'

The youth sat alone facing the camera. Behind him a large black fabric backdrop filled the screen. White Arabic writing was obscured by his head and shoulders. In place of the customary white *topi* he wore a black bandana. He was cross-legged. On his lap rested an AK47 assault rifle. He wore a suicide vest over his white shirt. His skinny knees were clad in white trousers. It was Tofo.

'Our people have a message for the West. Mirpur Plaza will be avenged. The 600 innocent victims of the evil colonialist West will not be silenced. They send their message from heaven and ask me to deliver it. Those who doubted will doubt no more. The 600 Muslims who died feeding the greed of fat Americans want to be heard and they want me to be their voice. They want me to tell the world that capitalist intervention in Bengal will not be tolerated. Every filthy non-believer who wears a designer shirt made in Bangladesh is responsible for their deaths. Every white businessman in Bangladesh is a legitimate target. They have made slaves of the Bengali people who die in their bondage serving the imperialist agenda. There will be no more globalisation in Bangladesh. No more factories where Bangladeshi women die to put money in the pockets of the West. Today Muslims avenge the deaths of the 600 and we begin the war against globalisation. Just as Bengalis did in the past whilst others watched the injustice and did nothing, today we act. Today we follow the brave tradition of Bengali uprising against evil imperialism. Today we strike at the symbol of Western influence in Bangladesh. We tire of seeing the guilty go free because of the influence of Western corruption. Today we begin to kill the guilty to avenge the innocent. And the West will see that we are prepared to die for this cause. The ultimate sacrifice will be made with honour and bravery so that the message of the 600 may be delivered in the only way that the West will understand. And where there is one prepared to give up their life for our cause, so there are many. Such is the commitment of our people to our cause. The messenger must remain brave and resolute in the face of death, for the messenger knows the value of the message. The messenger steps into the abyss and the messenger fears the abyss, yet still will the messenger deliver the message. Such are the messengers tested.'

Cadman laughed briefly, mockingly. The terrorist looked and sounded like the immature boy Cadman had listened to in a fake Turkish café near New Scotland Yard as he practised his childish philosophy. Cadman imagined him ostentatiously holding his fingertips together as he prattled on. Yet the boy was chilling; the threat seemed all the more dangerous for its dry and emotionless delivery.

'When was this uploaded? Can you tell?' Cadman demanded.

'Thirty minutes ago, Alex.'

Cadman dashed from the room and hurtled downstairs. Outside, he called Thorogood.

'Dave. It's Al. Have you seen the video?'

'I don't think so, Al. I don't know what you're talking about.'

'Tofo's posted a martyrdom video.'

'What? Where?'

'On YouTube. Half an hour ago, apparently.'

'Let me get back to you, Alex.'

'Dave…?' Thorogood had ended the call. Cadman tried him again, but got the busy tone. He called Pritchard, but he too was busy. 'Bloody hell!' he shouted out towards the lake.

Kanoski appeared. 'Alex, you've got a classroom of students waiting for their lesson up there.'

Cadman stared at Kanoski. 'Well, fuck off and teach them then!'

Kanoski hesitated for a moment, then said, 'OK, mate. Will do,' and he disappeared back into the building.

Cadman punched Thorogood's name into his phone. Still busy. A snake weaved its way covertly to the bank and disappeared in the blackness of the shadow of the wall. Cadman marched to the water's edge to try to spot it. The phone rattled into life.

'Yes, Dave.'

'I don't know how you did it, Alex, but you beat us all there. Everyone. Nobody had seen it. Well done, mate. Now get back to your lesson, would you? We're on the case.'

Thorogood ended the call. 'Get back to your bloody lesson,' Cadman said to himself. He dropped a pebble into the spot where he'd last seen the snake and it writhed out of its hiding place and headed back to the green water.

His mind took him involuntarily back to Mirpur Plaza. He'd been to Edgware Road Underground Station the day after the London suicide bombings took place in July 2005. The 163 injured commuters had been taken away for treatment, but the bodies of the six killed were still there. Plus the disintegrated remains of the bomber. And that was just one of four bombs that killed 56 people in total. But it was not to London that his mind now turned. It was to the devastation of Mirpur Plaza, where he had witnessed the cries of the dying. The survivors who died. This had brought home the horrors of terrorism to him. Mirpur Plaza may as well have been bombed. The suffering was equal to anything that terrorists had wreaked. Five hundred dead. How many injured? Akbar had suffered there and now Jasmina suffered her own torments. He pictured a beautiful lady with no legs opening a gift of a chocolate-coloured plait of hair. It was ludicrous.

And now Tofo wanted more death and torment. Cadman perched on the small wall and looked across the water. The snake had disappeared.

'I've taken them as far as I can, Alex.' Kanoski sat beside him and peered into the water. 'But we're going to need you to finish the lesson, mate.'

'Can't you do it?'

'Alex, you've been here an hour. I've given the students a break. I've done what I can, but how can I teach them to prepare for the aftermath? That's a copper's job.'

'Do you know who the terrorist in the video is, Sam?'

'No! Why should I? Some British Bangladeshi who feels polarised. Doesn't feel English, doesn't feel Bangladeshi. Feels victimised and starts to feel empathy with the underdog. Something like that?'

'Something like that. He calls himself Higher Ground in his Marxist chat room. Anti-globalisation and Islamist all wrapped in one.'

'Higher Ground? I thought he was a smart-arse little sod in the video.'

'He's Akbar's nephew.'

'What?'

'Tofo. That's what his family call him. A nickname, I suppose. Sounds like a make of toffee when I was a kid.'

'Akbar's nephew? What are you talking about, Alex?'

'He's Jasmina's cousin. He's the one who I met in London. He's the unforgiving type.'

'Oh shit.'

'Yes – oh shit.'

'And if we don't catch him pretty quick it looks like there'll be an aftermath to deal with, so I guess you're right. I think I'd better go and teach these kids how to prepare, don't you?'

'Is he dangerous?'

'What do you think? Did he look dangerous to you?'

'I don't know. Young. Sincere. Polarised. With an AK47 and a suicide vest. Dangerous, I'd say.'

Cadman heaved himself to his feet and started back to the shade of the portico. 'Come on,' he said. 'Let's teach.'

CHAPTER
TWENTY-THREE

'Nothing from your guys in London?' Kanoski asked as they packed away their laptops at the end of the day. The last of the students were still filing out of the door.

'No, Sam, nothing yet.'

'Alex, what do you think? I'm supposed to be meeting Mina this evening at the club.'

'I know. I've been thinking about that too. I wouldn't if I were you.'

'Do you think she's in on it?'

'Is she a terrorist? No, I don't think so. Do you?'

'No. But she's pretty messed up. She might know that her cousin is.'

'Well, if she didn't, she'll know by now. Where is she anyway?'

'I don't know. She was late opening up this morning, wasn't she? Then I don't think I saw her at morning tea.'

'Well, if I were you I wouldn't meet her tonight. She's probably got a surveillance team on her anyway. Shahjahan's a canny operator.'

'Shahjahan? What's he got to do with it?'

'I don't know. He warned me about the threat to Western interests though. He'll have her phone on and everything.

They'll be hoping she can lead them to him – innocent or not.'

'I didn't think you could tell me this stuff.'

'I couldn't if I knew. But this isn't my investigation. I'm guessing.'

Kanoski had reached the door ahead of Cadman and as he opened it Jasmina's voice echoed through the large foyer.

'Alex! Alex!' She was calling in panic. Cadman could hear her footsteps as she ran across the marble. Ignoring Kanoski, she dashed into the classroom and threw herself on Cadman. She was shaking all over. Her face was covered in moisture, her cheeks stained, her eyes red. 'Oh, Alex. Thank God you are still here. Have you seen the video? Of Tofo? I swear I had no idea, Alex. He didn't once tell me he was going to do that.' Her arms were wrapped around Cadman's torso and she hugged him and shivered. 'Oh, Tofo. What have you done? He's going to kill himself, Alex.'

'Well, he's not done it yet. Perhaps they'll find him before he gets the chance.'

She looked up hopefully, childishly. 'Are they looking, Alex? Who are? Can they find him? He has everything to live for.'

'The police are looking, Mina. The NSI.'

'But he's clever, Alex. Can they find him?'

'Perhaps he'll make some mistakes. He's inexperienced. Do you know where he is, Jasmina? You can help to save him.'

'No.' She bit her lip and wiped her eyes with her small, girlish fist. 'No. I knew he was in Dhaka, of course. He visited me a few times, but I don't know where he was staying. I was going to cook for him last night, but he called me and told me he could not come. He would come today for lunch, instead. I went home, but he did not come that time. I waited but still he did not come. I called him, but his phone just goes straight to message. Then, I got the tweet from the students and I saw him on the Internet. Like a terrorist, Alex. He's just a boy. He does not belong in Bangladesh. He doesn't even speak Bangla. He's an English boy.'

'Mina, they'll find him.'

'Do you think they can? They could not find Abu. He was not meant to do this. He was just here to give me support. To help me recover from… Oh, Alex! It was me! I made him do this. All my anger.'

'Don't talk like that, Mina. Your anger was natural. When Akbar died, I was very angry too.'

'He's just a boy, Alex. He has a whole life ahead of him. My uncle did everything to give Tofo a good life in London.'

'There may be something you can do to help. What phone numbers do you have for him? Do you know where he might be or where he was staying? Or who his friends were? The mob that attacked our car – who are they?'

'What? He was in the riot?'

'See if we can get a cup of tea. Let's go to your office and you can give me all the details you know that might help us track him down. You can save him, Mina.'

Kanoski looked up forlornly as Cadman walked past him, his arm around Jasmina, supporting her as they crossed the floor towards her office. He looked at Cadman and raised his shoulders and arms in question.

'Get some teas please, Sam,' Cadman ordered, 'We're going to be half an hour late leaving tonight. And speak to Frank. Tell him all about it. Get him to arrange a lift home for Jasmina.'

*

Forty-five minutes later, Cadman and Kanoski were with Ezaz on their way back to the hotel. They were in a three-vehicle convoy: a soft-top lorry of armed officers in front of them and one behind.

'Who arranged this, if Jasmina didn't?' Cadman asked.

'I did,' Kanoski said, proudly. 'Well, Frank did. But it was my idea. Good work, eh? Sir?'

'Good work, officer. Now, I must make that call.'

Kanoski scrutinised the pedestrian traffic through the window whilst Cadman called Thorogood. 'Alex! Is that him?' He craned his neck backwards. 'No. I thought…'

'Dave? I've spoken to the girl. She's given me a couple of phone numbers for Tofo. And the name of a guy who she thinks he was with when my car was torched. He's a Mirpur Plaza activist that Tofo met at the mosque.'

'For Christ's sake, Al. What are you doing? I told you not to speak to her. I might be your mate, but I'm also your bloody boss, you know. You just couldn't leave it alone, could…'

'Dave, shut up. Sir. I didn't disobey you. She came to me. She's distraught. She saw the video. She wants to help us find him before he kills anyone.'

'There he is!' Kanoski called. 'No, wait a minute. No.'

'Well, that's a bit different. Where is she now?'

'She's gone back to her flat. Is there a team with her?'

'I honestly don't know, Al. The NSI are certainly working on it with us. The Bangladeshi military attaché's here somewhere.'

'Well, she's done her bit to help us find him. Are you ready to take those details? You don't want me to go and use the bat-phone at the High Commission, do you, Dave?'

'No. No, this is urgent. I'll take them now.'

*

'Do you fancy a beer on the roof, Al?' It's been quite a day,' Kanoski suggested as they pulled up outside the hotel.

There were now two black-uniformed RAB officers on protection duty. One of them nodded almost imperceptibly as they squeezed by and Cadman caught a glimpse of his distorted reflection in the officer's sunglasses.

'That's reassuring anyway. They've doubled the guard,' Kanoski said.

'Fat lot of good they'll do against a suicide bomber.'

Kanoski looked puzzled. They were waiting for the lift, just a few metres in from the front glazed doors where the two menacing Rapid Action Battalion guards stood.

'There's no physical barrier. No distance. If a person-borne IED was directed here, the bomber would explode on the front steps before even being confronted, killing the guards, the porter, the receptionist...'

'And us,' Kanoski finished, 'unless we make it to the roof quick.'

'Do you think this building could withstand a bomb? I bet the whole lot would come tumbling down.' They stepped from the elevator into the heat of the early evening. 'You know this is the first time we've had a beer up here since the very first night of the very first course, Sam? Bloody hell, a lot has happened since then.' It was nearly dark and the blue glow of the pool illuminated the roof terrace. The army of barefoot workmen clambered around the bamboo scaffold all along one side of the hotel.

'Crikey, that building's gone up quickly,' Kanoski said.

'That's why they come down so quickly, I suppose,' Cadman replied.

The waiter arrived with two ice-cold Heinekens and poured them out ceremoniously, slowly. Cadman ached to get his lips around the glass. 'Cheers, Sam,' he said at last and they chinked their glasses together. Cadman was about to drink when his phone rang.

'Al? It's Dave. We've got him.'

'Hang on, Dave.' Cadman grabbed the waiter's waistcoat as he was picking up the empty cans. 'Two more,' he said. Raising his glass towards Kanoski he mouthed, 'They've got him' and guzzled his drink down in one uninterrupted pour.

Kanoski blew out a long breath of air. 'Thank God! We're safe.'

Cadman nodded and smiled. 'Sorry, Dave, carry on,' he said.

'The Bangladeshis have nicked Tofo in Dhaka,' Thorogood continued. 'It's just happened, so it's early days.'

'Weapons?'

'The AK47 and the suicide vest, both viable. There's peroxide in the flat. Looks like they made the explosives there. The AK47 had a full magazine on it.'

'Anyone else nicked?'

'One other. Might be the one the cousin told you about. Might be the one from the chat room – Daina. The locals know him. They've got a couple of laptops. And the video was filmed there by the look of things. There's a black flag with the white writing on it. Well done, mate. Looks like you've done your bit.'

'Can I tell his cousin, do you think, Dave? She's desperate to know he's safe. He is safe, isn't he?'

'Well, he's alive. No shots fired apparently. Yes, go on. Call her. She's a cop, after all. She might even know already. When you back?'

'Course ends tomorrow, Dave. I'm back at Heathrow about 7.00am Friday morning.'

'You'll be glad to see the back of the place, won't you?'

'I guess so. The place gets under your skin though.'

'Safe journey, Al. Give my love to Lee.'

Cadman dialled Jasmina immediately and she answered on the first ring.

'They've got him, Mina. Tofo's safe.'

She cried for a long time without speaking. Finally she said, 'Thank you so much, Alex. We are blessed that God brought you into our lives.'

'Well, I don't…'

'And tomorrow you will leave. I wish you a safe return to your family, Alex. But, as tomorrow is the last day, so I must meet with Samuel this evening. Don't come, Alex. It is important that he and I…'

'I understand, Mina. I'll wish you well for your meeting with Sam and we'll see you tomorrow.'

'*Insha'Allah.*'

*

'Are you going to meet Mina tonight then?' Cadman asked as the waiter poured their third beer.

'I guess I'll have to, it's the last chance. Are you sure she wants to?'

'She said so. She knows it's the last chance as well.'

'She's right. But I don't think I can tell her any good news. I'll go and get changed after this drink, I think. Ezaz and I can drop you off at Lee's on the way if you like. Do me a favour will you though, mate?'

'What's that?'

'Read my paper tonight. It's also the last chance for us to have a chat about it. I really do appreciate your views.'

'Who did you say I was like?'

'What do you mean?'

'Some detective out of a book who couldn't cope with terrorists?'

'Oh, Conrad. Chief Inspector Heat. Yes, that was a bit insulting wasn't it?'

'Just a tad.'

'Well, I was wrong, Alex. Cadman of the Yard always gets his man.'

CHAPTER
TWENTY-FOUR

'The American Embassy was closed today, honey,' Lee called out from the shower as Cadman changed into a sarong and T-shirt.

'I know. I meant to warn you. There was a threat to Westerners.'

'Not to worry. I saw it in the *Star*. They've arrested some terrorists apparently.'

'Yes. Two men.'

'Did you tell Jasmina about me today?'

'No, Lee. It's been a funny sort of day.'

'Welcome to Dhaka, Al.'

'Lee, the terrorist was Jasmina's cousin. The one I told you about.'

'Oh heavens, Al. That's different. I forgive you. Is she OK?'

'Yes, I think so. She helped us find him.'

Lee stepped naked from the shower and kissed the top of his head as he sat on the edge of the bed. 'Us? You were involved? You're quite a guy, Al.'

'It's been quite a day, Lee.'

'You want me to bring back some pizza?' She was pulling on the red silky blouse that Cadman liked.

'Bring back? Where are you going?'

'Just the club, honey. I need to call home.'

'Yes. Great. Perfect. That'll give me half an hour to read Sam's paper. You'll probably see him there with Jasmina – introduce yourself, if you like. You don't mind if I use your laptop, do you?'

'No, of course not, honey.'

Lee kissed the top of his head again and left the apartment. He could hear the lift mechanism as it arrived and then began to descend. He rested the laptop on his legs, found Kanoski's orange thumb drive and slotted it into the machine. There was just one little yellow folder. It was called 'DAINA'.

'Daina?' Cadman said aloud. 'Why would he call it Daina?' He pondered for a moment as to whether he'd let too much slip, that he had somehow leaked Daina's existence to Kanoski. He had made too many phone calls in Kanoski's presence. But he was sure he hadn't mentioned Daina. He opened the folder and found two sub-folders. The first was again called 'DAINA', the second, 'Pritilata'.

'*Have* I told him about Daina?' he questioned himself again, as he opened the single document in the sub-folder.

'DOGS AND INDIANS NOT ALLOWED'. The title was centred and written in large-font capital letters so that it covered most of the width of the page. The letters jumped out at him.

'Dogs And Indians Not Allowed – D, A, I, N, A,' he muttered.

He opened the second folder: 'Pritilata'. It contained five or six images. He clicked on the first one and saw the image of a woman. She was in bronze. Her face was strong and boyish. Proud and defiant. Full lips, thick eyebrows and a strong, straight nose. Her hair was short. She wore a sari. The sculptor had hollowed out her irises to create darkness, but the effect was that her eyes were dead. She was a bust, with no arms and no legs. It was a photograph of Pritilata's statue outside the European Club at Pahartali. It was like looking at a bronze sculpture of Jasmina.

'Oh. Oh no.'

Cadman collapsed back on the sofa and gripped his jaw between the palms of his hands.

'It's not over. She's Daina. She's the messenger! Tofo was talking about Daina delivering the message! Today – the club! Sam. And Lee!'

He picked up his phone, immediately saw that there was no signal and hurled it across the room. Crashing into the skirting board, it fell apart into three pieces: phone, battery and back plate. Jumping to his feet, he scooped all three parts up and ran to the door. He looked down at himself – a sarong and flip-flops. He thought about changing but instead flew out of the door. He called the lift and, as he waited, fumbled with the phone parts. His fingers seemed fatter than normal and useless, shaking and unable to coordinate. He dropped the battery trying to get it in and then the back plate.

'Hurry up!' he shouted to the lift and bashed the button again. At last he heard the whirring and clanking of the lift mechanism as it hauled the little steel box up towards the fifth floor. Again he tried to reassemble the phone, but dropped the phone itself as he tried to push the back plate in the wrong way, snapping one of the small plastic tabs that kept it in place. The lift stopped on the third floor.

'She's going to take Sam out at the club,' he muttered. 'She is Daina. Sam. Sam's the target. No one else. Not Lee.' These last words he repeated as he tried to slow his mind and his breathing, concentrating on trying to assemble the phone correctly. 'Not Lee. Not Lee.' At last he managed it, but the device would not hold together on its own because of the broken tab. The lift bell rang with a serene 'ding' and the doors slid open. He skipped in, clasping the phone together in his large fist. A small segment of slowly stretching white line appeared on a black screen as it rebooted. The lift stopped at the second floor and the doors opened to allow two suited businessmen in. Cadman prodded the button to close the door and when it didn't respond immediately he punched it three times with the side of his fist.

Sam's the enemy, not me. She won't kill Lee. Please don't kill Lee, Mina.

The lift descended painfully slowly, but finally settled to a halt and the doors juddered open. Cadman shot out sideways as they did so. He slapped across the foyer in his flip-flops and then was out through the revolving doors and into the heat and humidity. The sweat immediately began to bead on his face. The traffic was crawling, bumper to bumper. Commuters crammed into a grey bus looked sadly out at him as he stood wondering what to do. He ran along the road, dodging a rubbish heap. A big yellow-brown dog appeared from nowhere as he did so, barking viciously, its drooling fangs close to Cadman's bare calves. He skipped on and arrived at the first junction. Here he was in luck;

two rickshaw pullers were sitting on their machines and they both called out as they saw the white man approach. Cadman leapt into the nearest one and hollered. 'Club. Take me to the club.'

The puller's toothy grin evaporated. He looked over his shoulder at Cadman with complete blankness.

'Club!' Cadman shouted. 'For Europeans. White man's club.' He gestured towards his cheeks as he did so, but the mime did not help the puller in the least.

'Club!' Cadman shouted more loudly. 'Club, for Christ's sake.'

The puller in the other rickshaw barked something in Bangla and Cadman's puller looked over to him. They started to have a conversation.

'Club?' Cadman called out to the other man, 'Club?'

'Yes, sir. Club. I know,' the second puller said and Cadman was out of the first rickshaw and into the second. As he stepped up, his hand knocked against the outside of the seat and the back plate of the phone dropped to the road. Cadman jumped down, swept it up with the tips of his thick fingers and climbed back in.

'Club!' he ordered, as the puller stood up on his pedals and heaved them slowly out into the traffic. The first puller gesticulated and gibbered angrily as they edged away.

Sam's the target. Not Lee. She won't kill Lee.

They were stuck in a stream of traffic on the main road and the puller balanced on the pedals as he held their position, then made a big push to break the inertia only to travel a metre or so before having to hold again. Cadman's eyes swept up and down the road for an alternative solution, but there was none. A taxi or even Ezaz could not have done any more. Then the rickshaw squeezed into a side road and at last they made some progress.

Cadman worked to hold his nerve, telling himself to calm down, so that, once more, he could reassemble the phone. He got the back plate into position and again saw the slow line extending as the phone rebooted.

'Today we strike at the symbol of Western influence in Bangladesh.' Tofo's evil, emotionless voice rattled around Cadman's head. 'Today we kill the guilty to avenge the innocent.'

He thumped the ball of his free hand into his forehead over and over again as the puller dragged his heavy Western fare from the side road and into another busy main road. 'That's why she told me to stay away. She's the messenger. Pritilata, the IRA, Bengali uprising against the Empire.' His stomach churned and his heart thumped and the sweat ran into his eyes and soaked out into his T-shirt from his armpits, chest and back.

At last the phone was ready. He called Lee. 'The person you are trying to call is currently unavailable. Please try later.'

What does that mean? She's not there yet. If she was, she'd have connected to the WiFi. He went through his contacts and found Jasmina's number. *Call her. Tell her about Lee.* He started to dial but it suddenly occurred to him that the bomb might be triggered by her phone. He dialled Kanoski's number and he answered immediately.

'Sam? Are you there yet?' As he spoke, the rickshaw puller weaved expertly past three stationary cars and swung into an empty side road. Cadman realised that they were close. The road was one that he and Shahjahan had used when they were cruising the block around the club.

'Hi, Alex. Am I where?'

'The bloody club. Where else. Is Lee there?'

'Alright, calm down, mate. Yes, I'm here. It took ages to get in. There's extra security and they're searching everyone who comes in. Lee's not here, but she might be in the queue outside. Do you want me to go and see?'

'Is Mina there yet?'

'No. Typical – she's late.'

The rickshaw puller came to a halt at a T-junction and was held waiting to join yet another slow-moving road. Cadman stood and peered over the traffic. Two hundred metres away, he could see the entrance to the club. A small line of people were queuing. Amongst them he could see Lee in her bright red blouse.

'Lee!' he shouted. 'Lee!' But it was too far to be heard and the babble and chaos of Dhaka made shouting a useless means of communication. He leapt from the rickshaw, losing a flip-flop as he did so. He kicked off the other one and ran towards the club, dodging the lethal hanging wires, leaping over piles of rotten fruit skins and holes in the concrete.

Then he saw Jasmina. Stepping from a rickshaw outside the club. She wore a sari of yellow and gold that sparkled in the sunshine. The black rucksack on her back was in stark contrast. She approached the group standing at the door. She was next to Lee in her bright red. He was close. He could get there.

'Lee! Mina! Lee!!'

Lee's head turned towards him. There was a flash of orange as if the yellow and red had mixed. The rickshaw from which Jasmina had stepped lifted silently into the air, its puller leaping into a ludicrous back somersault. Two cars that had been stationary outside the club door rose up and rolled lengthways in mid-air, without making a sound. Cadman continued to run towards the door but was suddenly going backwards faster than he had been going forwards. He was naked. He was carried in a blast of burning air. Lumps flew past his face. Before he had made sense of it, there was a massive explosion of noise – an immense fat bass boom and, simultaneously, a thunderous sharp snap. It ripped through his ears and screamed away his sense. He hit something hard. He was still. Naked on this strange street in this strange world. Beside him an old man, a cigarette seller, lay bleeding from a place where his skinny arm had once been, clad only in a shredded pair of underpants. The remainder of his clothes had been blown away. The man groaned. Then there was again silence. But it didn't last long. There began a beautiful tinkling sound, like music, as broken glass rained down around them. A shard the size of a dinner plate drove into the cigarette seller's neck. Cadman faded away.

CHAPTER
TWENTY-FIVE

The metallic buzz drowned out everything. It conquered speech and traffic noise, music and laughter, barking and babbling. It never ceased. Day and night. Endless.

Kanoski and Cadman sat together at the breakfast table. The waiter brought Kanoski an omelette and he took it. They sat without speaking. Cadman did not eat. The Australian slid towards Cadman a copy of the *New Statesman* of four days earlier and Cadman read the front page article. It was an article that he had not seen.

A female suicide terrorist had attacked the European Club in Dhaka. Due to the success of the security net that had been placed over the city, she was unable to enter the club and instead detonated her bomb outside. Eighteen people were injured, including the RAB officers who were stationed at the entrance to the club. An American woman, whose full details are not yet known, had been killed outright. The bomber had also died at the scene; she had not yet been named. The police had reason to believe that the attack was carried out by a Marxist terror group that had posted a martyrdom video on the day of the bombing, expressing a desire to avenge the deaths of the 600 innocent victims of the Mirpur Plaza disaster. A police spokesman had condemned the despicable act of terrorism and added that Dhaka Metropolitan Police and RAB, working closely with the National Security Intelligence, were confident that they had arrested all terrorists concerned.

Cadman detached the front page and carefully folded around the article. Then, with fastidious attention to detail, he tore along the folds until he had separated the article from the rest of the page. Then he folded it into four and placed it in his jacket pocket with the others.

*

Kanoski stood and Cadman saw him shake hands with a man in a suit. Cadman looked up; it was Detective Superintendent Thorogood, who was now leaning forward and smiling into Cadman's face. Thorogood's mouth opened, but Cadman heard only the loud metallic buzz. Cadman had not known that his boss was in Bangladesh. The door porter stood behind Kanoski and Thorogood. He picked up Cadman's luggage and Cadman stood up and followed the three men outside. Ezaz opened the door and Cadman climbed into a seat at the back. He watched as Kanoski shook Thorogood's hand again and then Thorogood was in the car with them, leaving Kanoski standing with the porter outside the hotel. Kansoski raised an arm and they pulled into the traffic.

Daily Star, Bangladesh, October 2012

A new bronze sculpture of Pritilata Waddedar, the first Bengali woman to embrace martyrdom for freedom from British colonial rule, will be installed in the port city of Chittagong.

The statue will be adjacent to the then European Club, where a notorious signboard with the words 'Dogs and Indians are Not Allowed' hung at its main gate.

On 24 September 1932, a group of seven young members, led by Pritilata, launched the most desperate operation at the European Club.

Talking to the Daily Star, anti-colonial revolutionary Binod Binari Chowdhury said, 'I would like the history of courageous struggles of women like Pritilata to be disseminated to all corners of the country through such initiatives.'

Chittagong City Corporation Mayor, Mohammed Manjur Alam, told the Daily Star that it had been a long-standing demand of the people that a statue of Pritilata be installed in front of the European Club and it was a matter of pride for him that it had been installed in his tenure.

'If we do not safeguard the legacy of great characters like Pritilata, the next generation will forget our golden roots,' he said.